To my dear friend
Bonny!
Blessing
John 17:22-23

RAISING MESSIAH

A PROPHECY FOR MARY

K.C. LANGLEY

Copyright © 2020 K.C. Langley.

All rights reserved. No part of this book may be used or reproduced by any means, graphic, electronic, or mechanical, including photocopying, recording, taping or by any information storage retrieval system without the written permission of the author except in the case of brief quotations embodied in critical articles and reviews.

LifeRich Publishing is a registered trademark of The Reader's Digest Association, Inc.

LifeRich Publishing books may be ordered through booksellers or by contacting:

LifeRich Publishing
1663 Liberty Drive
Bloomington, IN 47403
www.liferichpublishing.com
844-686-9607

Because of the dynamic nature of the Internet, any web addresses or links contained in this book may have changed since publication and may no longer be valid. The views expressed in this work are solely those of the author and do not necessarily reflect the views of the publisher, and the publisher hereby disclaims any responsibility for them.

Any people depicted in stock imagery provided by Getty Images are models, and such images are being used for illustrative purposes only.
Certain stock imagery © Getty Images.

ISBN: 978-1-4897-3163-0 (sc)
ISBN: 978-1-4897-3164-7 (e)

Library of Congress Control Number: 2020920721

Print information available on the last page.

LifeRich Publishing rev. date: 10/20/2020

Acknowledgements

This book was only a glimmer until I was invited to the Church on the Mountain Crowley Lake Writer's Group. I'm indebted to them all. My greatest thanks go to my husband Jim. I'm also extremely grateful for my daughter Carrie Sanchez's diligence, for my friends Karen Close Goodman, Marilee Knight, and Judy Fowler, and my Pastor Peter Thomsen. Your support is amazing. Above and behind it all, my utmost thanks go to Father God, Jesus Christ, and Holy Spirit – the best inspiration of all.

...

This is a work of fiction. Just as there are gaps in the biblical narrative about Jesus, we know little about Mary's "missing years" – experiences and emotions that scripture omits. The Bible tells us that Anna the Prophet was 80 years old when she prophesied over Baby Jesus. Could Anna have prophesied over Mary as a young child? What dark powers would have come into play to keep this young girl from her destiny? Differing church traditions produce conflicting narratives about Mary's life and death. I conform to Protestant traditions in revealing the faith, strength, and courage of this amazing woman.

Map of Territory

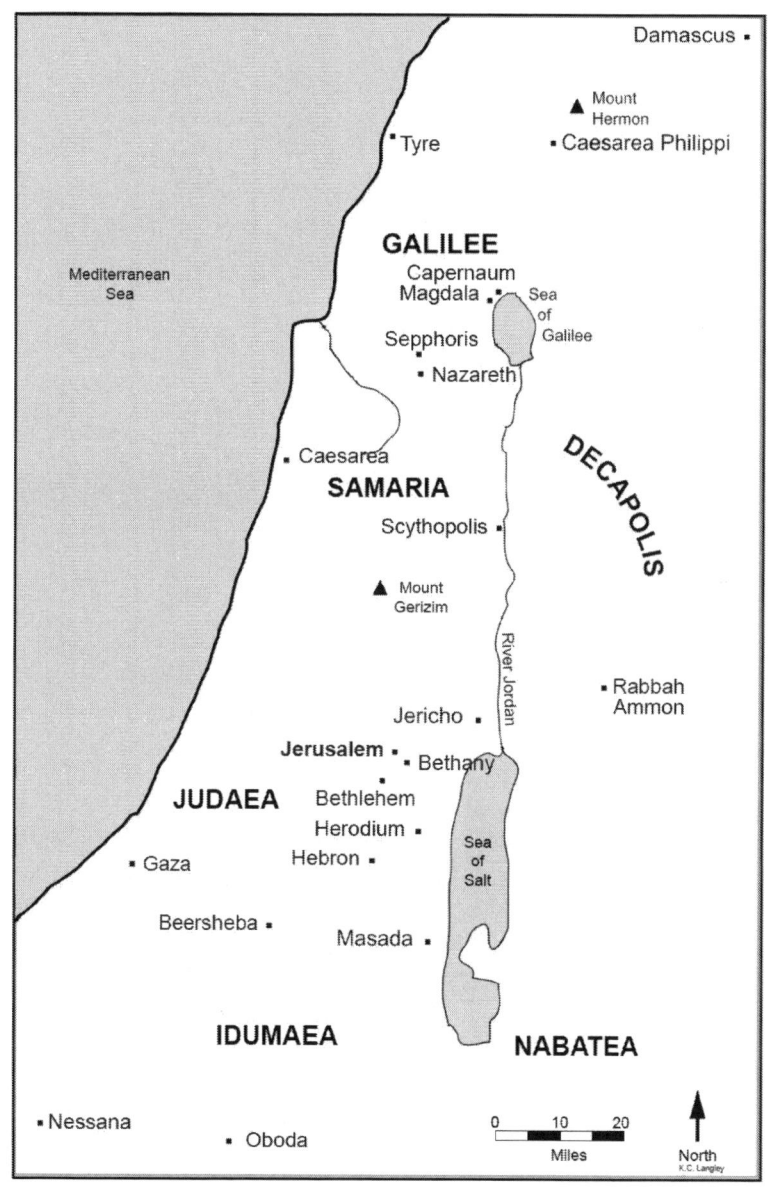

List of Persons in Order of Appearance

There are a number of repeated names in the Bible, including Mary, John, Josef (Joseph), and Anna or Hannah. Usually they are children named after a relative. A number 2 after the name refers to the second person mentioned who has that name, etc. In a few cases the names are altered slightly to help distinguish different people, such as Hannah and Anna and Josef and Josey. I have sometimes used a more Hebrew version rather than the Greek names of the New Testament, such as replacing James with Jacob.

*Fictional character

Herod	King of Judah
Mary	Future mother of Jesus
Mama/Hannah	Mary's mother
Elizabeth	Mama's cousin
Papa/Heli	Mary's father
Taoma*	Papa's friend
Anna	Prophetess at the Temple
Abigail*	Taoma's daughter
Caleb* & Gideon*	Taoma's sons
Josef	Young builder

Widow Rachel*	Neighbor in Nazareth
Orli*	Taoma's wife/ Abigail's mother
Nahor*	Shepherd
Daniel*	Taoma's 3rd son
Salome/Sali	Mary's sister
Samuel*	Hannah's cousin
Zechariah	Elizabeth's husband
Piltai* & Yael*	Elizabeth's neighbors
Aaron*	Nazareth synagogue president
Josef 2	Hannah's brother from Arimathea
Ari*	Merchant from Jericho
Hiram*	Innkeeper in Jericho
Isaac*	Childhood friend of Josef
Deborah*	Wife of Isaac
Jacob	Josef's father
Jacob* 2	Josef's brother
Cleopas	Josef's brother
Matthias*	Friend of Josef
Susannah*	Wife of Matthias
Serai*	Daughter of Matthias and Susannah
Bernice*	Guest of Matthias and Susannah
Jesus	Mary's first child
Simeon	Witness for Jesus
Sharon*	Samaritan wife
Boutros*	Nabatean trader
Faizan*	Brother to Boutros
Elias*	Young Jewish trader
Yefet*	Husband to Sharon
Amali*	Egyptian neighbor

Lara*	Amaili's daughter
Deborah 2*	Mary's first daughter
Huldah*	Mary's second daughter
Jacob 3	Mary & Josef's son
Judah	Mary and Josef's son
Zebedee	Salome's husband
Noah & Avner*	Zebedee's sons
Jacob 4	Salome's first son (later known as James)
Eleazar*	Capernaum official
Jairus	Eleazar's son
Josey	Mary and Josef's son
Mary 2	Wife of Cleopas
Simon	Mary & Josef's son
Uriah*	Farmer Davon's son
John	Salome's second son
Esther*	Mary & Josef's third daughter
Solomon*	Father of the bride in Cana
Gideon*	Taoma's grandson
Levi*	Nazareth's new synagogue president
Tirtzah*	Levi's wife
Micah*	Levi's son
Benjamin*	Esther's husband
Naomi* & Danny*	Deborah's children
Reuben*	Innkeeper's son

Chapter 1

Jerusalem
10th year of Herod's Reign

Deep grumbling grabbed little Mary's attention from the two kittens at her feet. A chilly gust blew chips of stone as two massive blocks careened toward her from the top of the narrow alley, slamming from side to side. She looked for an open door. Nothing. At the bottom of the hill, her mother scrambled up the street, hands flailing, and her mouth opened in a garbled wail.

Mary turned back. One basalt block hurtled straight at her and she froze. "Help!"

Someone gripped her arm. As he whisked her up and away, she glimpsed people below scattering like leaves blasted by wind. She found herself inside a barren room. There was not a table, bench or cabinet.

"I will let you down now," whispered the man who had lifted her through his window.

Mary studied the beardless face rimmed with rusty crinkled hair. Sobs erupted and her body trembled.

"I won't hurt you."

The man's voice gentled her, but she ached for her mother's arms. "I need to find my mama." They both turned as fists rapped on his door.

"Mary? Give me my child! Mary, are you in…?" Coughing choked the words.

Mary tugged at the door. "I'm here, Mama," she called. The man reached past her and unlatched the door.

"Praise the Almighty." Clutching Mary, Hannah sobbed through strangled breaths. "Didn't you hear me? Those stones would have killed you."

"This man saved me, Mama."

Hannah released Mary and hugged the man, then backed away, red-faced, as she tugged her headscarf over her braids. She touched his arm. "May the good Lord bless you, sir. You were just where we needed you to be. Did you see that cart wheel split? Someone said that's what caused the blocks to spill."

"I barely noticed the shouts; the battering against the walls grabbed my attention. When I looked, your daughter was right below me."

"I'm grateful you pulled my daughter from danger. Just like an angel, you are."

"Think nothing of it. I was where I needed to be."

"We are indebted to you. Mary, did you say, 'Thank you'?"

A chattering crowd waited outside the door. The cobbler stepped forward and swept Mary onto his shoulders. All were sharing what they saw, what they heard, where they were as the blocks tumbled toward them.

Mary was eager to tell Papa.

That night Papa shook his head. "One more reason to move, don't you agree, Hannah?."

"Move where, Papa? Why?"

"Away from here and the dust that makes your mama cough. Away from constant pounding all night as Herod satisfies his ego with higher buildings." He patted Mary's head. "Away from mysterious broken cart wheels."

"Mys- what?"

"Mysterious means strange. When others told me what happened, I ran to investigate. That's one thing I build, Mary, cart wheels. That one had my mark on it. I know it was well built. The wheel shouldn't have split apart. It's not safe here anymore."

"But I love living where I can be close to our temple. This is where I belong; Anna, the sweeper, said so."

Papa wrapped her in a hug. "You belong with us, little one."

Mary's lips quivered. "But Papa, our temple is here." *My heart is telling me to live next to the temple.*

By the end of the week, her mother's coughing wouldn't stop. "Mama, I brought you some honey."

Hannah's weak smile dissolved the knot in Mary's stomach. She reached for the damp rag and wiped the dust from her mother's forehead.

"What's the good news Papa is bringing?"

"We'll learn soon enough, dear one."

Mary opened the door and peeked along the street. Young men wheeling carts shouted their wares. Mothers balancing baskets on their head led clusters of squawking children. Soldiers hollered at strings of groaning bodies as they hauled loads of sand or stone to patch towering walls. Gray dust sifted into every crack of building and crease of skin.

The clamor faded as she dragged the door closed and turned around. A cloudy mist was settling on their table. She looked at her feet. "I'm sorry, Mama. I only peeked to see if Papa was coming." She grabbed the cloth and brushed at the fresh layer of grit.

"It's all right, sweet Mary."

The tall shadow of the temple had just stretched across the room when Papa burst in. "Taoma and I decided! Our families leave two days after Sabbath."

"So soon, Heli?" Mama propped herself on her elbows. "I hope I get all our possessions packed by then. I'm depending on your brawny arms to carry everything."

"Are we going to see Mama's cousin Elizabeth in Ein Karem?"

Papa scooped her and swung her around. "We're moving to Nazareth with Taoma and his family." He reached down and lifted her mother's chin. "Don't worry. We'll buy a donkey to help us."

Mary clung to her father. "Who's that man and why is he making you move?"

"Taoma has been my best friend since I was a young boy, but he stayed in Bethlehem and I moved here when my parents died. If we live in Nazareth, it means your mother won't become sick from the grime of stones being shaped or lose sleep from the noise of builders stacking and chipping."

"But you're a builder, Papa."

He sat beside Mama and placed Mary on his knees. "We're going to a village called Nazareth, where I can choose the buildings I want to build and design the furniture and bowls I love to make. I resent King Herod forcing me to build his palaces and porticos." He reached over and smoothed her mother's hair. "And maybe your dear mama will get well enough and have another baby."

"Where is Nazareth? How will we get to the temple? Can my friends come too?" Her questions poured out while they ate their soup. As her father carefully answered each one, Mama's eyes took on sparkles and Mary's head sunk lower.

Her mother pulled her close. "Why so troubled, precious one?"

"I'll miss helping at the temple."

"I'm sure the priests will find someone else to help that lady sweep the courtyards."

"I don't think so; and she told me." She slapped her hand over her mouth and wiped drippy eyes.

Her father's forehead wrinkled. "What nonsense has she been telling you?"

Mary's heartbeat quickened. "She gets to talk to our Father in heaven all the time when she's working, and I want to do that, too. I love being at the temple." She squeezed her mother's hand. "Mama, can't I stay and sweep the courtyards. Would you miss me too much if I helped that poor lady?"

Papa stared at her mother. "Hannah, where did all this come from?"

"Not I." Mama smiled. "Heli, you're the one who has been teaching her about the Lord, training her to repeat the verses and light the Sabbath candles. You're dancing when you go to worship Yahweh. It's no wonder she wants to stay here."

Papa patted his knees, and Mary climbed on his lap. He took a deep breath. "Mary, your mother and I love you dearly. You delight us, daughter, but hopefully in Nazareth, the Lord would bless our family with one or two more children." He looked across at Mama and she nodded. "Your mother became with child two times before you were born, and each time, the babies she bore died. I don't think you remember two years ago that there was another baby." His voice caught and tears welled. "I held a tiny boy in my large calloused hand; he took his first and last breaths within minutes. You are our only surviving child. My heart swells when I teach you Yahweh's laws and the stories of our heroes and the songs of praise."

His gaze passed above her. "I used to wish I was born into a priestly family like your mother's. Few young girls receive the teaching you do. I long for another child, perhaps a son to teach, someday." He hugged her and looked at Mama.

Mary sat hushed and frowning as she realized what her father meant. *I can't leave the temple* throbbed in her mind.

"Your father and I were thinking; if we're in a healthier place, I might birth healthier babies."

"Must we move so far away?" Mary slipped off her father's lap to hold her mother's hand. "Let's live near your cousin Elizabeth in Ein Karem. We'd walk along the creek, Mama; you'd like to do that. And it's shady and cool, and there isn't any dust." Her head whirled, and she winced at the thought of leaving Jerusalem. This was their sacred city. Jerusalem was the best place to serve the Holy One, like Anna did.

"What about moving to Bethlehem, Papa? That's where you used to live." She had to change her father's mind. "Remember when you told me the prophets said the Messiah would be born in Bethlehem? If we lived there, waiting on him and sweeping his floors would be even easier."

Mama looked at Papa.

He pressed his lips together. "Mary, the decision is already made. We're going to Nazareth. I'm depending on you to help your mother pack and get ready to move." His smile erupted. "Oh, I forgot to tell you. Taoma has a little girl about your age. Abigail. Just think how fun that would be. Even better, I'll build us a bigger house with its own courtyard." His voice swelled, the way it did when he sang the songs of King David. His eyes were gleaming, just as they did when she and her mother lit the candles on the Sabbath.

Mama grabbed her hands. "I will heal there. And what do you think of our raising our own chickens, Mary? The yard has room for a coop." Now gleams lit her mother's eyes. "Someday, your father might make me a full-size loom, and I can teach you to weave. That will be much better than little lap looms."

The melody in her mother's voice loosened the pinching in Mary's chest. When she went to bed, she asked Papa, "Will Nazareth be more beautiful than Jerusalem?"

"Nothing is more glorious than the temple of the Lord, Mary." He glanced at her mother, breathing raggedly in her sleep. "Except your mother." His lips touched the top of her head. "And you."

Dust and heat, sores from the straps on her pack, and more hills to climb. A teasing sliver of blue glittered from the Jordan River far below. Mary longed for the spring water of the Bethesda pools by their home in Jerusalem. She clenched her lips so her complaints didn't reach Mama's ears. She hadn't told her parents, but she had promised Anna she would return to help her as soon as possible. Now she grumbled at the idea of traveling this miserable road again. She thought she would have the company of a playmate, but it had taken Mama longer to pack, so Taoma's family had gone ahead without them. Now her companion was a dusty donkey Papa had named Balaam.

The three of them paused above the next stream crossing, then headed for the sycamore trees on the left where two merchants with a camel were resting. While Papa led the donkey down the river bank, her mother unwrapped locusts and dried figs. Mary propped her pack against a boulder and slumped against it, studying the camel. An icy gust swept through. Wouldn't it be wonderful to travel above all the dust? No sore feet.

A sharp sting woke her. Her left hand was tingling. She shook it and the pain exploded. "Mama! It burns." Tears spouted and Mary tried to stand up, but her head was whirling. She sunk to the ground. The merchants were starting toward her as her father climbed from the riverbank. It felt like she was lying in a fire.

Chapter 2

A bulging moon swayed and ducked behind filmy gray wisps that draped the blackness. Mary's tunic stuck to her, heavy and hot. Her heart skipped to an unknown song, and her mind couldn't comprehend the words that floated through it. Mary tried to roll on her side to wake her mother who was sleeping against her, rugs cocooned her body. "Mama. Papa." Her frail words caused her mother to surge from her blanket.

"Praise the Mighty One, everyone. She's awake. Hallelujah; my darling is awake." Around them, other long mounds wriggled, and heads emerged.

Mary's father knelt by her. "Hold still, dear one. Don't move quickly."

"I'm dizzy and my hand hurts, Papa. There's something wrapped around it, and I can't get it off. I want to go home." Papa wiped her face with his kerchief and kissed her cheek.

"She's still very warm, but better. Hannah, hand me the water while I prop her."

Water dripped on her chin when Mary tried to swallow, so her father gently wiped her and gave her another drink. "Slowly, slowly. You're still weak."

Human shadows drew closer, and Mary tried to understand what they were saying. The words made no sense. She turned to her mother. "What happened to me?"

"It was a scorpion bite. Without the ministrations of these kind travelers, we would have lost you." Mama beamed at the two men now standing at Mary's feet. She beckoned them. "Would you be so kind as to examine Mary's hand again?"

One man knelt beside her. His snowy turban covered all but a few reddish curls, and the moonlight rested on his pale jaw and open hand. *He must have a little girl of his own.* Relaxing, Mary placed her aching hand in his. He tenderly unwrapped the cloths and moved her hard, swollen arm into the silver glow.

"Is she better? Are we past danger?" Her mother sucked her breath. The man nodded, and Mama jumped up and hugged Papa.

The other merchant handed a flask to his friend.

"What are you doing?" Her mother frowned.

He smiled with his eyes while he poured. "This vinegar will clean the resin we put on her hand. Resin pulls out the poison. Messy, isn't it?" He poured from the flask.

"She'll recover?"

"Yes, honored lady. She will be fine. Fortune smiled on us. We treated her quickly enough to sweat out the poison."

The other merchant laid his hand on her father's shoulder. "You would do well to stay another day for her to sweat more and rest."

Mary's eyelids flickered shut, and the surrounding murmuring faded.

No other travelers were camping by the river when Mary woke. Beside her, Mama was weaving on the lap loom. Long shadows spread toward the meandering tree line of the Jordan.

"Where's Papa?"

Her mother set down her shuttle and moved the loom aside. "He's hunting for locusts and grasshoppers." She laughed at Mary's frown. "It's what travelers eat when they don't reach their town by nightfall." She pulled the rug from Mary's arm. "Let's see if you can rise without getting dizzy." She knelt by Mary and helped her to her knees. "Take a moment to get your balance before you try to walk."

"I don't want to travel anymore. Can we go back to Jerusalem?"

Mama handed her the water skin. The water was as warm as Mary's mouth. Her hands quivered, and most of it landed in her lap.

"Is your mouth still numb? Here; let me help."

Papa came down the hill above her with a bulging sack. "Mary, my love; are you well?" She nodded. "Good. We'll eat and then go on until dark. We can make good time now that the heat is lessening. Soon we'll be in Nazareth."

Seven days later, Mary stood at the base of another hill staring at the cluster of homes squatting on top. How green and cool Nazareth looked. There couldn't be more than twenty or thirty homes. She couldn't even distinguish a synagogue. How would they worship? And would Mama truly be healed here? Mary thought back over the last two weeks. She shook her head; there wasn't a single time that her mother had coughed.

Papa removed two small sacks from the donkey and held them out. "Let's keep going. If you and your Mama each take a little more weight from Balaam here, we can reach Nazareth before dark." He wiped Mary's sweat-streaked cheeks. "When the last group of travelers passed us yesterday, I told them to leave word with Taoma that we would arrive tonight. I'm guessing his wife Orli will have a hot meal ready for us and bread with yeast."

"Papa, I hope you aren't teasing me. I would love some fluffy bread, and I can't wait to meet Abigail." Since the scorpion bite, Mary tried to think of good things about Nazareth so her mother and father wouldn't worry about her. She set her heart on Abigail.

"Then let's put our climbing legs to work." He gave her a quick kiss and picked up the donkey's lead.

...

Abigail. She was quiet and calm. She could recite wonderful stories from the scriptures. She loved to play with dolls, and sing songs about the Lord. That was the Abigail Mary had imagined. That Abigail had not moved to Nazareth.

Taoma's Abigail wasn't interested in being a playmate. She liked to tag after her brothers, especially Caleb. She repeated everything he said as though it was scripture itself. "Caleb can recite all the books of the prophets and play the lute and sing King David's songs."

Mary's eyes climbed into her eyebrows. "Do you know the alphabet proverb of a godly wife? My papa says that about my mama all the time, and he taught it to me."

"No, I haven't heard that one. It must not be very important."

Mary blinked. "It's the sayings about a woman who reveres the Lord."

"Caleb knows more important sayings than that. He makes his own."

"What proverbs have you learned?"

"My father says I don't need to learn them, as long as Caleb and my brothers do. Papa says my husband will teach me what I need to know when I'm married, just as he taught my mother."

Mary fidgeted. As soon as Abigail left to find her brothers, she went behind their tent where her father and his new helper Josef were stacking stones for their house. "Papa, is it proper for me to learn our scriptures?"

Her father lay down his chisel and dusted his hands. He lifted Mary onto a low olive branch and wiped his sweaty face. "That's a crucial question, isn't it?"

She nodded, struck by his rare seriousness.

"Have we ever talked about the women who have played an important part in the history of our people?"

"Yes." His silence prompted her to recall his lessons. "Miriam!"

"Why Miriam?"

"She watched over Moses when he was a baby, and later she led the women with singing and dancing when our people left Egypt."

"Any other reason for Miriam?"

Giggling erupted. "I'm named for her." She squinted, remembering other women from her father's lessons. "Rahab. She hid the spies so our people could capture Jericho." Her father smiled, waiting. "The judge, Deborah, and that other one, the prophetess; is it Hildah?" Her father shook his head. "I know, Papa, I know; it's Huldah. She was the one who prophesied over King Josiah when his scribes and priests couldn't hear from heaven."

"At supper tonight, I want you to tell me two more names of women who hold a special place in the story of our people. We are the people of the Book, all of us - men and women." He lifted Mary from the branch and dusted the back of her tunic. "You may ask your mother to help you." Giving her father a quick hug, she ran to the tent.

Mary brought the grapes and bread to the low table and knelt between her parents. "Why don't Abigail's mama and papa teach her about our scriptures? I don't think she knows any of them. How will she be a good mama when she grows up?"

"I'm sure she will be a very loving mother," Mama said. "You know how much she loves her parents and how devoted she is to Caleb and Gideon."

Her face brightened. "I love my parents more than the sun and the moon and the stars, but not as much as the Holy One. Papa, didn't you tell me the Holy One will always send help when we need it? He sent Moses to our people. He sent Abigail to King David. Mama also reminded me of one more woman: Eve, and the scroll of Beginnings says someday a woman will have a baby who will defeat Satan."

Papa tugged her braids. "What do you remember about Queen Esther?"

"It would have been scary to be her."

"She was very brave and obedient, wasn't she?"

"Papa, do you think Anna is a prophetess like Huldah was?"

"Anna? We don't know an Anna." He laughed.

"Do you mean Anna, the sweeper in Jerusalem?" Mama said. She looked over Mary's head. "Some people at the temple call her a prophetess."

Papa shook his head and hugged Mary. "It's not likely the Lord of Heaven is sending us prophets anymore, or prophetesses, although we need them, little one." He ran his fingers through his hair. "What we need even more is our Messiah.

That night Mary's thoughts tumbled as she hunted for sleep. The life of their people was in jeopardy from the Romans, and there were more Romans in Galilee than in Jerusalem. Her parents sometimes talked about King Herod's evil ways when they thought she was asleep. *Can I be as brave as Queen Esther when I grow up? Can I be the servant Anna said I would be? Sometimes prophets were wrong. What if Anna is wrong? What if Anna isn't a prophet?* The unsettling thoughts kept sleep at bay.

"It's time I taught you to weave," Mary's mother said a few days later. "I visited with Abigail's mother Orli at the well yesterday. I know you hoped to play with Abigail, but she's still busy with her brothers."

Sparkles lit Mary's eyes. The full-sized loom against the side of the tent was her father's latest project. She ran her hand up and down the smooth oak frame.

"Ha-ha; not yet, my darling. I'll start you with my lap loom. You've already been such a help for me with carding and spinning. Would you like to make a sash for your tunic?"

"Yes. Then I'll make one for Abigail."

"I'm sure she'd like that."

"Then tomorrow will you teach me how to use your new loom?"

"Let's see how well you work today."

At the end of the day, her fingers cramped and her back ached. "It didn't seem this hard when you were weaving, Mama. I wanted to give a sash to Abigail tomorrow, but mine is crooked, and I couldn't get all the yarns tight. I'm too tired to make Abigail's."

"You've made a fine start. Do you want to practice more tomorrow before you make Abigail's?"

Mary nodded solemnly.

The next afternoon Mary was inspecting the new chicken coop her father had made when Abigail walked over.

"Can you play?"

"Where did your brothers go?" Mary said, going back in the tent.

Abigail followed her. "Papa took them to the vineyard. At last, the vineyards belong to us. They have to help him all the time, now that he made the last payment. Today they're learning to trim the grapes."

Mary's mother turned from her loom. "You must feel lonely without them."

"Mama wouldn't let me go with them. She says I have to help her more. This morning I had to wash clothes and sweep while she was mending and cooking."

Mary picked up her woven sash. Tentatively, she showed it to Abigail. "See what I made."

Abigail stretched it. "Oh, I can weave, too. But my sashes are straight." She handed it back. "I'll make one for you."

Mary stuffed the sash back in the basket, swiped her eyes, and glanced at her mother. "Uh, thank you," she mumbled. Her eyes darted around the tent. "See the new loom my father made. Now my mother can make cloth to sell."

Abigail's mouth opened. "That's a beautiful loom. I didn't know your father could make something like that."

Hannah pulled Abigail to her with a hug. "Abigail, did you know that my husband and your father are longtime friends?" Abigail nodded. "We agreed to come to Nazareth together so we could help one another make a new life. Your father is growing grapes and selling wine, and Mary's father will make a better wine press and help him build more rooms on your house. I'm making cloth and your mother dyes it. We all find something to do that will help the others." She grabbed a hand of each girl and drew them to her. "You both are kind children. Our Father in heaven has put wonderful talents in each of you, yes?"

Abigail squirmed and Mary shrugged her shoulders.

"Mary, why don't you take your dolly outside to play with Abigail?"

When she snuggled under her blanket that night, Mary grabbed her mother's arm. "Are we going to have sheep, too?"

"We need their wool, and we need the meat afterwards for our sacrifices and for food."

"Can I have a lamb of my very own?"

"Yes, but baby lambs grow up, Mary. I don't want you to get too attached. Raising a lamb isn't like playing with your dolls."

A few weeks later, late in the morning, Papa peered in the tent's door, brushing dust from his tunic. "Is it too early to eat?"

"Heli, have you noticed our girl using the lap loom? She is learning so quickly."

"She'll have scarves and coverings for all of us before I finish our house, won't she?" He tickled Mary and brushed her mother's cheek. Mama handed him a loaf of bread and some cheese. He stuffed them in his mouth. "Do you have some bread and cheese I can take to Josef?" Food in his hands, he slipped away. The clunking of stones began again.

"I miss talking with Papa. He's so tired at night he forgets to pray the prayers with me."

"Once, Mary; he forgot one time. But Taoma's neighbor's son from Bethlehem is only here for a month."

"I don't like Josef."

"Mary! Shame on you. He's a wonderful assistant for your father, and he's a quick learner."

"But he's ugly."

"Because of his wrinkled scar? That's just on the outside. Better to have a scarred face than a scarred heart. We don't judge people by their looks; what counts is their kindness or generosity." She took the lap loom from Mary.

Mary looked up, jutting her lip. "Papa spends all his time with him. He doesn't do things with me anymore."

"Papa is trying to build a workshop for himself and a house for us as fast as he can so we can move out of this tent. Josef is helping him. Anything that helps your father makes life easier for you and me. Have you thought about Josef? Do you think he enjoys being away from his family?"

Mary shook her head.

"In a few days the workshop will be ready; then we can move in there. We've finished gathering the stones, so the construction of the house will go faster." At Mary's bright face, Mama said. "But don't think you'll have more time with your Papa. With the house finished, he'll be making stools, carts, everything."

"Then Josef can go home, and I can be his helper!"

After eight more Sabbaths, squared logs covered with brush and mud replaced the leaky canopy of skins, shutters swung together at night on iron hinges, plaster covered the walls, and rolled wool blankets pillowed smooth benches.

Papa declared a festival, and neighbors Mary had never seen before streamed into the courtyard. Widow Rachel, whom she had met at the well, brought figs and apples and her flute. The family who lived at the top of the street brought stewed eggplant and tambourines, and Caleb trailed his parents, playing his lute.

"Oh good," Mary whispered to Abigail, "sesame buns and dates and dried fish."

"My father brought his wines," Abigail said. "He told me it's like wine Father Abraham made from vines he and his nephew and the other Sumer people planted a long, long time ago."

Taoma caught Abigail's eye and threaded his way to the girls, waving a small jug in each hand. "Do you want Abraham's wine or Lot's?" They grimaced as they sipped. "I've started pruning my vines a new way," he said. "Wait until I restore their health; then my wine will be unmatched." He clicked the two jugs and wandered over to other neighbors.

Her eyes succumbed, and Mary fell asleep on a bench while dancing swirled around her.

Chapter 3

Papa rose before sunrise to tell Josef goodbye before he left for Bethlehem. Grabbing the broom, Mary swept the floor and straightened the sleeping mats.

"You finished your chores early today," Mama said. "Do you want to use my loom?"

Mary stroked the loom. She had spun enough yarn to attach the warp threads the night before. "May I see Papa's workshop first?"

At her mother's smile, she slipped away. Her father built the workshop against the back of the house and, like the house, the window was on the south side. She waved to her father inside as she passed. He lay down his plane and waited for her. He tenderly placed a wooden box in her hands. "I have a lesson to teach you. Smell this small chest, Mary. Each tree has its own perfume; can you tell me which wood I used?"

She sniffed and shook her head. "Is this olive wood?"

"Olive has a strong fragrance, but it also has varied shades of brown and you'll see the twisted curves of the branches." He held out a paddle. "Like this piece here. Try again."

Mary wrinkled her nose. "Cedar?"

"Excellent. Doesn't it smell like our Lord's house in Jerusalem? King Solomon built the very first temple with the cedars of Lebanon, and King Herod has used cedar. Now what about this sappy branch?"

She shook her head. "I don't know any other trees."

"This one is pine; we eat their nuts. You'll soon learn to tell them apart."

"I want to be your helper."

"Why don't your mother and I share your abilities? You help her with cooking and weaving. You can help me now by cleaning. Why don't you sweep the sawdust?"

Mary spun, her face gleaming until the swirling grit prompted a sneeze. "Papa, I think I should sweep first and then dance."

Mama laughed when Mary came back jabbering about what her father was making and what she wanted to build.

"You aren't coughing anymore, Mama. You used to cough when you laughed." Mary hugged her mother. "And I can tell you are eating better." She patted her mother's belly.

"That's not from more food, Mary. A baby is growing there."

Mary covered her mouth and tears swelled until they slid down her cheeks. "Oh Mama." She placed her arms around her mother, then dropped them suddenly. "I'm sorry."

"What do you mean? This is a good thing; having a baby is a blessing."

"It's so sad to lose another baby, though."

"I will not lose this one, Mary. With you and Papa, and Orli to help, all will go well."

"How can I help? I don't know what to do."

"When the time comes, in three or four more months, I will tell you. And you can pray. Prayer is always most important. For now, we need to make soup. Rich foods every night aren't healthy."

"Papa said I should first help you every day before I help him. Do you think I'll ever play with Abigail again?"

"Oh, yes."

...

"Mary, come quickly." Papa grabbed Mary's hand and pulled her along the street. "I want you to see this." He took her to a stable at the bottom of the hill and pointed inside. "It's your lamb. It's being born right now. Nahor the shepherd sent word."

"Is this the mother sheep we bought?"

"No, we are only purchasing the lamb. The ewe comes from good stock, but this is her first lambing."

Mary examined the beardless man in the gray leather tunic. "My customers like to verify they're getting the lamb from the ewe they chose;

that's why I invited you to see the birth. We don't always bring the sheep off the hills." He smiled at her and motioned her closer. "Your Papa told me you wanted a lamb to raise. That's a lot of work. Ask my uncle here." He motioned to an old humpbacked man in the corner.

"You're right; sheep are a lot of work. People baby them too much, like Nahor here. Leave the dams in the field to drop the lambs themselves. That's what I always did."

"Uncle, you're right that the ewes do fine by themselves. I've found, though, that with first-time mothers, I don't lose as many of them or their babes if I watch over them. When I see their swelling, I bring them in."

The uncle glared and cleared his throat. "Nonsense."

Mary crept next to Nahor. "Why is the mama sheep groaning and squealing?"

"I think one of the lamb's legs is backward. I have to help her. That's why I'm going to reach in and straighten it."

"Won't that hurt the mama?"

"Not much. It's better than having the lamb and its mama die. Let me step outside to rinse my hand here that got in the droppings."

Tears rolled down Mary's pinched face while she prayed for the bleating ewe and her baby. Abruptly, the uncle bounded forward, knelt on the ground, and reached into the ewe. With a squeal from the panting animal, Nahor extracted a slimy body and lay it against the panting sheep. "There. It's done." He narrowed his eyes at Mary's father and jutted his chin, then wiped his hands and arms on his cloak. He stomped from the shed as Nahor came in.

The shepherd looked at the lamb and its mother and shook his head. He frowned. "Not quite how I wanted to do it," he said, shaking his head. "That lamb looks like a wet towel, doesn't it?"

"What happens to it now?" She feared asking if it was dead. Her father put his arm around her.

Nahor patted the ewe. "We wait to see what the mama does, whether she licks it or rejects it."

Mary held her breath as the ewe wavered, eyeing the sodden body. A slight shudder in the lamb evidenced life, and Nahor nudged the ewe. She staggered closer, bending toward her lamb. "Do it; do it," whispered the shepherd, cradling the tiny head.

Her father knelt beside her, and Mary leaned against him. Her chest heaved as she prayed aloud. "Save my lamb, dear Lord; save him." The ewe took one more step forward and began stroking the lamb with her tongue. "Thank you, dear Lord. See, Papa, the Holy One even cares for little lambs." She buried her head against his shoulder. "I'm so happy. I have a lamb of my very own."

"You know that the lamb has to stay with its mother until it's weaned, Mary."

"That's all right, Papa. But can I go out on the hills and watch it sometimes?"

Nahor smiled. "I think I can keep the herd in this area for a few more weeks. The grasses have benefitted from our early spring showers."

Six nights later, Nahor came to the door with the lamb in his arms. "I am grieved to tell you that the ewe became sick and died. The problem now is our young one here needs a new mama. Would your daughter be willing?"

Mary pushed between her parents. "I can do this; I'm willing." She held out her arms.

Nahor hesitated until her father nodded. "There's a milk goat up the street; can we use its milk?"

"Yes; that will do. The lamb is heavier now," the shepherd said. "He's growing fast. Let me show you how to feed him with this wineskin."

Her eyes bulged as she concentrated on Nahor's instructions. "I must sit to hold him." She plopped on the floor and made a nest for the lamb. "Can I hold him now?"

The lamb bleated and scooted away. "Wait! Come back." She jumped up and scrambled after him.

"Let me settle him. He's used to being fed by me, and he's not used to you yet."

...

Mary was falling asleep during the evening prayers after a fortnight of tending Moses. (She named him that because the lamb, like their famous leader, was taken from his mother and raised in another family, she informed every visitor.) While Mary swept, collected eggs from the chickens, and fetched water, Moses, like a dutiful son, trotted beside her until the day he was no longer so docile, stepping on the eggs, chewing on her mother's balls of yarn, and knocking over her father's pile of lumber.

"It's time to send Moses out to the pastures," Papa said. "He's getting too big for us to keep here, and he needs to feed on the hills with the rest of the herd."

Mary covered her face to hide her tears.

"You knew this day would come, Mary. He's still your lamb, and you'll get to see him when we collect his wool."

"I'm afraid he'll forget me."

"He won't forget you, but he has another purpose now." Papa pulled on his chin. "There's another responsibility I have for you now." He cleared his throat. "Passover is only ten days off. It's time to leave."

"I can't wait. I've missed the temple so much. This will be wonderful. Now I won't mind leaving Moses."

Her father looked away, then down at his feet.

"Papa, you know I've been practicing all the climbing psalms to sing when we go up that Amen road." Her father's chortle stopped her. "Why are you laughing?"

"You're more right than you realize. The road that goes up from Jericho is the Adummim, but we sing lots of 'Amens' at the end of our songs, don't we?" His smile warmed her.

"I want to sing the one about being in exile and coming back to Jerusalem. Don't you feel like we've been in exile in Nazareth?"

"I need your help for a very crucial task, Mary." He closed his eyes and grimaced.

"Do you want me to carry a pack? I'm stronger now; I can carry a lot."

His silence pushed against her until he cleared his throat. "Your mother can't travel at the risk of losing the baby. I need you to stay home with her."

"Oh." Mary pressed her fingers against her eyelids and her shoulders heaved.

Her father pulled her against his chest. "I'm trusting you."

"What if the baby comes?"

"I don't think that will happen; it's still too soon. If it does, go to Abigail's house; Orli will be here. She just had her baby a few weeks ago; she'll know what to do." He stooped and took her hands. "Will you do this for me?"

The sun inched across the sky the first day after her father left. Mary missed his humming psalms. In spite of the little sweet-cake Mama helped her bake, the hours were hollow; even getting to work on the lap loom held no allure.

"Don't you want to play with Abigail? You don't need to stay with me every moment." Her mother sat and took a deep breath.

"I'm fine. Abigail must be cleaning the house for her mother. I haven't even seen them outside."

"Don't you want to fetch some water? Then you can visit with the other women and girls who stayed home."

"Papa and I did that yesterday, and the only lady there was Widow Rachel. She said all the others have gone to Passover." Mary turned away to hide her frown. At her mother's quick grunt, she swung back. "What's that?"

"It's nothing; only my body reminding me there's a baby inside."

"It's too soon for the baby to come; Papa said so."

Mama turned away and Mary's suspicions rose. "Should I get Abigail's mother?"

"No, Mary; I'm fine. There are other signs when a baby comes, and this one isn't ready for at least two months, more likely three. Come here; we need to card more wool. Would you like to make a blanket for the baby? You can have it ready to show Papa when he returns."

Mary stayed by her mother's side for the next few days, and she ran each time she left to fetch water or buy grain. No twitches or squeaks or groans troubled her mother. "See, Mary; the baby is safe. Why don't you ask Abigail to come play this afternoon? We haven't seen her since last Sabbath. She must be busy helping her mother with their new baby."

Mary skipped from the house. Low dark clouds circled Nazareth, hiding the fields below. The air lay damp and a faint odor of wood ash drifted past. She slowed her step and crossed her arms to rub heat into her skin. Most of the homes had shuttered doors and windows, even Abigail's house. Only Widow Rachel's house down the street had a plume of smoke rising. *Were they saving firewood for this evening's supper?* Tendrils of fog crept up the hill from the vineyards. Mary wrapped her stole tighter and rapped on Abigail's door. There was still no answer after the second try. She walked around the house; no sounds anywhere. She knocked once more before turning back home.

"I don't know where they are, Mama. They may have gone to visit neighbors."

"Never mind, then. We'll work on yarn for the baby's blanket."

Mary shifted a bristly handful of wool from hand to hand. "Why does it take so long to prepare this? If I could comb Moses' coat every day, it wouldn't be all this work. I never knew sheep could get so much straw and bugs on them." She pushed the ball into soapy water and picked up the stirring stick.

Her mother reached into the basket, grabbed a bundle of clean dry wool with one hand and leaned down to the floor for her carding combs. "Ugh! Oh no." She grasped her gown, using it to swab water seeping down her legs. "Mary," she gasped. "Get someone. Anyone." She hobbled toward the sleeping mat and jerked it onto the floor. Mary froze. Her mother turned back. "Now. Please hurry." She grabbed some towels and sunk onto the mattress.

Chapter 4

Mary left the house and looked for a neighbor in the street. At the top of the hill, two Roman soldiers staggered from an alehouse, shouting slurred calls to those still inside. The fog had rolled up the hill, hiding and then revealing buildings like a game of peek-a-boo.

"Ho, we have company in the frigid mists," bellowed one man. "A sweet young girl." The taller soldier stumbled, righted himself, and started toward Mary.

Who else is home? Who has a light on? A dim flicker came from Widow Rachel's. Mary ran. *At least the widow would know what to do.* She pounded on the door. No sound. The men called from five houses away. "Wait, little miss, are you alone? We'll help you."

A steady thumping from the widow's cane came from inside. "Who's there?"

"Widow Rachel, it's me, Mary. My mother is having her baby. She needs help."

The door scraped open. "Mary? What's wrong?"

"The baby is coming and my mother needs someone to help. I tried to get Abigail's mama, but no one's home. Can you come?" Mary felt a prickling in her back.

The soldiers had stopped beside her. "We'll help this girl get home. Leave her with us."

"Off with you. You have no business here." The widow waved her cane at them. "Go away now." They laughed as she pulled Mary inside and shut the door. "What can I do, dear? I never had a child myself. I haven't even been to a baby's birth for ten years."

"Where is Orli? Mama said I was to get her. Is she at the market?"

"They wanted to show little Daniel to their family in Bethlehem, so they all went to Jerusalem."

"We have to do something."

Rachel stared at Mary. "You're right." She banked her fire, grabbed a wrap, and pushed Mary ahead of her out the door.

The tapping of her cane echoed off stone walls as they hurried up the street. "I'm scared," Mary whispered.

"There's no reason to be afraid. Babies are born all the time."

"But Mama has lost all the others since me. That's why we moved to Nazareth." She choked back tears. "So she could have another baby."

"Are you praying, Mary?"

"Yes."

"Then that's enough. The good Lord knows what He's doing."

A feeble bleat reached them when they opened the door. "Mama, are you all right?" Mary tiptoed to her mother. The wet bundle on her stomach looked like her lamb Moses when he was born.

Hannah smiled wanly at their neighbor. "Greetings, Rachel. I believe I need some help with the birth cord. There's a knife on the shelf over there and some yarn by the loom. And could you see that Mary brings us some jugs of water?"

The widow grabbed the knife and held it until Mama indicated the place to cut. They both looked at Mary. "Let her see. She may need to know herself someday."

"I'd be of more help to you if others had asked me to attend them at childbirth." Rachel grimaced as she made the cut under Mama's direction. She pointed to Mary. "Now you can fetch the water." Mary started to the kitchen. "Wait," Rachel called out. "Bring the salt too. We're supposed to rub it on the baby to purge the skin."

Her mother's loud "No" halted Mary. Hannah looked fiercely at Rachel. "My first two babies were early and the midwife salted them heavily. They died. I didn't let anyone salt Mary here, and I'm not rubbing it on this child. You can bring the water now, sweetheart."

When Mary returned, the baby snuggled against her mother's breast, and the soggy blanket was replaced with one of the new ones her mother had woven. Mary tiptoed closer. "Is it a boy or a girl?"

"It's a little girl, sweet like you."

The widow gently touched the soft skin. "Did you and Heli pick a name?"

Mama tucked her head. "We had discussed a name for a boy," she said. She straightened and smiled at Mary. "I think we should let you choose the baby's name, Mary. You were a wonderful help for me today - more than most little girls of seven years. We'll see if your father agrees when he gets home."

"This will be a wonderful surprise, won't it, Mama?"

"Yes, it surely will be."

"I want to name her Salome, because she will bring you and Papa peace."

...

In her first year, Salome fed and slept and grew, and Mary spent more time with her father when he wasn't chipping stone at the quarry. "Don't you need me to sweep again? Do you want me to sort the woods? I can tell cedar from pine and almond wood from olive now."

"I have to work outside to make these door frames, Mary."

"Can I help inside, though? When I'm in your workshop, I feel like I'm back at the temple." Papa waved his hand toward her. "Go on, then."

Mary slipped around the door and closed her eyes. She inhaled deeply. The rich scents of pine and cedar surrounded her like perfume. She looked around to see what new woods her father had brought in. A long gray branch leaned in the corner. *Was this locust?* On the shelf beside it were three goblets. She gently lifted one and slid her fingers around the bowl, stroking the slender stem. The pale wood suggested apple.

Her father came in the shop, grinning widely at the goblet in her hand. "You know I enjoy making special pieces like the goblets and ladles."

"I love to watch you use the plane, especially when the curly strips float away from the logs. They're like tawny wings. I think you make the eagles jealous, Papa."

"You're wrong there, darling. No one can create like our heavenly Father."

"I'm sorry, Papa; I didn't mean disrespect."

Mary ran her hand over the satiny curves. "There's not one speck of sawdust on this one, Papa. Is it ready for the finish?"

When Heli began the last step of applying the citron resin, the fragrance hovered around them, and the sense that they were in the temple was complete.

At bedtime, while her mother sang lullabies to Salome, Papa taught Mary psalms and scriptures. *If only Abigail loved repeating the Lord's word.*

"Do you know what my papa taught me last night?" was her usual remark when she met Abigail at the well.

"No, but I'm sure you'll tell me." Abigail filled her jugs while Mary recited verses.

A week later, Mary met her friend at the well again. "You'll never guess what my father reminded me last night."

"Did King David win another battle, or was it Samson's battle?" Abigail simpered.

"No, this is better." Mary set her jugs next to the well until Abigail looked at her. "The holy scriptures say the Messiah will be born in Bethlehem. That's where you're from."

"So?" Abigail tossed her head and filled her jugs.

"What if it's someone you know? It might be your cousin Leah."

"Leah doesn't have a husband; she can't have a baby yet."

"My Papa laughed when he told me. He said when he was a boy, he and his friends would tease each other, saying their sisters wouldn't have a chance because they were too bossy." She stepped up to the well. "Maybe that's why he married my mother; she's from Jerusalem."

"It won't be us either then," Abigail said. "I wouldn't want to have the Messiah as my son. He would probably boss me around."

"But what if you got to be the Queen Mother, Abigail? What if it's one of your girlfriends in Bethlehem? Maybe they would invite you to their palace."

When Mary finished drawing water, the girls each lifted a jug to her head and held the other to her chest as they climbed home.

"I would be happy just sweeping the floors of Messiah's palace. Can you imagine how wonderful it would be to meet him?" Mary said.

Abigail sputtered. "He'll want nothing to do with country girls like us."

...

"Did you trade Salome for another girl?" Abigail asked Mary's mother one afternoon. "This little girl looks like Salome, and she knows who we are, but I don't know who she is."

When Salome learned to walk, she ran. When she learned to talk, she shouted. She fascinated Abigail, who only had brothers, and she and Mary drew closer as Abigail came regularly to help entertain the little girl.

Mama shook her head and smiled. "What a wonder she is, but such a contradiction from her peaceful name. We have to move water jugs away and anything else we don't want broken or in a tangle. You'll see, Abigail. Soon the entire neighborhood will grab for their jugs and baskets when they see Salome appear."

"Mama, what gives her that energy? Do you think some nomads switched her on us? She's like a whirlwind, rushing and yelling wherever she goes." Mary held up her hands. "I try to be her protection, but she's always twenty paces ahead of me. I fear when she runs into Papa's workshop. She dashes under his workbench and runs out again. What if she knocks over goblets or spills the resin?"

Mama shook her head. "I know the Lord of Heaven's Armies has a wonderful plan for Salome, just as he has for you."

"Did Anna, the sweeper, tell you?"

"What are you talking about?"

Mary looked away as she spoke. "Never mind, Mama." Blushing, she quickly inserted the shuttle through the weft. "How is my weaving looking?"

"Hmm, you were doing well until this last row. See here where you skipped three?"

She ducked her head. "I'm sorry."

...

At least once a week at dinner-time Papa put his hands on his knees and sighed. "We should have named her Thunder or Stormy instead of Peace."

"Maybe she just has to grow into her name, Papa."

Mama's remark about a plan for Salome's life troubled Mary. She pondered Salome's behavior. Her sister was always thinking up adventures. If Mama asked Salome to bring in the eggs, she climbed the small fig tree to reach the roof and then jumped onto the shed and slid into the chicken yard.

In contrast, Mary daydreamed lazily, content to see angel wings in the wispy clouds overhead. *Was this the future Anna the prophetess had predicted? How could chasing after her sister prepare her to serve in the temple? We climb trees together,* she thought, *but Salome scrambles from branch to branch while I make up songs about pomegranate blossoms in spring or eagles soaring.* When there were visitors, Sali stood in the center of the room singing through her little collection of songs until Mama shushed her and sent her outside.

As busy as Sali was during the day, at night she loved to hear the stories about the heroes. "Mary, sing me David's song about defeating his enemies. Open the heavens, Yahweh. Hurl your lightning bolts and scatter your enemies! Shoot your arrows and confuse them."

Finally, after an adventure or two, Salome was happy just to chirp refrains of "His loving kindness endures forever" until she settled to sleep. Mary would continue to sing to herself, resting in the Lord's love for little ones, making her own verses about His mercy and faithfulness to humble people like her parents.

"Why is Salome playing with Abigail's little brother and his friends? Why isn't she helping at home?" Papa complained regularly, but the more he watched his youngest daughter, and the more he tasted her dry breads and put on the dingy clothes that she helped wash, the more he shrugged his shoulders and told Mary, "She'll learn someday."

Her father's work was so well made, after a few years people came from Cana and Sepphoris. As a builder, he had orders for everything from carts to houses, rakes to bowls. Each morning began with "Please, Hannah, let me have Mary's help again today." Mary couldn't keep up. Although her father taught her to chisel platters and bowls, she didn't have the strength he needed for lifting cart wheels. Within another year, his shop became crowded with benches needing repair and logs to be planed for window frames as jobs piled up around him.

That Spring, when the family went to Jerusalem for Passover, Father met with former friends from Bethlehem. Three months later, his new helper began working in his shop, boarding with Widow Rachel.

"Josef? Mama, why Josef?"

"Your father knows best. Josef is a strong, capable man, and a hard worker."

A week later when Josef had returned to the widow's home for the evening, Mary whined. "Why is Josef here, Papa? You don't need him; you have me to help."

Her father gave a crooked smile. "I need help hauling the large timbers and lifting the stone blocks, and I have much more work."

Putting his arm around her shoulder early one morning, Papa said, "Mary, my workshop is small for three people. Your mother needs more help, and you have much to learn. She has many things she hasn't taught you yet." He shrugged. "And someday you will want your children to rise up and call you 'Blessed.'" He wrapped his arms around her.

"You don't need me anymore."

He took a deep breath. "It's more than that. Mama will explain. You can ask her."

Mary shook her head and turned away. "Wait!" She grabbed his tunic. "Papa, will you still teach me King David's songs?"

"That won't change, dear Mary."

Just like women were excluded from going inside the temple in Jerusalem, she felt banished from her sacred retreat. Mary stood silently. The scent of cedar seemed to waft across her. She pictured the latest set of trays the innkeeper had ordered. She squeezed her fist as if she were gripping the plane. Her chest felt bruised.

A light brushing sound drew her around. Her mother stood a few feet away, arms outstretched. "Your papa is a wonderful man, and I know you will miss working with him." Mary fell into her mother's hug, sobbing.

Chapter 5

Josef clung to the shadows or slipped outside if Mary was around. "What a strange man," she told her mother. "He takes his midday meal from Father and goes to the back side to eat alone." Even on Sabbath, he stayed away from most people and stood against the wall by himself. Mary heard some women at the well whispering that Josef was in his twenties and not betrothed yet. Her father praised his helper's work and bragged to friends about his skill.

"I have been remiss," Papa said one evening. "Mary, I taught you our scriptures and the alphabet, but I've neglected teaching Salome. Would you be willing to teach your sister?"

Mary giggled as she pictured her fidgety sister. "If you teach her how to sit still, I won't mind, Papa. I'll spend the daylight learning what Mama has for me to do and teach her in the evenings."

When the two girls climbed into their loft that night, Mary whispered to Salome. "I thought I knew everything Mama does for us; I hadn't paid attention before."

"She just grinds the grain and makes our meals and washes cloths and weaves. What else is there?"

"I've helped her with the baking and cleaning and washing and even making candles. Who cleans the oil lamps? And what about all the information she knows, like where to buy the best grains or which merchant has the freshest fruit or which one will try to weight the scales?"

"Will I learn all that someday, too?" Salome scratched her head.

"And butchering chickens." She wrapped her arm over Sali's shoulder. "You have six years already; I'm almost twice as old as you. Try to learn something each month."

"I wish the only chore I had was going to the well to fetch water, unless it's the third time on a hot day!" Sali yawned. "Will you tell me the story about Moses and Pharaoh tonight, Mary?"

...

"Mama, I'm jealous of Sali." Mary pulled the linens from the soapy water, wringing them into a long tight rope before carrying them over to the wall. "When I was little, Papa took me along to deliver stools or tables, but now he takes Sali while Josef stays and works in the workshop."

"The time you spent helping your father was precious. You're missing that, aren't you?" Her mother sighed.

Mary looked up. Her mother was looking down the hill at the road leading to Jerusalem. "Mama, do you miss Jerusalem? Do you miss living behind our temple?" A fleeting image of a woman sweeping flitted through Mary's mind. "There are people at the temple I wish I could see, too."

Mama tilted her head at Mary. "Do you remember when I used to cough from the dust?" Mary nodded. "Now I have two healthy girls and a wonderful, handsome husband who has a successful business. The Lord has blessed me in several ways." She grabbed an end of the wet cloth and helped Mary spread it open.

...

"I love working with wool, Mama. Fancy stitching is too tedious." Mary held the tunic she was embroidering. "Who needs pretty clothes?"

"We all do, Mary. Sometimes there are special occasions." Her mother took the linen robe and spread it across her lap. "Look how even your stitches are now. Would you like me to show you how to embroider pomegranates and daises? Rows of leaves and lilies are tiring. The thread colors aren't as vibrant, either."

"I'd rather weave. It's so much faster." Mary picked up a thick ball of yarn and rubbed it against her cheek. "I'm so glad you still want me making blankets. We're going to have plenty for winter."

The next day Mary was walking back from the market with Abigail. "Does your mother have you decorating tunics with those intricate designs and piling blankets for winter?"

"They're for our dowry. Haven't you noticed? My father and yours have been giving us earrings for our birthdays the last two years. Those are for our dowry, too."

"Dowry? I've never heard that word before."

Abigail looked sideways at her and snickered. "You're joking, aren't you?" At Mary's puzzled face, Abigail listed steps that lay ahead for girls their age: the betrothal, the waiting, the wedding, and – yes, the coming together as one.

Pale-faced, Mary shuffled into her house. She placed the fresh fish in the clay pot and slid it in the oven. She glanced at her mother and took a deep breath.

"Mama, what is happening? Am I preparing for betrothal?"

"Ah, Abigail is quicker than I am." She smiled and embraced Mary. "My parents betrothed me when I was thirteen. Since you are that age now, it's time for us to make an alliance to ready you for marriage." Prickles studded Mary's heart while she formed a protest. No reason surfaced to block her parents' plans.

The next day, Mary hurried through her chores so she and her friend would have time to talk. Marriage! Who would even look at them? "We'll marry someone from Nazareth, won't we?" she said. They began naming the older boys in the neighborhood.

"I hope I have a young husband, but my mother said they're looking for a man with wealth, and none of the young men have much money yet. Also, older men are more stable." She frowned.

Whether it was a wedding, a funeral, or a new birth, whenever the community gathered, the two girls inspected the bachelors with sidelong glances and whispers behind their hands, trying to guess which handsome neighbor or traveling merchant would be their match. Would it be a tradesman in Nazareth or a fisherman from the sea? Would it be Abigail's brother Caleb or Gideon for Mary or someone her father's age?

"My parents told me they're looking for someone older for me because they feel I'm too flighty for a younger man," Abigail announced. "I hope that doesn't mean Farmer Obed; he has a daughter my age. Neither would I want Josef. He acts so strange around people."

"You're right. Nobody would want him."

"My mother said the custom was for the man to find the woman he wanted and make arrangements with her father. We girls have no say." Tears slid down Abigail's face. "I can't help worrying about all the older men around us, especially those who have already buried one wife."

Mary squeezed her hand. "I'll pray for you." She tilted her head. "I can trust my father. He knows me so well, and he knows who would take care of me the best. Still, I also hope it won't be Josef - or your brother Gideon; you've already told me he snores." The girls giggled.

Abigail and Mary were talking at the well a few weeks later when Widow Rachel came up behind them. "Who is the fortunate young girl who gets Josef for a husband?" She raised her eyebrows.

The girls wrinkled their noses and looked at each other.

"You wouldn't get a kinder man. He even helps me feed my chickens and collect the eggs." She nodded in Mary's direction. "That's why he doesn't come over to work for your father until later, Mary." She turned back to Abigail. "Appearances aren't everything, girls." She clucked at them to move aside as she filled her first jug. Mary took the second jug, filled it, and followed the widow to her house. Intrigued with the last remark, Mary hoped she would say more, but the old woman nodded her thanks and turned away as Mary placed the jug inside the doorway.

Mama drew Mary aside before daybreak the next morning and delivered surprising news. Mary's heart tumbled. "Josef?" She scowled. "Mama, he's not from around here. His family are strangers."

"Taoma knows his family, and your father met them in Jerusalem at the Feast of Tabernacles last year."

You've seen how he acts; he's like a mute; he doesn't visit with other people. Papa doesn't know him well enough!" She rattled off her objections, but her mother's face remained stony. Mary left the house. Did her mother's look mean she didn't approve of her outburst or didn't approve of Josef as a match for her daughter? Her mother would do what her father said. She also knew her mother was unhappy with Mary's complaints. Maybe she could plead her case with her father.

She scurried to the workshop, knowing Josef didn't arrive until well after daylight. Papa is reasonable, she thought, and he adored her. She could easily persuade him to change his mind. She rehearsed her complaints.

Josef would not be a good fit for her. Josef didn't attend any of the usual festivities, and he never spoke or read in the synagogue. He didn't sing the psalms the way Father did.

Her steps slowed when she heard Papa talking. Men would frequently bring work, like a hayfork needing repair, before they went out to the fields. She padded respectfully inside and stopped short. Her father wasn't speaking with a customer; he was speaking with Josef.

Mary's shadow blocked the doorway's dim light, and they both turned to greet her. In the muted light of the workshop, Josef appeared both poised and thoughtful, holding his hand over his mouth and chin.

"Josef," Papa began, "It's time you two became better acquainted. Mary, Josef and his father asked at Passover that he be betrothed to you. They were so pleased that I've raised such a devout daughter. I agreed. Josef will be the perfect husband for you, because he's a builder like me and will take good care of you. That's why I invited Josef to come work with me, so he would get to know you better." Her father's enormous grin dissolved her hopes.

Abigail had forewarned her. It was the groom that approved the bride. It was Josef who had to approve of *her*. Her stomach twisted, and he felt the pressure rise against the back of her eyes. What could she say that wouldn't embarrass her father? To say she was grateful was a lie. She glanced sideways at her father. Her lips trembled. Taking a deep breath, she pasted on a smile. "I pray that I will be a worthy wife, J-Josef."

A shiver swept through Mary's body and her knees knocked together. She lowered her head. With a chuckle, her father waved her away. She went to the door, but turned back to ask her father if a wedding date was determined. The sun had risen and flooded the workshop. Josef had let his hand drop from his chin, and his pink, puckered scar shone in the morning's light.

Covering her mouth before anyone heard her gasp, Mary ran to their tree and climbed it faster than Salome ever had. Tears streaming, she could hardly see which branch to grasp. *Who cares if he's kind; everyone will laugh at me. They'll say my parents didn't know what they were doing.* She'd heard little boys call him Scarface. *Were there other names people had for him? How could her parents make such a decision?*

Had Papa really decided Josef was the right one for her, or that she was the right one for Josef? She had always trusted her father. Why was it so hard to trust him now?

Mary dropped from the tree and found her mother sweeping the courtyard. "Have you and Papa been planning this very long?"

"Yes, that's why we met his parents in Jerusalem. It was the day you'd gone to the temple to find that caretaker. We asked you to come right back to the inn. This arrangement almost didn't happen because you weren't there."

"When I was looking for Anna?"

"That must have been the time. You told us you would come right back, so we didn't tell you we had an appointment with Josef and his parents. When your lady wasn't there, you didn't check with us; you went looking for her."

"I had to ask her a question about something she had for me to do."

Her father came up, and Mama sat Mary on the bench. "What nonsense is this? Why didn't you tell us?" Mama looked at Heli and shook her head. "We must speak to the temple officials next time." She nodded to Papa. "Why doesn't this woman mind her own work? She shouldn't be telling other people's children what to do. Who knows what strange things she puts in little girls' heads?" She tapped Mary's chest. "There's no question as important as your future."

Mary wanted to remind them that Anna predicted something about her future too, but by now her memory was fuzzy. She felt uneasy explaining it now.

Numb, she ate supper with few words while Sali babbled. Just before she climbed to the loft after her little sister, she knelt in front of her father. "Why Josef, Papa?"

Her father's eyes narrowed. "He is a righteous man; he knows the Torah."

How could her father conceive that a deformed man was good enough for her? What will Abigail say? Will she laugh? Mary squeezed her eyes shut so Papa wouldn't see her tears.

Her parents announced the betrothal the next day. The men congratulated Josef and Heli. The women smiled at Hannah and teased her about forthcoming grandchildren. Abigail's eyebrows rose.

Chapter 6

For two weeks, days and nights blended into gray duty. Mary pasted a smile on her face each morning. Her mother constantly reminded her to be grateful. Her father frowned at her. Josef avoided her, but one day there was a delicate white lily on the bench outside where she usually carded wool and another day two polished twigs, one of cedar and one of almond wood. At the end of the second week, she dragged herself up to the loft, dreading her ritual of recounting stories for Sali.

They snuggled under the covers, and Mary rubbed her sister's back. Mary gave a short laugh.

"What's funny?" Salome asked.

"This makes me feel more like a mother tonight, and sometime soon, after Josef and I marry, I will be one." She gulped, suddenly remembering Abigail's lesson of how men and women conceived babies. She pictured her own mother nursing Salome.

"What story are you telling me tonight?"

Mary pondered. What stories of husbands and wives and mothers and babies could she relate? She'd recently told Sali about Moses in the rushes and David and his children. Oh yes, there was Ruth, who became the great-grandmother of King David. Usually she didn't think much about their own lineage from the songwriter she loved so much. *How did Ruth feel about marrying Boaz? Wasn't Ruth merely obeying her kind mother-in-law? Wasn't Josef also from David's line? Obedience.* Mary took a deep breath and said a quick prayer that the long story would put her sister right to sleep.

"Now sing for me," Sali yawned, only half-asleep. She had been climbing trees again today and playing tag with the neighbor boys after the midday meal.

As she reflected on the Lord and His creatures, Mary crooned about the deer panting for water, and she realized how her own heart desired to grow closer to the Lord and meet with Him. Her soul, like the psalmist's, was distressed, not with fears of the enemy but with doubts about Josef. Sali was already sleeping when Mary sang about her soul being sad. "Put your hope in God," she reminded herself in a whisper, leaving the melody behind. "For I will yet praise him, my Savior and my God."

She should have asked her mother if she and Salome could sleep on the roof. The summer heat had made the sleeping loft stifling, and singing about deer seeking water made her thirsty, so she crept down the ladder.

When she poured a drink, a rustling sound alerted her. Mice in the rafters again? As she looked around, a golden glow formed at the front door. She trembled. "Papa!" she attempted, but her fright choked the word. Her father's snores continued behind their curtain.

A muscular being taller than the doorway stood before her. His glaring white tunic was belted with a golden sash. Dazzling rays spread over his shoulders like wings. His eyes were bright green gems. *Is that what emeralds look like?*

Her stomach flipped and churned. Unable to scream for help, she perspired and shivered at the same time. Suddenly, the angel smiled and boomed, "Rejoice, you highly favored one! The Lord is with you."

The radiance on the creature's face grew, and Mary was breathing erratically. The angel continued, "Don't be afraid, Mary, for you have found favor with God. Behold, you will conceive in your womb and give birth to a son, and shall name him 'Jesus.'"

Mary struggled to make sense of his words while the angel, as calm as if he were visiting with her father and mother over wine, continued to share the royal future of a child she would be raising.

Two questions burned inside her. Dare she ask? Two weeks ago she'd heard that Zechariah, the husband of her mother's cousin Elizabeth, was struck mute for questioning an angel who had appeared to him. Mary began to speak, halted, and then plunged forward. "If it isn't too disrespectful, will you tell me how this can happen? I have never been with a man before." The angel's smile widened until the room was diffused with gold. How could this brilliant glow and their conversation not wake her parents?

"The Holy Spirit will come on you, and the power of the Most High will overshadow you. Also, the holy one who is born from you will be called the Son of God. You seem to be aware how that happens," he said. Mary held her breath. The angel flicked his hand toward the south. "Elizabeth, your relative, also has conceived a son in her old age; and this is the sixth month with her, who was called barren. For nothing spoken by God is impossible."

With a jolt in her soul, Mary opened her mind to this strange idea. Her body felt weightless. She couldn't tell if she was laughing or crying. "Yes, yes!" Her heart felt as if it were bursting. "I want to be the Lord's servant. Let it be done to me according to your word." She closed her eyes for a silent prayer, and when she opened them, her ethereal visitor had disappeared. Light from his appearance slowly faded, while her own spirit filled with a light of its own. The beautiful song that welled within her made her feel like a dove's feather floating in the breeze.

Yearning to dance with joy, she slipped out to the courtyard. The astounding notion of the Lord selecting someone so insignificant overwhelmed her. A fountain of warmth made her heart pound, and she felt lifted off her feet. She twirled across the courtyard.

Oh, it truly seemed a great and magnificent thing the Mighty One had done in choosing her to bear that child! She puzzled over how God's Spirit could make it happen, but the thrill in her soul assured her that it would. This night of the angelic visit, both amazing and humbling, a night of glory and promise and hope, this night, Mary imagined, would make everything wonderful and good.

When the last glow of the angel faded, Mary tiptoed inside and peeked behind her parents' curtain. To her surprise, Papa was already awake. Her eyes met his.

"Mary, tell me; is it true? I had a dream about you." He stood and drew her against his chest.

"What happened? What is it?" Mama asked, rubbing her forehead.

"Yahweh is bestowing an incredible favor on this precious girl," he replied, and he described the unusual honor given to her.

Mary's excitement grew like a wildfire. Papa would help; Mama would be her support. Salome would love playing with the baby, and so would Abigail.

"Now I can tell you the secret Anna gave me."

"What are you talking about? What Anna? What does that have to do with your dream?" Her father's eyes bored into her.

"Anna, the sweeper at the temple. Just before we moved here, she told me the Lord of Heaven's Armies had a strange task for me. I would be a special caretaker. It's why I didn't want to move here; she said I would take care of the Holy One's temple." She scratched her head. "I still don't quite understand how my baby could be a king, but I guess Yahweh will figure that out."

Mama clenched her hands. "I don't know if this is good, Heli; Mary has a difficult burden to bear. The neighbors.… Josef. How do we explain a, a baby?"

Flames of exultation turned to icy daggers. Mary's stomach lurched. Mama was right; her betrothed wouldn't believe in angels. He wouldn't give credence to the secret Anna gave her. He might even know that this special child was to be born in Bethlehem. How could that happen now? He would disown her and break off his promise. She would be dishonored, maybe even banished.

"Papa, what about *him*?"

Her face flushed. She had thought she was the only one embarrassed by the betrothal; now she couldn't bear to contemplate what Josef would say.

"Sh, sh, sh. We have faith, just as Abraham had." Papa drew her against his chest and stroked her head. "By faith he obeyed the Lord and prepared to sacrifice his son. Moses, too, had faith the Lord would rescue his people from Egypt, remember? And all the others I've taught you. I will speak with Josef. I will explain about my dream as well as yours." Her father gave her a tight squeeze. "Now go back to sleep. We'll talk more in the morning."

Mary climbed the ladder, hearing Papa's murmurs as he explained to her mother the astounding news. She squirmed until her nightdress was a sweaty tangle, finally going back down and tapping her father's shoulder. He sat up instantly. "Are you all right?"

"May I sleep on the rooftop?"

Papa stroked her head. "Yes. Here; take this blanket."

Mary spread the blanket and lay on her back. A wide cloudy stream poured across the dark vault overhead, so bright no other stars stood out. *Will my baby come down on a trail of stars?* The more she wondered, the more she worried. *What if Josef leaves me? What if people make my family leave Nazareth?*

Finally picturing the angel, she burst into worship, and the praises lifted her above the fears. Over and over, the angel's parting words sang, "Nothing shall be impossible for God."

...

If only it had been like that. Her father's shoulders were slumped when he came in for the evening meal. He looked at Mama, then told Salome to sweep the workshop.

"What is it? What's wrong?" Mama grabbed Heli with one hand and pulled him to the bench.

Papa looked at the floor.

"Josef wants time to pray and 'think about it.' It was like talking to a stone wall. He went to Widow Rachel's for a couple hours, then came back to say he's leaving Nazareth tomorrow to have some time alone, but he'd finish today's work."

"Did you tell him about the angel? Did you tell him Mary has never been alone with a man?" Mama wrapped Mary in her arms.

"There's more," he said. "Josef worked without a word the rest of the day, while I did everything I could to explain, to tell him about Mary's dream as well as my own." Papa put his head in his hands, mumbling words.

"Speak up; I didn't understand, Heli."

"Josef's last words were to quote King Solomon: 'A worthy woman is the crown of her husband, but a disgraceful wife is as rottenness in his bones.' I struggled to reply, and he threw the name 'Bethlehem' over his shoulder and left."

...

Mary dwelt on her father's comment about Josef's righteousness. It haunted her and sullied her joy. Now *her* righteousness was questioned! How could she have known that her vivid experience would take her from mountaintops of delight and plummet her to despair? One day she exulted in intense belonging, while in the next she was floundering in betrayal and pain.

While she waited for the precious swelling in her belly to begin, Mary fretted over what people would say when they found she was pregnant and abandoned. Josef had not said he had abandoned her, but what if he did? The community would label her a harlot.

Josef and Mary were promised in marriage, but Josef disappeared. Neighbors asked her mother where he was, then whispered behind their hands. Would Abigail avoid her as well? Her friend hadn't come to the well or the market with her lately. Mary wondered if even her dear Mama secretly doubted what Papa and she recognized, and if Salome wondered why people were shunning her. How could she survive this? No one speaking to her. Neighbors averted their gaze when she walked by or let words slip out as they passed in the road: "shameful," "wanton." What should have been a joyful season became agony. Summer's sticky heat had given her an excuse to stay indoors, away from accusing eyes, but harvest time was here.

Their Hebrew new year began two days ago. Usually the synagogue president asked her father to blow the ram's horn because of his virtuous character and devotion to the Holy One. This year, while Papa waited nervously in the courtyard for the invitation, the shofar resounded from the synagogue. Mary's soul shattered at the look on his face when he realized they rejected him. Would the community also deny their family the upcoming celebrations at the Feast of Booths? Salome had been dragging palm fronds and dead tree limbs next to the house for the past three days. Was that in vain?

The scraping of the courtyard gate and shouts outside brought Mama to the door. "Samuel? What are you doing here? Come in. Mary, go get your father; tell him my cousin Samuel is here."

The burly man hugged her mother and took Mary's hand. "This can't be little Mary. Must be, though, since I haven't had the pleasure of seeing you for eight or ten years." Long ebony locks dipped below his shoulders and bristly whiskers covered his nose and bright eyes. "Do you remember Elizabeth who lives in Ein Karem?" Mary nodded. "She's my sister. It sorrows me I don't see her much, myself," he said, turning back to Mama. "The Lord willing, this trip south, I will repent of my neglect and pay her and her esteemed husband a call. It's irresponsible to be neglectful of family."

"Mary, get your father. Tell him Samuel is here."

Mary rushed out but stopped short with a scream. "Aiee!"

"I'm coming," Samuel called, quickly joining her outside. He placed himself between Mary and a camel, whose head was now sticking over the high wall.

"Please forgive me, Mary. I failed to tell you about my business partner, Sheba," he said. The dusty beast nibbled at Samuel's chest when he came through the gate and pawed at the ground. Thick ropes held several coarse packs on its hump, Every little boy and girl playing outside was chattering, making an arc around it. The boys were daring each other to run over and touch it.

"Will she bite?" Mary cowered behind Samuel.

"She has no reason to maul or maim you." Samuel motioned with his head toward the boys and raised his voice. "She may be disposed to place a toe on the head of some impolite ruffian, though." The boys scattered as Samuel pushed the camel back and pulled Mary under the long neck. "We can let Sheba repose; let's fetch your father."

"Is this Samuel?" Papa enveloped him. "It's been five years since I've seen you, and that was in Jerusalem. What a welcome surprise. What brings you to Nazareth? You rarely bring your goods this far north, as I recall."

"The roads are much improved; that's the only beneficial remark I can make about our Roman overlords." He shook his shaggy head. "The taxation is outrageous; I'm compelled to acquire a prodigious variety of goods." He lowered his voice. "You mustn't tell anyone: I've even had to supply Herod's castles with everything from candlesticks to carpets, along with a plethora of exotic food."

"We're pleased to have you. Well-traveled visitors such as you are a rarity in Nazareth, and family even rarer. We must celebrate. Mary, tell your mother we'll have a party in Samuel's honor tonight."

Only Rachel joined them, bringing a platter of nuts and figs. While Samuel regaled the rest of the family with tales from his travels, their neighbor gently asked Mary about the items she had been weaving and embroidering. When their neighbor left, Mary crept up to bed, staring at the ceiling for hours until the house quieted and settled to sleep.

"Your mother and I talked with Samuel last night. We have a plan," Papa announced the next morning when Mary joined him and her mother. "It's likely this will ease the situation." Mary noticed he didn't use the word "solve." "We want to send you to Elizabeth, who is also expecting a miraculous baby. Your mother and I have talked about this before, but we couldn't agree how to carry it out. We discussed this with Samuel last night, and he has agreed to help."

Her mother's voice wobbled, and she pulled Mary on her lap. "A girl needs to be with her mother at a time like this. I'm not convinced this is a good thing." She sniffed and wiped tears.

"It's a workable plan, Hannah, thanks to Samuel."

Mary kept her head down and twisted her hands.

"You'll be away from Nazareth, safe from talk and gossip, at least for several weeks," her father continued. "Cousin Elizabeth is married to a Levitical priest. That will give you some much-needed righteous covering."

The life growing inside Mary wasn't noticeable. Perhaps no one in Ein Karem had heard the rumors.

"But what if Zechariah refuses her?" Now it was Mama twisting her hands.

Mary's spirit crashed to the floor with those words, reminders of what she, herself, wondered.

Chapter 7

"We know you are pure and righteous, Mary." Papa pulled her to his chest. "Living with Zechariah will reassure others that you're not embarrassed to be in the presence of a priest."

Mama grabbed her hand, and a bleak smile softened the wrinkles in her forehead. "I'm upset, not because of any shame; there is none to be had. Only ....." She wiped the tear streaks. "I'm relieved that you can be with another mother-to-be, with someone who is herself pregnant and who can tell you what to expect. I just wanted to be that woman, and to hold you and reassure you."

"What if your cousin Elizabeth refuses to see me or care for me, or her husband says no? I don't even know what to call her; is she my cousin or my aunt?"

Her father wrapped his arm around her. "Actually, she is a cousin, but because she is the same generation as your mother and I, you can call her *Aunt*, and call Zechariah and Samuel here *Uncle*. Those are little things. I want you to be assured that the Holy One will prepare the way."

Mary studied her hands. Would Elizabeth understand? What about Zechariah? They both were such godly people, but even in Nazareth, people heard that Zechariah was struck mute when the holy messenger came to him. At least *he* shouldn't rail at her. Pondering the old priest's infamous retort, Mary breathed a sigh that her own reaction to the angel was to break into thanksgiving instead of disbelief. She looked at her family and this extraordinary relative. "Do we have to leave today? May I pray about it?"

Samuel walked over and patted her shoulder. "You have rightly spoken. I am not discomfited by prolonging my respite, nor is Sheba. We'll leave the day after tomorrow; every journey necessitates ample and prayerful preparation." A broad grin lit his face.

Before dawn two days later, Mary hugged her parents and Salome goodbye. Her mother darted in the house immediately, and Mary guessed her mother wanted to hide her tears. Mary's flowed openly as she trailed Samuel and Sheba. She doubted Samuel heard her own sobs, but she noticed he picked up their pace when her sobbing turned to sniffles.

"It will be cooler at Elizabeth's," Samuel said when they stopped for water. He handed Mary dried fish and a bun before sitting on a rock.

Mary nodded. Maybe the Ein Karem climate would be cooler, but would her welcome be cool? The morning sun slicing across Mt. Gilboa turned its barren slopes to silver. Mary sighed. Was that a favorable sign? She had never taken this route before, and the trip was already drudgery. The road through Samaria was shorter and more traveled, but also had more hills to climb. After a few minutes, Samuel rose, tightened the ropes over the merchandise, and picked up the camel's lead. Mary readjusted her knapsack, pulled the scarf from her head, and fell in behind Sheba's twitching tail.

It must have been her deep sigh. Samuel stopped Sheba and motioned. "Come up and walk by me. I don't normally have the gratification of anyone's company, so I'm wont to make nary a whisper except to cluck at Sheba."

Her smile growing, Mary trotted past Sheba. Within a furlong, the sun was burning away the chill and Samuel began to entertain her. As if he were the honored speaker before the council of priests, Samuel regaled Mary with the beauty of the hills and valleys and the abundance of waters of their homeland.

"See the towers on that mountain? That's Mt. Gerizim." He shook his head at Mary's shudder. "Just because Samaritans live in this territory doesn't mean the mountain has no importance for us Jews. These people claim they possess the original land given to our people when we left Egypt."

At Mary's wide eyes, he added, "Don't tell the priests in Jerusalem, but Samaritans believe our Ark of the Covenant safely rests in a hidden cave somewhere on Mt. Gerizim, that it has rested there for 600 years."

Uncle Samuel sprinkled his conversation with historical tidbits of their people, starting with Father Abraham's journey from Ur clear up to Herod's victories and Rome's advances. As each day passed, Mary grew more thrilled with the territory the baby in her belly would someday rule.

When he wasn't spouting tales of battles Yahweh had won, Samuel boasted of the Holy One's answers to his prayers and the joys of spending time with his family and friends. Through the next few days, each town or village they passed evoked stories of families he'd traded with there, as well as of victories won and lost. Mary's heart lightened.

As they approached the hills north of Jerusalem, Samuel confided that he had finally bought a house where he could rest between trips. "This is my secret, Mary, to be held in strictest confidence."

Mary blanched, afraid to ask why.

With a laugh, Samuel patted her shoulder. "I've bought a house in Bethlehem. I've kept the news from my esteemed sister because she'll be overwrought that I'm not settling on her side of the city."

"Why Bethlehem, then?"

"It's because of business. Much of my trade is with Herod. I'm delivering to all his palaces, except for Masada. (Who desires to climb that awful mountain?) Bethlehem is a short distance from Jerusalem and his Herodium Palace and close to the route to Jericho." He shrugged his shoulders. "It's a business decision; houses are too costly in Jerusalem."

All Mary's fears had lifted and her hopes brightened until they came along the narrow road to Ein Karem. On the hillside grapevines, red and green leaves as big as platters made her think of people holding their hands over their mouths as they whispered about her. Embarrassment squeezed her heart.

Someone must have seen them in town while Samuel made arrangements to stable Sheba. As they walked down the footpath hugging the hillside, they saw her mother's cousin waiting for them in front of her house. Mary watched, holding back while Samuel embraced his sister.

"Sister, the transformation is remarkable. This beautiful face that was creased and forlorn is glowing and carefree." Elizabeth broke into a grin.

Mary stepped forward. "Aunt Elizabeth, greetings from my mother and father." She reached to embrace her aunt but was interrupted by Elizabeth's ecstatic squeal.

"Blessed are you among women, and blessed is the fruit of your womb! Why am I so favored, that the mother of my Lord should come to me? When the voice of your greeting came into my ears, the baby leaped in my womb for joy! Blessed is she who believed!"

Who could have told her this news? Mary stared at Samuel. His mouth had fallen open.

Elizabeth called for her husband, then turned back. "May you be blessed, for there will be a fulfillment of the things which have been spoken to you from the Lord." She pulled Mary close and squeezed her tightly.

How did she know all this? Mary's fears evaporated; the tension she was carrying melted away.

Once again, tears ran down Mary's cheeks, and fragments of various psalms flowed from her heart, lifting like butterflies rising off flowers. Zechariah came to the door and Mary's praises tumbled out. "My soul magnifies the Lord. My spirit has rejoiced in God my Savior, for he has looked at the humble state of his servant. All generations will call me blessed, for he who is mighty has done great things for me. Holy is his name. He is so merciful."

Phrase after phrase of adoration flowed. Samuel stood behind her, gleaming as if he had produced this behavior.

Sinking to her knees, bubbles of joy made Mary laugh. "He has filled the hungry with good things. He has sent the rich away empty." She looked up at Elizabeth. "Aunt Elizabeth, aren't I the one who is rich? This is so hard to believe!" Without consciously forming them, more words flowed. "He has given help to Israel, his servant, that he might remember mercy, as he spoke to our fathers, to Abraham and his offspring forever." Finally, exhausted, she dropped her head to her knees. Samuel scooped her up and brought her inside to a couch where she fell into a deep sleep. When she awoke the next evening, Samuel and Sheba had left.

...

Living with Elizabeth and Zechariah was like living in a temple, Mary imagined. The words "justice" and "righteousness" were in their daily prayers. At night together, Elizabeth and Mary recited and discussed prophecies about the Messiah. Zechariah would clap his hands enthusiastically when they found the scriptures that were his favorites, and he would shake his head and wave his hands downward when they tried to make other verses fit the predictions.

"How do you think our son will prepare the hearts of our people?" Elizabeth asked Zechariah one night while they all ate soup.

Mary rested her chin in her hand. "How will *my* son inspire them to establish the new kingdom of Israel?" She turned to Zechariah. "Will we actually see our people in control of our own land?" He shrugged his shoulders, noiselessly working his mouth.

"Ah, young one," Elizabeth said solemnly, "In that day that the nations will seek the root of Jesse, who stands as a banner of the peoples; and his resting place will be glorious. Yahweh's Spirit will rest on him: the spirit of wisdom and understanding, the spirit of counsel and might. Only the good Lord knows the set up."

Mary's heart fluttered. Ah, to dream of such a day and realize that her son would bring it to pass!

The grape pickers left, taking their songs with them. The fan-shaped leaves of the vines crumbled and fell, exposing dreary trunks. Zechariah disappeared early one morning and returned several hours later with a fragile scroll, as crinkled and yellow as the mulberry leaves rotting on the path. Spreading the scroll on the table following their midday meal, he pointed to himself, then the scroll, and then himself again.

"You copied this?" Mary said. He shook his head no, pointed to himself again and demonstrated writing the text.

Elizabeth peered over his shoulder. "These are the writings of the prophet Zechariah, my husband's namesake. Remember, we were trying to think of which other prophets told about Messiah."

Delicately, he unrolled the scroll. His blue-veined hands gently moved down the page until he reached a particular portion. Having housed Mary four weeks by then, Elizabeth and Zechariah knew Heli had taught Mary to read, as well as memorize the scriptures. Twinkling eyes peered at her and smiled tenderly.

"I may read? Is that what you mean?" Zechariah nodded and showed her where to start.

Never before had Mary been allowed to handle the words of the Holy One. She started to weep, then she panicked, afraid that a teardrop would mar this priceless parchment. Elizabeth quickly handed her a cloth, and, with a hiccup, she took a deep breath and read.

"Soon I am going to bring my servant, the Branch." She read a little further, "and I will remove the sins of this land in a single day." Mary looked up in confusion. Zechariah opened the scroll further, pointing again. "Yes, He will build the temple of the Lord. Then He will receive royal honor and will rule as king from his throne. He will also serve as priest from there, and there will be perfect harmony." She waited, her heart quickening while her uncle's gnarled fingers searched for another passage. "Behold, your King comes to you! He is righteous, and having salvation; lowly, and riding on a donkey, even on a colt, the foal of a donkey." She looked up. "How can that be?"

Zechariah touched two or three more verses on the scroll, shook his head, and swiftly moved on before Mary could decipher the words. An expansive smile lit his face as his finger lingered on one last verse, and Mary read aloud. "Yahweh will be King over all the earth. In that day Yahweh will be one, and his name one."

He lifted his eyes to Mary, and she barely heard his whisper. "His Name alone will be worshiped." A shiver ran through her. She gently returned the fragile scroll to her uncle and sat back, eyes closed. What did that mean, Yahweh will be one? Is there more than one Yahweh?

That evening as the sun slid into bed behind the rolling western slopes, she pondered all the prophecies. Would all these oracles apply to this tiny baby developing inside her? A few minutes later, she excused herself and retreated to her little curtained alcove.

Sleep didn't come. Her eyes wide, staring toward the night that existed beyond the ceiling of this little home, she puzzled over those prophecies. If her son was to be the Messiah and the one who brought all people together, how could he be the Lord and His name one, as well? How could the Holy One be in the heavens and still place His son in her arms? The Lord of Hosts created their world, and so His son would be His heir? Her son, the heir of creation? Her head could not contain such thoughts. It seemed unlawful even to think them.

What about the other predictions? Were there others she couldn't remember or didn't know? Why did Zechariah skip over some passages? She turned in bed so many times, the coverings were in tangles. Exhausted, she recited the words that had always brought her comfort, the words that began: "Hear, Israel: Yahweh is our God. Yahweh is one. You shall love Yahweh your God with all your heart, with all your soul, and with all your might."

When she approached the sentence that said, "You shall teach them diligently to your children," she paused and tried to imagine the little child growing within, whom she would teach. She choked, took several deep breaths, and began praying again until sleep smothered her thoughts. Her dreams, though, were peaceful. For the next few days, all the discussions about the prophecies kept her from dwelling on Josef and what he was thinking.

Each morning Mary wanted to skip down the path to the well, but Elizabeth was tiring with her increased swelling. Instead, they shuffled along the lanes under barren fig trees. Shoulder to shoulder, the gnarled grape vines wrote their script across the hills, inviting winter to hurry through and restore the white blossoms of springtime. Each day Mary hoped to wander far enough along the hills that she could see the tumbling Sorek River spread across the plains into the great sea, but Elizabeth lacked endurance, and Mary didn't want to venture alone.

If only there were other girls she could visit here. If only she could go into Jerusalem! She would find Anna, the prophetess, and tell her about the angel and the dream. *Was Anna still alive?* Anticipation tickled her chest. *Would her aunt and uncle allow her to go by herself? Of course not. Perhaps Uncle Zechariah would be called to a meeting at the temple. No, he couldn't speak yet.* She ran her hands through her hair. *Was their someone else in Ein Karem she could join?*

Two days later a message came for Zechariah. He glanced at it and handed it to his wife.

"They want you at the High Council meeting? What can you do since you can't speak?"

"Let me take a message for you." Mary bounced from the bench.

"You can't go alone, Mary." Elizabeth shook her head with a knowing expression. "Though I realize it must be lonely spending so much time with two people as slow and settled as we are."

"Not at all, I love being with you here."

"Mary." Her aunt tilted her head, and Mary blushed.

Elizabeth turned back to her husband. "Why don't we send your message with Piltai when they bring their oils to market this week?"

Mary studied her hands, trying to hold back her plea. Elizabeth touched her shoulder. "You'd like to join them, wouldn't you?"

She jumped up and hugged her aunt. "Yes, please." She could look for Anna, after all. She tossed and turned all night worrying she wouldn't hear Piltai's knock on the door.

Wrapped in cloaks, Piltai and Yael arrived just as gray sky lightened to pale blue. Both of them had plump cheeks and round bellies. Yael hugged her tightly. "It must be very hard for you to wait so long for your husband to finish his travels, you just newly betrothed."

Mary nodded and smiled weakly, wondering what story Elizabeth concocted. "Let me know how I can help you," she said. "I need to go to the temple to deliver some messages. That won't take you out of your way, will it?"

"You can stay with me at the market and we'll send Piltai. It's especially crowded since many people are coming to celebrate the Festival of Lights."

"But there's a woman I have to see." Mary swallowed her excitement. "There's a woman I'm hoping to meet at the temple."

Yael frowned.

"The lady who cleans. Anna." Mary held her breath.

"I don't know her." Yael stroked her chin. "Grab a cloak. We'll see if there's time after we sell our goods."

As they entered the city, a leaf-rattling wind arose, setting fabrics flying and bowls and food trays tumbling. Carts bumped against each other as merchants chased after their merchandise and dashed for the best corner on the square. Twice, Yael yanked Mary from being squashed between two colliding wheels.

"I thought you grew up in Jerusalem."

A flush blossomed on Mary's cheeks. "Yes, that's true, but I had only six years when we left. I must have forgotten everyone's eagerness in the markets." A screech jerked her around. Instantly, her mind flashed to monstrous gray blocks bouncing toward her, but there was no hill here. She shivered, madly searching through the frenzy for the source of danger. The roadbed was vibrating. Piltai and Yael had been swallowed by the crowd.

Mary whipped around so quickly that her shawl slipped to her sandals. She tripped on it and crumbled to the street. Spewing ribbons of foam team, a team of black stallions stormed toward her dragging an empty chariot. The cobblestones trembled beneath her. Screams of warning echoed from the walls. "Lord in heaven!" Mary wrapped her arms across the precious gift inside, curled her body, and squeezed her eyes shut. Something bumped against her and she rolled to the side.

Squatting beside Yael, Mary rubbed her bruised knees. The runaway team had caused the couple's cart to overturn. After Yael had soothed her shaking, Mary helped them sweep away shattered clay as they trod carefully around the oily paving stones. She placed herself between the couple, holding her abdomen. Her eyes darted from side to side, and she flinched at every loud voice that called out in the street as they continued toward the shopping square.

Piltai groaned when they reached the market pavilions. "All the spaces are taken. How can we sell the little we have left?" He waved his hand over the few barrels of olives and dried spikenard. "We should go back home. We won't make enough money to pay for our breakfast, let alone the fee for a space."

"Surely there will be latecomers that we can entice down here." Yael clung to his arm to prevent his leaving. "We're already here. There's no need to bring back what little we have left. We'll sell from the cart. This way we'll avoid the pavilion fee."

She turned to Mary leaning against the cart wheel. "Mary, we won't be going to the temple today." She looked down at Mary's belly and then stared, eyes narrowed. "Especially with the condition you're in." She waited for Mary to speak.

Mary's face burned. She didn't think Elizabeth had told any neighbors about the baby, but her robe didn't always hide her early swelling. She looked at her feet and then back up to meet Yael's gaze. What if they *did* let her go? Was Jerusalem safe? She gulped. "What about Zechariah's message?"

"He said not to worry if we couldn't go." Yael set her hands on her hips.

Seven or eight soldiers just released from duty swaggered by, pointing at Mary. "What's for sale today, Beauty?" said the one in front. The others laughed and made kissing sounds.

Mary ducked her head and wrapped her arms around her body. An hour later, she followed the cart back to Ein Karem.

Chapter 8

Her father had said he would come for her after two or three months. Elizabeth would soon deliver her baby; where was he? Before sunset, Mary served the afternoon meal to Elizabeth and Zechariah, cleaned the kitchen, and wrapped a blanket over her shoulders. She stood behind the cottage facing west. The shorter days left her with too much night. The bright fire of the earlier times reading the scriptures had turned to abandoned coals. As Elizabeth's spirits rose in expectation of her son's birth, Mary's own fell lower. She had scarcely spoken about Josef, and Elizabeth had known not to mention him. Zechariah and Elizabeth's fond attentions did little to warm Mary's heart or muffle her questions. Had Josef ever returned? What was going on in his mind? Would he divorce her? What were the neighbors in Nazareth saying? Was she disgraced? Would anyone ever marry her if Josef refused?

The sun dipped behind the farthest ridge and sucked the day's luster. Dew on the grasses became a curtain of fog. As she turned to go inside, a faint bray fluttered toward her. A man and donkey appeared through the bleak haze. The next gust carried a hoarse "Mary."

"Papa!" She ran to greet him, falling into his arms. "At last." She burst into tears and buried her head in her father's chest.

"Mary, Mary," he crooned. "You will be fine. It's good news. On the way home, we'll talk. For now, I will enjoy my visit with our generous relatives." Mary clamped her lips and helped her father bring old Balaam under the lean-to.

Once in the house, Papa gently kissed Elizabeth's hand and grasped Zechariah's arm, pulling him into a tight embrace. Then he put his arm over Mary's shoulder and took a deep breath. "Hannah and I are grateful and humbled that you would care for our precious daughter. We trust she hasn't disappointed you?"

"The good Lord has revealed to us the special calling on her life." Elizabeth said. "We are honored that our son will know the Lord himself and prepare the way for him, to give knowledge of salvation to his people by the remission of their sins and rejoice in their Messiah."

Heli's eyes widened and his hand slapped his chest. "You know Mary's special assignment?"

"Yes, and my son knows it as well. He turned in my womb at your daughter's first appearance at our door."

Heli wiped the sudden tears away and hugged Elizabeth. "My daughter was truly brought here by the Mighty One. I'm deeply touched and grateful for your hospitality and loving care."

"Well then, now, let us feed you and give you a good night's rest. I'm sure Mary is anxious to be on the road before daybreak."

As soon as they could no longer see Zechariah and Elizabeth waving them farewell, Mary slid off Balaam's back and grabbed her father's cloak. "Papa, I have to know. What has Josef done? Have you seen him? Have you had any word from him?"

"Yes, my darling. I have spoken with him. Would you believe that Josef had a dream too?"

"Can that be?" The knot in her stomach loosened. "You must tell me everything."

Papa chuckled. "You have become as insistent and hurried as your sister."

"But Papa, I have to know what's coming."

"'Those who wait for Yahweh will renew their strength. They will mount up with wings like eagles. They will run, and not be weary. They will walk, and not faint.' We have a slow trip home; why don't you get back up on our humble friend here and I'll tell you as we continue."

Her father made sense, of course. She climbed back on Balaam and raised her arms. Small puffs of wooly clouds scooted across the heavens, echoing her "Hallelujahs".

Their panting donkey stopped of his own accord atop a small hill, and Father handed the wine flask to Mary.

"You'll be as surprised as we were," her father said, after she'd had a few swallows. "Josef had gone into the countryside for more than a month to pray and fast. See, he is a godly man – just the one you need. He had become fond of you, and he was so hurt to learn you were with child, any child. He had finally decided to divorce you quietly."

Papa stopped at her sudden cry and wiped the tears from her cheeks. "Wait. Wait. Hear the rest! An angel came to him in a dream and told him not to be afraid. Who knew he was afraid? Not I. But he was. The angel confirmed what we knew; that you conceived your baby by the Spirit of the Lord, and you will have a son which you are to name Jesus, and he will be our salvation."

Mary had only one other pent-up question, one she was too embarrassed to ask. Who will the baby look like? Will he look like her? Papa? Maybe the angel.

As they continued home, her father shared more of the plans he and Josef had made. Her dowry was to be a home for them. Not only that, but – such a gift of the Lord – Josef had started helping her father begin the construction on the north side of the house. Mary loved the idea of making a home added onto her parents; it would be their own compound to accommodate more family. She felt blessed that she wouldn't have to live with strangers.

Homecoming was a joy and a relief. Mary gasped when Salome ran into her arms; she teetered from the impact. "Sali, you're almost as tall as I am." Her sister giggled; then her face reddened as she became aware of Mary's fuller stomach. She stepped away quickly.

"It's fine; it's fine. You haven't hurt him." Mary's soothing words only sent her sister back to their mother's side. Mary froze, focusing only on her mother's eyes, waiting for her to move.

With a sob, Mama stepped forward and pulled Mary into her arms. "I was afraid you would resent me for sending you to Elizabeth's. I was so lonely without you." She glanced at Salome. "This girl doesn't sit still long enough to share a pleasant conversation, or even to finish five rows on the loom." She motioned Sali to join their embrace. "Now we're all together again."

Papa cleared his throat. "Your mother and I have made plans for your wedding in Nazareth," he said. "We'll have a small ceremony, and then Josef will take you to Bethlehem to meet his family. Then ..."

Hannah held up her hand. "There's been a change since you left." Mama looked over Mary's shoulder at neighbors who had slowed their steps as they passed. "Let's all come inside; I'm sure you're famished." She led them inside and lit a fire under a pot of lentils before turning to face her husband.

"Josef has received a message from his mother and father to break the betrothal to Mary and return home immediately."

A chill settled over Mary. What was this? Josef would also be penalized? *It gives us something in common,* she thought. It was little consolation.

In addition, Abigail avoided her. She wouldn't even wave back. She and her mother were never at the well when Mary and Mama were there. Rachel seemed to be the only woman in the neighborhood who wasn't embarrassed to be seen with them.

"Mama, do you know why Abigail's family is avoiding me?"

Her mother put her fingers over her mouth and nodded. "I was hoping I wouldn't have to tell you." She took Mary's hands in hers. "You remember that Josef went away?" Mary nodded. "When he came back, before he had the dream, Abigail's papa went to him and asked Josef to marry her. I think they are embarrassed now."

"But he chose me when he had the dream. Or the angel told him to."

"Yes."

"My feelings are still tumbling in my heart, Mama. I know Papa has decided this is the right man. What do you think? How well did you know Papa before *you* were married?"

"I had never met your Papa, but I trusted my father to make the right choice. As you know, it has been a worthy alliance." She pulled Mary into a hug and whispered. "I can tell you, though, that Josef is the answer to *my* prayers for you."

Confusing thoughts badgered Mary. Did Josef still want to marry her or was he merely afraid of an angel? Before her own angel came (she didn't know if the same one came to Josef), the man had tender feelings for her even though she hadn't warmly welcomed them. Had she started to care for Josef or did she only want a father for her baby? One thing Mary learned from Elizabeth and Zechariah was that the Holy One of Israel doesn't force people to do His will.

She was still trying to grasp how to trust that plan herself. What else could she do? Her father had absolute trust; he and her mother went ahead with the plans for the wedding.

Some people in the neighborhood were still gossiping about her disgraceful condition. Just three weeks before the wedding, two boys, about nine or ten years old, were laughing among themselves when Mary and Salome were at the well. Just as the girls bent over to fill their jugs, a stone whizzed over Mary's head, then another hit her in the back. "Ow!" Red heat crept from her chest to her ears.

At Mary's cry, Salome whirled around and saw the boys picking up more stones. Arms swinging, screaming for them to stop, she stormed them like a mother lion protecting her cubs. "Leave Mary alone!" She grabbed the smaller boy by the ear. "She has a special baby; you'll be sorry!"

Mary didn't know if she was more shocked at what Sali knew about her baby or at her courage in attacking three boys. The boys scattered in different directions; Mary sobbed. Her ferocious sister immediately turned tender and gently led her home.

A week before their wedding, Father asked Salome and Mary to talk with him before they went to bed. "I have a plan, and, unusual as it is, I would like your opinion." Their heads tilted to the side, and they huddled at his feet. They were female, they were immature; why would Father need their advice? Before speaking, Papa motioned Mama to come and sit beside him. Once settled, she reached over and held his hand.

"My dearly loved and faithful wife is my light; she is all I have ever needed. When she requests something of me, I consider it very carefully." Mary and Sali glanced at each. "While it is not necessary for a man to have a male heir, your mother is – we are – concerned about protection for both of you girls."

Immediately Mary's mind flitted back to the boys throwing rocks at her. She thought they had kept what happened a secret. *O, Holy One*, she prayed silently, *protect me from the strife of tongues.*

Was Papa afraid of evil tongues hurting them? They must have heard some local gossip. Softly he began. "With your mother's suggestion, I have decided to adopt Josef as my son, our son." Seeing Mary's face blanch, he hurried on. "Mary, I would like your permission as well, since when there is no male heir, daughters may inherit."

Heat rose from her chest to her face. Why would she be worthy to inherit? It was the law, but she knew of no one who had ever given property to a daughter.

Her father spoke softly. "Josef's family has been reluctant to see him as well as you." When Mary frowned, Papa spoke louder. "When I pass away, this property, including the rooms Josef has built with me, needs to stay as a home for your mother and you girls, as long as you need it. Josef needs a secure future as well, especially for the sake of your little baby, Mary."

She squirmed and her eyes widened. Hadn't they surprised the neighbors enough already?

"I didn't discuss this with Josef yet; I was waiting for approval from you two."

Slowly her mind comprehended what her heart was coveting: Safety, reassurance, support. And yes, peace. Then her thoughts swung back to the neighbors. This was one more eye-raising complication before their ceremony.

"Of course, Papa. Whatever you think is best," Mary said, and Salome nodded, her face more serious than Mary had ever seen.

"It's not only my opinion. From the beginning, our forefather Moses taught that a man shall leave his father and mother and hold fast to his wife. I shall work out the details with Josef and tell our synagogue leaders."

Salome wrinkled her forehead. "But won't this make people talk even more?"

"This is not their decision. It is mine and your mother's, and I want to avoid any confrontations in the future."

"We won't stop the townspeople from talking," Mama said as she stood, "but we can stop them from thwarting the Lord's protection."

The next morning, Mary listened as Mama and Salome began designing the simple ceremony.

"Does Josef know if his brothers are coming?" her sister said.

"I'll go ask." Mary went around to the workshop, hoping her father would be there, too. She hadn't yet been with Josef alone; they had barely spoken.

"Is my father nearby?"

Josef looked up from a cedar plank and set down the plane. "Can I help you?" A lopsided smile tweaked his face. "I promise I won't bite." At her blush, he erased the smile. "I'm sorry, but your father left to purchase more nails." He took a step toward her.

"I – we were ...." Her tongue stuck. She looked around the room to see if there was a stool or some item she could put between Josef and herself, and her eyes stopped on a large oak chest. The lid was carved with lilies, and a garland of apple blossoms engraved the sides. "It's beautiful! I've never seen that before. Did my father make that?" Her hands flew to her mouth.

"No." He turned toward the chest. "I did. It was meant to be a surprise for you."

Mary slowly looked up to face him. Prickles touched the back of her eyes and she blinked hard. "It's so beautiful, it's worthy of a temple."

"Yes." Josef cleared his throat. "Did you have a question I can answer?"

No parade of groomsmen or bridesmaids began the ceremony. Josef had hoped his brothers would come, but word was sent they couldn't get away: "Everyone is 'ill-disposed' in Bethlehem." Josef struggled to believe them. Abigail's family talked about a cousin's wedding in Capernaum that would call them away. There was no long week of festivities and no bouquets of summer flowers, though Sali did her best to decorate the house with bowls of pomegranates and garlands of fir branches.

The day before the service, Mama handed Mary a roll of linen. Hands trembling, she unwrapped the package. A violet silk veil embroidered with red pomegranates slid over her hands. "Oh, Mama; this is exquisite. Did you make it?"

A wide smile stretched across Mama's face, and she nodded. "I wore this at my wedding. It's my joy and pleasure to see you wear this."

Papa came up behind Mama. "Now it's my turn." He held out shiny copper earrings and grinned. "No, I didn't wear these at my wedding."

The next evening as Salome and Mama were lighting the lanterns in the courtyard, two guests arrived at the gate. Her father had begged – or maybe bribed – their synagogue president, Aaron, to come. A stranger came, too; a stranger to Mary, but not to her mother. Mama's face gleamed.

"Heli, this is the special surprise you had for me, isn't it? I knew you had a secret. Mary, Salome, Josef, this is another Josef, my brother, my little brother, not in size but in years. I'm ten years his senior." Her voice tinkled as she wrapped her arms around the stocky man. The men clasped arms.

Even though Uncle Josef produced a precious smile for her mother, Mary backed away from him, afraid he or the synagogue official would ask too much about her, especially after Uncle Josef announced he was eagerly preparing for the priesthood.

Papa stepped into the silence. "Brother Josef. How grateful I am you made this long trip. Our bridal couple will be doubly blessed by your presence." He spread out his arms. "Now that our last guest is here, let's get these two people married." He pulled Josef under the canopy he had erected. "Let's bless the marriage of these two young people. Come, everyone." He reached for Mary.

Mary's trembling caused her new earrings to tinkle. She pulled the silky veil over her ears, forced a smile on her face, and stepped under the canopy.

Papa extolled Josef's hard work and precision in building. Mama detailed Mary's prowess with sewing and weaving and cooking. Papa's eyes were moist when he described Mary's devotion to the holy scriptures and how well she memorized verses.

Josef stood poised facing her, his shoulders taut. He took a deep breath. "Mary."

Her name hung in the air before her veil. Mary thought, with one breath he could blow it away and her marriage would be over. "My wife." The release of breaths around her vibrated in the silence.

Aaron saw everyone looking at him, and he blushed. "This family is faithful in attending….. Knocking began at the courtyard door, rising in intensity. Mary's heart flipped upside down. Was someone coming to drag her out to be stoned? Papa's head jerked nervously.

A reed flute trilled, and a high voice warbled. "Heli, open the door!" Father threw the door wide, to be hugged by Widow Rachel. The crowd behind Rachel cheered. Abigail and her family – Orli, Taoma, Caleb with his lute, and Gideon and Daniel with a cheerful gaggle of her father's customers – pushed into the courtyard, and Aaron quickly declared Mary and Josef married.

"We don't understand this whole situation," Mary heard Taoma tell her father, "but Josef is a good worker, a kindhearted man, and if he says this is right, that convinces me. More than that, we know you, Heli, and we know you are a righteous man! Let's celebrate!" Cradling bottles, he swaggered past the others. "What's a wedding without wine?" A trio of women bringing a lamb roast and pastries followed him.

No, it wasn't the whole village, but it was a beautiful celebration. Mama turned away so the neighbors wouldn't see her tears, then turned back to pass out plates and cups. Mary pulled the veil closer around her face, so no one saw her tears either, or the blush that had come when Taoma glanced at her when he mentioned righteousness. Sali? She was laughing and twirling around in circles, flitting from one person to another, as if she had personally planned the entire celebration. Maybe she did.

The only awkwardness came because there was no bridal chamber prepared where the marriage would have been consummated. The neighborhood musicians played a few songs, but when no one started to dance, her father began a round of toasts.

After the toasts, Rachel gave Mary and her family a warm hug and announced the sun had set, and she going home to bed. That seemed to be the signal for Aaron, Taoma, and the others to offer more wishes along with their farewells.

A hush settled on the family that remained, and all eyes turned to Josef, who took Mary's hand. "Your father and I," he looked at Papa, who nodded. "We thought it would be," another word hanging now, "*easier* if I stayed with Widow Rachel for a while." He let out his breath and twisted his hands. "There isn't room for both of us there."

"Of course," Mama said nervously. "Go ahead, Josef. It won't be long until your room is finished here." At his nod, she added, "We'll expect you to have meals with us, with your wife."

Josef nodded and grasped forearms with Mary's father and uncle. Quickly he kissed Mary's forehead and left.

Then there were the five of them, looking at each other awkwardly until Mama said, "Winter nights are cold, Brother, so I can't send you to the rooftop. I've made a pallet for you in the workshop. It's time we all went to bed."

Immediately, Uncle Josef extended good wishes and darted around the house.

Sali laughed at his hasty exit. "Maybe he's embarrassed at being in the midst of the strangest wedding he's ever attended," she whispered to Mary.

Mama took a daughter in each hand and pulled them into the house.

Chapter 9

The sun held little warmth, but Mary enjoyed the increasing hours of daylight. She sat alone in the courtyard carding wool when Josef entered. He squatted beside her and waited till she put the paddles down.

"We've had very little chance to talk, and there are two considerations I want you to know."

Mary held her breath.

"I feel we should wait to come together as man and wife until after the baby comes."

A flush rose on her cheeks, but she let out her breath. "And the other?"

He stood and leaned against the loom. "I'd love to bring you to Bethlehem; I want you to meet my parents,"

Her eyebrows slid together. "You think they've changed their minds?" She picked up a clutch of wool and picked at some pieces of grass. "I thought we were going to wait until after the baby is born."

"Yes, that's what we agreed." He stroked her cheek. "I just want my parents to know what a sweet wife I have. I'm proud of the woman I married, the mother of my child."

Josef's fervor pierced her heart, and Mary tilted her face to study him. His blush accentuated the scar, the scar she realized she had stopped noticing. "Oh." Her hands flew to her lips. "Did you just say, 'Mother of *your* child?'"

"Sweet woman," he said, "If this child is to be the Savior of our people, then the child belongs to me as well."

...

Fat rain drops were splattering the dust in front of the house when Taoma stopped by. Mary led him around to the workshop and slipped inside just as the wind drove a cloudburst against their backs.

"Josef? Heli?" The two men turned to Taoma, their eyes widening. "Weren't you both born in Bethlehem?"

Her father and husband looked at each other, furrows creasing their brows, and Josef nodded.

"There's a census from Imperial Rome, although I think it's at Herod's request."

"So?" Her father put down his mallet. "What does that have to do with Bethlehem?"

"Every male must go to his birthplace to register, no exceptions. I'm leaving tomorrow with my two older boys; Daniel isn't old enough to register, so he'll stay with Orli and Abigail."

"Why do you think Herod wants that?" Josef said.

"I'm guessing he wants to show Rome how many people he has to govern, so he'll get more money or roads or soldiers to keep us all oppressed." Taoma grimaced. "I'm alerting a few others and then going home to pack." He waved farewell.

Papa, Josef, and Mary delivered the news to her mother.

"How will you register? You have so much work," she said. They looked at each other, worry tightening their jaws.

"I'll leave for Bethlehem tomorrow," Papa said. "I can travel through Samaria and be back in less than a fortnight. Praise be to Yahweh that Josef is here to watch over the rest of the family; he can keep the work going and be preparing for his own trip." He folded his arms across his chest.

Still carding her wool, her mother shook her head. "Not Samaria; they're half-breeds. You can't trust them to give you a fair price on food or lodging."

"I must go that road to save time. There will be plenty of us taking the shortest route. I'll stay in a group." He reached over and squeezed her hand. "I promise." She glared back.

"We don't have many choices, Hannah."

"You're right." She set the wool aside and stood, hands on hips. "Salome, get your father's warm clothes together. Mary, kill and pluck two chickens. Grab any eggs you see. I'll boil them." She reached for the grain sack and poured out the barley. "Your father needs a hearty meal tonight."

Her father left in the rain early the next morning. The others watched him till the road turned at the bottom of the hill.

"Mary, it's imperative we leave the moment he returns," said Josef. "I want you with me. I'll dispatch a runner to my parents today, explaining we'll need to stay with them while I register. The circumstances will convince them. The runner will be back before your father."

Ten days later, the answer came back: "No."

Mary's shoulders sank. "I'll stay in Nazareth. Then you can see your family."

Josef pulled her against his chest. "Mary, I am grieved and embarrassed by my parents' behavior. If only they knew you and your integrity and your righteous behavior. I want them to meet you and have the privilege of meeting the mother of this unique child." Josef raised his voice. "I will not leave you. I have to register, and I want us to go together."

Her robe concealed her shaking knees. "You're sure you won't leave me home? Even in Bethlehem, we'll need to find a place to stay." Mary reached an arm around to massage her back. "Besides, won't we be going again when my time comes?"

"What do you mean?"

"The prophecies say the Messiah will be born in Bethlehem. That means another trip there."

"My family will make room for us when we arrive at their door. You'll see."

She sighed; she was moving slower, and the baby was turning and twisting. Many other people would be on the roads, staying at whatever lodging they could find. Shelters would likely be just as difficult to find in Bethlehem. Seven months ago, Josef had doubted her. Mary's only hope now was that an angel would visit his parents.

Her father stumbled in the doorway two days later. "Rain made sloppy, boggy areas in the valleys. In the hills, they washed away soil and pebbles." He sat on the courtyard bench to remove his sandals. Mary handed him hot tea, and Mama handed him a rag to wipe his mud-caked feet. When he finished, he pointed at Josef. "Leave your wife at home."

Mary turned to see Josef looking at her. *This is a test. Do I obey my father or my husband? Do I have the strength to make two trips to Bethlehem? Her heart beat faster.* She turned to her mother. Hannah was holding her breath, her eyes down. "It will be longer, but we can take the eastern road through Galilee," said Mary, facing her father. "I want to go with my husband; I'll be fine." Her eyes shifted to her mother, catching a smile so fleeting she doubted seeing it.

"Then take Balaam," her father said.

"Thank you, Papa, but he would slow us down, and I'd be too uncomfortable riding him. I'll be fine; the baby isn't due for a couple months yet."

...

Light as dove feathers, snow was falling as they left Nazareth. Woolen strips wrapped Mary's legs, but her sandaled toes tingled. They tramped for two hours before stopping. The weather warmed as they travelled south. As they approached Magdala and Scythopolis, Josef found modest lodging on the outskirts. "I'm as conservative as I can with our finances, but I didn't expect the prices to be higher than when we go to the festivals."

"Temperatures are rising; we have blankets for sleeping outside.

...

"You must be grateful for the gentler terrain." Josef gazed back at the road behind them. He turned around quickly, catching Mary rubbing her legs. "What's wrong?" She shook her head. "It looks like your legs are swelling."

"Babies can cause that, I've heard. I'll be fine."

"Another day and we'll be in Jericho. I think we should spend an extra night there."

"At the foot of Herod's palaces?" Mary shuddered. "Can't we hurry through and stop on the other side? Just the sound of his name makes me shudder."

"We go up the Adummim road from Jericho. I want to make the climb refreshed."

Her shoulders drooped.

Josef studied her. "Why don't I decide when we get to Jericho?" He stood and glanced again at Mary's legs.

Two parties of travelers passed by, exchanging greetings and laughter. Josef bent for his pack and caught Mary yawning as he rose. He looked at the travelers, then at the sky, and then back at Mary. "Would you like to spend the night here? We can sleep under that sycamore." She nodded.

Eerie howling woke Mary. The black sky was gone, but the sun seemed to have stayed asleep. Branches overhead were groaning and wind gusts tugged at their blanket. She shook Josef awake. "The winds have come up. Something doesn't sound right; I can't even tell north from south." She coughed to clear her throat and spit out dust.

As they looked around, dim light gradually spread, but no sun rose. "It's a dust storm; this will be nasty," Josef said.

"Can we wait it out?"

"Not likely." Josef swiped dust from his eyes and chased after their tumbling knapsack.

They hurriedly munched on dates and dried meat while watching clouds as dark as leather boil on the eastern skyline. "Let's fill our water skins from that stream and get to Jericho while we can see the road. Do you have an extra scarf I can tie over my mouth?"

As if the entire sky garrisoned an army amassed to attack, debris-laden dust clouds assaulted Mary and Josef. They ran down the road from one copse of trees to another, their arms shielding their face from the seeds and stalk, grit and grain propelled by each volley. Dirt lodged between their teeth; smudges covered Mary's face where she'd wiped tears from her cheeks.

...

The few people remaining on the road at the outskirts of Jericho were little more than silhouettes in the yellow haze. Whenever Mary and Josef veered from the extravagant edifices of Herod and his predecessors, the more dust and wind they encountered. "I feel those winds are pushing us to the palaces. It frightens me," Mary said as they came closer.

"They're enormous. How could Herod have built so much since the last time I was here?"

"Lots of slave labor."

"Look further down the street. They've built a covered walkway that connects the palaces."

Josef shrugged. "He must think he's too good to cross the road the rest of us use."

"Can we stop below it and rest?"

"I thought you wanted to get as far away from Herod as possible."

Mary bent to rub her leg. "Just a little break? The dust isn't swirling over here. There's no wind and we can see. It must be why all the carts and people are going this way."

Josef pointed a block ahead to a stone bench under the left side of the arch. "There's a resting spot waiting for you."

A grating rumble echoed from wall to wall, and panicked roars burst from the crowd. The screams echoed off the walls on each side. "Look up! Get back!" With a convulsive growl, colossal blocks began falling a couple reed-lengths away.

Mary jerked at the memory of granite blocks smashing toward her. Her leg slipped out from under her, and she collapsed on the pavement.

"Mary, get up!"

"I can't; something's wrong with my ankle." Mary began crawling toward Josef.

As Josef tried to lift her, a hand snatched at his pack, pulling him backward. "Stop. Let go! What are you doing?" he called over his shoulder.

The kerchief-covered man tugged harder as Josef reached again for Mary. When the thief cut the straps, the pack slid away, and Josef landed on top of his wife. Falling stones were bouncing off the pile and skidding closer. Barely upright, Josef dragged Mary to a side street. In seconds, half the arch filled the road before them.

Parts of crushed bodies were exposed in the spreading rubble: a leg here, a man buried to his torso there, an upturned cart just beyond them; all were tangled among cursing men and crying women and children. Groans and screams echoed from the high walls as frantic friends and family called for each other. Agonized screeches of crippled horses and tormented moans of oxen increased the turmoil.

Josef helped Mary to her feet, but she stumbled on her first step, sobbing and shivering.

"Mary, is the baby safe? Was the baby hurt?"

"Yes, yes."

"Oh, Lord of Heaven's Armies! Forgive us!" Josef reached to steady her.

"Wait; I mean, yes, the baby is safe. And, no, no harm has come to the baby, but I twisted my ankle when I fell."

Panting heavily, Josef surveyed the road. Grey dust billowed from the piles of rubble in the street. "Will you be safe if I leave you for a moment? There's a splintered cart over there; I see a stick of wood you can use for a crutch."

"Yes, please. That would help." Mary backed against a wall. Her body quivered and she coughed to clear the ashy air.

She leaned on the stick, and Josef supported her other arm as she hobbled to a small inn two blocks away. Inside, he set her on a bench at the back and pulled the money sack from his neck, counting the few coins.

"We'll have two bowls of soup," he said to the heavy set man behind the counter. He placed his money on the bar and brought the bowls to Mary. "The longer it takes us to drink this, the more time we have to calm our nerves and rest." She nodded.

As the broth soothed her insides, Mary's trembling subsided.

"How is your ankle?"

Mary wriggled her foot. "Much better."

Around them, more customers trickled inside, shaking off their dusty cloaks, and Mary and Josef listened to the chatter.

"The road is a disaster."

"How will they clear the rubble? Those last stones were massive."

"Did you see the horse that was harnessed to a cart? Crushed under a column."

"It was my horse and cart that were smashed." The gray-haired man buried his face in his hands. "I was fortunate I wasn't in it, but what will I tell my wife?" he mumbled.

All the customers were caught up in stories of the carnage they saw, the stones they escaped, and the screams they heard. The innkeeper hustled back and forth with cups of ale and flasks of wine.

Josef nudged Mary and pulled her makeshift cane under the table. He emptied his bowl. "You were right to be wary of Jericho, Mary. If you feel stable enough, let's leave as soon as you finish."

"What about our packs, our blanket, our food? We have nothing left but your coins and these clothes." She plucked at her cloak, filthy from their struggles against the dust storm and her falling in the street.

Her husband's shoulders sagged, and he tugged his ear. "I don't know. I don't even have the energy to pray."

Mary closed her eyes. "Oh, Holy One, I don't want to complain. Thank you for rescuing us and my baby. Please be our refuge, our strength, our help in this trouble."

"Therefore we won't be afraid, though the earth changes, though the mountains are shaken into the heart of the seas." Josef patted Mary's knee. "Thank you for reminding me who is watching us."

By now, ale and wine made most of the other patrons raucous. Two tables away, a customer turned to Josef and Mary. "We haven't heard *your* story. Did you see any of the catastrophe caused by Herod's folly?"

What a kind voice. Mary looked up from her empty bowl. The man's face was narrow and devoid of whiskers. Gentle eyes peered beneath dark orange curls.

Josef kept his eyes on his soup bowl. "Yes."

"What? You're not going to tell me the details? Your brief answer makes me even more curious. And your dirty cloaks are crying to be explained. From your accent, I'm guessing you're from the Holy City. Are you going to Jerusalem to register?"

"We thank the Holy One that our lives have been spared," said Mary. She whispered to Josef, "Don't tell him anything."

"We're going to Bethlehem," he said, with a quick glare at Mary.

She shrugged her shoulders and smiled at the man. "A thief stole our food and coverings right off my husband's back while he was pulling me away from the danger."

By now the men and women at the neighboring tables had turned their attention to Josef and Mary. The man who had been speaking to them stood, his lanky frame stooping under the low ceiling. He crossed to them and placed his hands on their table. "Oh yes; I saw that happen. I can help you," he said, whiffs of ale accompanying his words.

Under the table, Mary grasped Josef's hand. He turned to her and she begged him with her eyes

"I'm sorry, but I don't have enough funds to pay you."

The stranger pounded their table, causing their bowls to jump. "I'm not asking for money, friend. I want to help you. I'm bringing figs and dates to Jerusalem. If you can carry two my bags, there'll be room for your wife in my cart. Don't you think that baby in her belly would like a ride?"

Mary broke into tears and her hands flew to cover her face.

Josef reached to shake the man's hand. "I'm Josef, son of Jacob. I'm grateful, and I think that was also a 'Yes' from my wife."

"Call me Ari. Born near here, under the big, blue heavens." His body swayed with his laugh, and his friends laughed with him. He raised his hand and waved for the innkeeper. "Serve these young people a bowl of beans. On me."

"You mustn't." Josef's face reddened, and he lowered his voice. "We can't pay."

Ari took the bowls from the innkeeper. "Hiram, these are my special friends. Whatever they need, I'll take care of it." He pushed Josef's pouch away. "This is my gift for your son."

Mary jerked back. "How did you…? I mean, wh-what makes you think it's a boy?"

"If it isn't, I'd be surprised. Forget I said anything."

Josef's stomach clenched and his face turned white. "I've changed my mind. We don't know you. We'd best be going." He stood and helped Mary to her feet. "Thank you for the food. Come, Mary." He pulled her toward the door.

In two strides, Ari laid his sinewy hands on Josef's back. "Don't be stubborn. Your wife is exhausted, and you need me. First, I'm putting you up in a room here tonight. You couldn't get even halfway to Jerusalem this afternoon. Then we'll leave at dawn."

Josef sputtered and Mary sank against the wall while Ari approached the innkeeper and handed him coins. He came back and stood in Josef's face. "You are a good man, and your wife is an honorable woman." Hiram waved them over and led them to a small room at the back, and Ari trailed behind. "I'll wake you before daybreak, so we get a bite before we leave."

The next morning, Mary stretched her arms and yawned at the knock on their door. "I don't know how this happened, but I'm glad it did."

"I have to admit, we couldn't have made it to Jerusalem last night." Josef opened the door to Hiram, and they followed him through the inn.

"See you next time, Hiram," Ari hollered over his shoulder. "Be sure to take care of this couple whenever they come by." He led Josef and Mary out to his cart and donkey. "Now, let's make that climb to Jerusalem."

...

Mary's eyebrows rose when she recognized the tune Ari was humming. Josef was walking beside the cart, and when he turned to her, she knew he had heard it too.

When the family climbed the road for the festivals in Jerusalem other times, they sang all the traditional songs of ascent together. How she loved King David's psalms about their holy city. She added the words to Ari's melody and sang along. "I will lift up my eyes to the hills. Where does my help come from? My help comes from Yahweh, who made heaven and earth. He will not allow your foot to be moved. Yahweh will keep you from all evil. He will keep your soul. Yahweh will keep your going out and your coming in, from this time forward, and forever more."

How appropriate. Had Ari chosen that one for her sake? She faced Josef with a crooked grin. The sun hid behind a low, drab sky. The dust storm had passed, but the hill was covered with loose sand and torn branches that covered the paving stones. The donkey stumbled toward the shoulder, and Mary lurched for a sack teetering on the edge of the cart. Ari kept his eyes forward and his steps steady, and the donkey lined up behind him.

At the halfway point, Ari motioned them to a stop.

"Do you sing the ascent songs every trip?" Mary stretched her legs and rearranged her position.

A grin stretched across his face. "No; I never do. But this trip I have a passenger who needed to sing them."

"It's very kind of you. You're right; I needed them."

Ari spread his hands. "It's nothing. They're only songs. Makes me feel good." He dug in his pack and produced dates and almonds. "Here. Let's have a bite and move on. We want to arrive before dark, and it would be miserable if the winds come up again."

Their spirits rose when the temple appeared above them, back-lit by deep gold rays that split umber clouds. Josef began the song, "I was glad when they said to me, 'Let's go to Yahweh's house!'"

"Josef," Mary blurted, "I think that's a sign that we should first go to the temple before turning toward Bethlehem." *If only Anna would be there.*

"Then just ahead is where I'll leave you two. I'm off to Bethany."

"Where can we find you, Ari? I want to repay you for all you've done for us, and I don't have enough coins with me right now."

"Don't think of it, Josef. I was happy to help."

"Can we find you at the inn in Jericho? We'll pass through on the way back to Nazareth."

"That's as good a place as any." Ari wrapped Josef in a hug. He placed his left hand on Mary's head as he took her other hand. "Be very cautious, young lady. May the Holy One always be with you and your young one there." He swiped his eyes. "I hope we'll meet again someday." Ari picked up the donkey's lead and plodded on toward the Huldah gates.

Mary's heart pounded at the thought of seeing Anna. Was she still alive? Would she remember her? As they climbed the steps, Josef asked everyone they passed, but no one had seen her that day. Mary tugged Josef's sleeve. "Can you keep looking? Everyone is so used to her, they don't even notice her."

After passing from person to person, Josef returned to the column where Mary leaned. "Mary, let's go. It appears there's no lodging left here; we must head for Bethlehem while we still have light."

"Won't you ask that couple? They might have seen Anna. At least, we can ask if there's room for us where they're staying."

"Pardon me." The man turned. "Isaac! It's me, Josef." The men embraced. "Mary, this is one of my oldest friends."

"And my wife Deborah and our baby." Isaac grinned and patted his wife's belly. "The midwife tells her it will be a girl."

"We're expecting too, and we're quite sure ours will be a boy," Mary said.

"Well then, let's betroth them now, and save us all the formalities later." Isaac laughed. The chuckles lightened their spirits until Isaac explained they were going back to Bethlehem that night since there was no lodging left.

"Then that's where we'll go. We need a place to stay."

"Josef, you'll be staying at your father's house, of course."

Josef nodded his head. "That's our plan." Fatigue clouded Mary's mind, and she gave up her hopes of seeing Anna.

...

"Josef, can we go slower?" Mary grabbed her side.

"Can't you keep up? Isaac and Deborah are out-distancing us."

"My stomach hurts."

"Me too. We're just hungry." He stopped at the top of the hill where a road cut off to the Herodium palace. "Do you want me to buy some bread or fruit? That inn is still open. We could eat as we go."

"No, I'm not hungry." Mary sat on the wall beside the inn. With a yawn, she crossed her arms to rub warmth into them.

"How much longer?"

"Usually it's no time at all to Bethlehem, but now it's dark and we don't have the advantage of smooth paving stones."

She didn't move.

"Look. Can't you see that twinkling? That's Bethlehem. We'll be settled in before the first watch is over."

Mary plodded steadily behind Josef, focusing on his footsteps. When he stopped, she looked up.

"See the third house. That's where we're going."

"It's on a hill. I didn't know that."

"All of Bethlehem is on hills. You've never been here before? Hasn't your father brought you?"

"No, his family came to us in Jerusalem. I think because of my mother's health." She took several deep breaths. "Why are these houses so tall? They climb the hill."

"We keep the animals inside at night and sleep in the rooms above them. The animals stay safe from predators, and it's warmer for all of us in winter. The downstairs is like your courtyard in Nazareth."

Josef led Mary to the largest cluster of homes. She quickly re-braided her hair and straightened her headscarf while they waited for a response to Josef's knocking.

Josef's father Jacob opened the door. His eyes darted from Josef to scrape Mary's body. He stepped back and slammed the door.

Josef blew out his breath. "I wasn't expecting that." He glanced at Mary, who was clutching her side. "You have a side-ache?" She nodded. "Let's ask my brothers; Cleopas, the youngest, lives with my brother Jacob now."

"Don't they live next door?"

"I want to try." Jacob's eyes lit when he recognized Josef, but as soon as he saw Mary, he shook his head and pushed the door.

Josef stepped into the slim opening. "Jacob, don't turn us away. You have to help us. Mary isn't feeling well."

"You've brought us shame, Josef, or rather, *she* did."

"That's not true. You don't understand." Josef saw his younger brother Cleopas peering over Jacob's shoulder. "Cleopas, *you* believe me, don't you?" Jacob pushed Josef back and closed the door.

Mary cringed as she heard the bolt slam into place.

"How could this be?" Josef threw his arms in the air. "It makes me angry. This is my family! I'm not a criminal; we're not lepers." He moaned. "If only they had had a dream." He grabbed his jaw. "We'll go to the inn, then," he said, shaking his head.

Dispirited, Mary plodded behind him, gripping her stomach. She wrapped her shawl tighter around her head as a breeze shimmied up the hill. Ahead of them, a cluster of men argued at the doorway of the inn, their donkeys a noisy chorus. Josef brought Mary to a low wall. "Wait here; I'll be right back." Within minutes, he returned, shaking his head. "No room. I pleaded, told them of your condition."

Mary stomped her feet to warm them. Tears slid down her face, but she was too tired to wipe them away.

"You must be more disheartened than I am. Let me just think a moment." Suddenly, Josef pulled her up. "I forgot about my friend, Matthias. He and his wife have an extra room. They aren't on any of the main roads, so perhaps he has a place for us. They're only a little farther up this road."

"Up this hill?" Mary massaged her stomach. Her cramp was throbbing with her heartbeat. Her eyes widened, and she covered her mouth as the thought exploded that her precious baby was about to arrive. Mute, she trudged behind Josef while her heart thumped harder.

Five minutes later, Josef began pounding on a door where a dim spot of light leaked. Half a face peered around the door. "No room! Go away!" the voice growled, shoving the door at them.

Swiftly wedging his foot in the way, Josef barked, "Matthias. It's me, Josef!"

"Josef?" The door opened to the width of his body. "Friend, what are you doing here? I thought you were in Nazareth." Peering over Josef's shoulder, Matthias squinted at Mary's half-bent form. "Did you come to register? Why aren't you staying with your family?" He leaned around Josef to examine Mary as the widened door poured light from the room. A sheep and donkey were staring at her.

Mary cringed behind Josef and brushed at the dried mud trimming her cloak.

"It's a long story. I'll tell you in the morning; but, do you have a room for us?"

"You're joking. No one has rooms anymore; we let out our guest room."

"But my wife...." Josef looked back at Mary and began kneading his hands.

Mary kept her head down. *Had the brief encounter with his family brought back his reservations about marrying her? Would he abandon her now, faced with all this opposition?*

Chapter 10

At Mary's next groan, Josef's face paled as he turned back to Matthias. "Her time is close, if not imminent."

"What! You can't be serious, Josef."

Mary grasped Josef's arm. "Please, is there a shed? A cave even?" Sweat beaded her face, and words stuck in her throat. Why couldn't she be outspoken like Sali? Thoughts of her whirlwind sister prompted her. "Is there a woman here who can help me?" She pushed around Josef and called over Matthias's shoulder. "Please, I don't want to have this baby on your doorstep!" Josef grasped Matthias's arm.

Instantly, a woman and young girl appeared. The woman took one look at Mary and grabbed some bedding. "Matthias, start moving the animals out. Serai, boil a pot of water. You, dear one, come over here." She guided Mary inside the room to a bench covered with rugs, pulling off the dusty cloak as they walked. "Set here for a moment, and then I can help you. I'm Susannah." She headed toward a chest against the wall.

The animals' wary eyes watched Mary as Matthias leapt into action, grabbing a wooden pigeon cage with one hand and pulling the donkey past her into the night. A young boy tugged at the protesting sheep, dragging it outside. Mary doubled over with her next pain.

When she looked up again, she noticed a man and woman huddled against the wall on the balcony area at the back. These must be the guests who had filled the spare room. The woman watched her for a few moments and then asked Susannah, "I've had two babies of my own. May I help?" Susannah nodded eagerly, coming to Mary with cloths and bedding. Her husband slipped away to join the men outside.

Susannah's daughter Serai took other children away—where, Mary didn't care. The rustling noises faded, and the room was becoming quieter. Another cramp spread across Mary's belly.

"If you can stay there and take some deep breaths, I'll make a pallet for you," Susannah said.

Waves of pain washed over Mary. She watched Susannah prepare the mattress. The other woman, Bernice, helped her carry it to the opposite wall. The two women murmured as they gathered water jugs and more cloths.

"Please tell me what to do next." Mary groaned. "Everything my mother told me has evaporated." Her mind froze as each cramp rolled over her belly. In between, her thoughts were skipping. *Thank the Lord, we aren't still on the road. Food. I can't eat a thing. Where did Josef and his friend go? I wish my mother were here.*

Susannah and Bernice carefully positioned Mary on a stool in the corner and began massaging her belly.

...

"He's here; my baby is here." Mary cuddled her son, kissing the top of his wet head.

"Oh, look at the little Josef." Bernice cooed and touched his chin.

"Let me have him, Mary." Susannah reached for the baby. "We'll clean him up and get some salt onto him. I think I have enough."

"No; wait! You don't understand. His name is Jesus. It's Jesus, and I don't want any salt on him."

"You have to salt a baby or it won't breathe right," Bernice said through clenched teeth.

"Now, why don't I bring Josef in here to see his son?" Susannah whispered to Bernice, who went back upstairs.

"Yes, please bring Josef. He'll tell you his name. But no salt; my mama's babies who were scrubbed in salt died. She told me she wouldn't do that to mine."

"I'll let you sleep a few moments first." Susannah disappeared.

Fighting sleep, Mary clung to her son. She gazed into Jesus' tiny puckered face. *He's not as beautiful as I thought he would be. Wouldn't you think that the King of Israel would be handsome like Saul and David* were? She hadn't paid much attention to what babies looked like before, other than her sister, but not too many people would be chirping and clucking over him. He was just what little boys looked like, she decided. He was *her* baby, and she would give him all the attention he needed.

Jesus slept, tucked against her side, her only solace for the achy loneliness she felt for her mother. She lay on a mat on the stone floor. Susannah had piled some blankets in the straw-filled depression beside her where the animals were fed. How tempting to settle the baby into that manger. The pungent scent of the animals tickled her nose, reminding her of her lamb Moses when he lived with them. What a sweet memory. Her head nodded, and she pinched herself to stay awake.

"My sweet wife. And look at that little man."

"Do you like him?" Mary smiled weakly.

Josef tilted his head. "Why wouldn't I like him?" He turned to Susannah hovering behind him. "What was it you wanted me to ask Mary? The salting?"

"Josef, I can explain." Mary struggled to sit up.

"Never mind. But we did warn her." Susannah shook her head and took a deep breath. "Josef, you can see we're already crowded here. Do you think you can move to your parents' house tomorrow?"

Josef looked at Mary, and she shook her head.

"Have you talked to Matthias about this?"

Jesus snuffled and mewed. Suddenly, he burst into fussy squeaking. Mary fumbled at lowering the top of her robe to feed him, unsure how to help him latch on. Jesus rooted around her chest, trying to find something to suck until he broke into a wail.

"Humph. Here, let me show you." Susannah knelt and guided his mouth.

Mary's face grew warm. "I'm sorry. It's been a few years since my sister was little. We weren't expecting him to come so soon. I thought my mother would be with me." She gulped, holding back a sob.

Susannah studied Mary before taking a deep breath. "I apologize for my behavior. I'm a better hostess than this. Don't worry about leaving just yet, and I won't do anything you don't want me to do." She stroked Mary's hair, then brought her some water.

Matthias came in the door and whispered to his wife before turning to Josef. "Let's all get some sleep."

As soon as Susannah left, Josef pulled another blanket off the bench and lay beside Mary, slipping his arm under her head and falling instantly asleep. Jesus dozed on Mary's chest. Her eyes drooped, and she ached from her discomfort. With a yawn, she pulled the blanket close to the baby's head.

A soft lowing and bleating filtered in the home from the donkey and sheep protesting their removal, but Jesus was snuggled between Josef and herself. Mary's heart squeezed. He wasn't swaddled in the cloths Elizabeth and she had prepared; he wasn't wrapped in one of the warm blankets her mother had woven. *I will just have to wait a few weeks*, she thought. She rolled the baby to her other side, wiggling so she could feed him, and lay him in the padded feeding trough.

Shouts outside, pounding on the door, sheep squalling! Josef jumped up, and Matthias stumbled from his room. "What's wrong? Who's there? Josef, what did you do?"

Loud voices from outside accompanied more pounding on the door, now waking the baby. His bird-like squeals added to the commotion.

Mary held him to her chest and wrapped the blanket around her shoulders, hiding Jesus inside. As Matthias moved to the door, she slipped him back into the manger and concealed him by sitting in front of it, blocking him from harm and drafts.

The pounding began again, and Matthias and Josef conferred on whether to open up. "I'll open it," Matthias said. "Whoever's out there is too noisy to be a thief."

Their mouths fell open at the group of ragged shepherds. One of them cradled a little lamb in his arms. "Is this the place? Do you have a baby in a manger? We were told the new King was born tonight in Bethlehem."

Another man pushed forward. "We tried other homes, but they didn't have a baby."

"And we saw the animals under the shed, not inside, so we wondered."

"Is he here?"

"Can we see him?"

The questions tumbled into the room. Matthias waved them back. "Get away from here! You're crazy! We're all trying to sleep here." He advanced, shoving the man in front.

Chapter 11

"Wait, Matthias!" Josef grabbed his arm. "You don't understand. We couldn't tell you."

"What are you talking about?" Matthias frowned. Susannah stood behind him, her arm latched through his elbow.

The shepherd at the front interrupted. "The angels told us! We were out in the fields with the herd, and the sky suddenly filled with light, like a thousand lightning strikes, and voices shouting about the Holy One's glory, and peace to all the people."

"They said he would be lying in a manger," said another. "Born today, in David's city, a Savior, who is Christ the Lord. We want to see the Savior of Israel."

A boney youth, carrying a lamb, interrupted, "He's here, isn't he?" All eyes turned at a squall from Jesus; Mary scooped her son up and turned him away from their sight.

"There he is! I see him! Can you believe it? The angels came to us, poor, wretched shepherds. They promised us, 'You will find a baby wrapped in strips of cloth, lying in a feeding trough' and here he is: the Messiah!"

Matthias put his hands to his head, eyes blazing. He looked at Josef and then his eyes pierced Mary. "Who are you? Are you a witch? A devil?" He started toward her, reaching to grab her arm.

Susannah pulled his sleeve. "Wait! Don't you remember the prophecies?" Then she turned back to Josef and Mary. "But Josef, the prophecy says the Savior is to be born to a virgin."

Jesus was still fussing, so Mary turned from the crowd and scooted into the corner. Josef sighed deeply and began the account. She didn't hear all his words, but he admitted his own disbelief until the angel came to him. She blushed when he explained that his family wouldn't believe that she was pure and had never been with a man, not even Josef.

"Ah," said Matthias, as his eyes met Susannah's. "And the child is Immanuel—God with us." He brushed at tears. "Jesus: the one who saves now lives with us? Lord, forgive us." He turned away and covered his face.

There was whispering among the shepherds, and the oldest shepherd trembled as he stepped toward Mary. "I… I brought a gift. I was going to bring it to my wife for the child she is expecting, but I want to give it to the Messiah." He held out a sheepskin of purest white, and Josef handed it down to Mary.

She pressed it against her cheek. "It's so soft! I'm grateful, and I'm sure my own little lamb here will enjoy it."

"We both thank you," Josef said, patting the man's shoulder.

At Josef's words, the shepherds crept farther into the room to kneel at Mary's feet. She looked up and saw that, behind those dirty young men, Matthias and Susannah were kneeling as well, then Josef. Tears clouded her vision and dripped onto her swollen breasts. She gulped and whispered to Josef, "You believe me, and you truly believe the angel now, don't you?"

He nodded.

The next morning, Josef took Matthias and Susannah to visit his parents. They returned and Josef was fuming. "You would think all of us could convince my parents of our royal baby, but no. My father cannot conceive that the Messiah would be born in a simple room and not a palace, especially without anyone's prior notice, including his." He paced in front of Mary while she fed the baby. "It didn't help that mere shepherds were the first visitors."

"What do we do now?"

"First, I register." Josef yawned. "Why don't we stay in Bethlehem a few weeks to give my parents a chance to know you?"

"We need to wait, at least for my purification, but let's think; I don't want to impose on Matthias and Susannah any longer. Do you know anyone who has a house to let?" She studied her husband's shaking head. "Then we pray."

Josef lifted his arms to heaven.

In the midst of his praises, Mary shouted. "Uncle Samuel."

"Who?"

"My mother's cousin, the one who brought me to Elizabeth and Zechariah's. You met him in Na ...." Her words fell as she remembered Josef had disappeared when Samuel had come. "He lives here in Bethlehem when he isn't traveling, and he knows about Jesus. My father told him about our dreams, and he was with me when Elizabeth's baby, John, leapt in her womb. I told you about that, didn't I?"

"Your father told me. Matthias must know him."

"He likely has a cave or stable for Sheba we could share."

Josef tilted his head.

"His camel; her name is Sheba." Mary smiled.

"Samuel, the merchant? Yes, we all know where he lives," Matthias said. "Bethlehem looks like a little city with all these relatives come back to register, but there are only 40 or 50 families who live here all the time, except for Samuel, who doesn't stay very long. I don't know when I last saw him, but let's go look." Matthias and Josef left, and Mary fell asleep.

She woke to Jesus' cries. Feeding him was easier now, but changing his messy cloths was awkward, Mary hating to disturb Susannah and her family and have them wash the laundry she or her mother should do. How she missed her mother. She shook her head over the fading dream. Would her other dreams fade too?

Josef burst in the door, breathing hard. "We found him." He took deep breaths. "I almost missed him."

Matthias squeezed in around him. "Just in time. He was leading Sheba out of town, on his way to Egypt."

"Oh no. I was hoping we could stay with him."

Josef squeezed Mary and ran his finger over Jesus's soft cheek. "We can. He's letting us use his house as long as we need it. He even turned around to make his house presentable for you. He'll delay his trip a few days."

"Praise the Holy One!" Jesus jerked at Mary's shout and started whimpering. "Don't fuss, little one. This is good news." She rocked him in her arms, and he settled to sleep.

A few days after the move, Mary stood in front of Samuel and took a deep breath. "Uncle Samuel, knowing I was unmarried when Jesus was growing in me, how could you be so kind, so generous?"

His teeth gleamed through the dark whiskers. "Little Mary, the prophet Isaiah told us our Messiah would be born to a virgin. I realized that the virgin would have to be somebody's daughter and that the Lord of Hosts would obviously pick the sweetest, purest girl He could find. Since you're the sweetest, purest girl I know, I wasn't taken aback with His choice." He patted Mary on the head and his eyes misted with tears. "Now, be at peace and make my home your home."

The first two weeks with the baby finally became calmer, but not much easier. Mary's strength was weakened by the accident in Jericho, the climb to Bethlehem, the birth among strangers, the commotion of the shepherds, as well as moving into Samuel's home. Days passed, and still no word of welcome came from Josef's parents.

Josef shrugged his shoulders. "What more can I do?"

To earn a living while they stayed in Bethlehem, Josef took in carpentry jobs, setting up a workshop on one side of Sheba's cave. He proudly handed the money to Samuel when he came back from Egypt. "Here's our rent."

"No, that will not happen!" Samuel pushed Josef's hands away. "I cannot take money from my family; this house is yours, just as it is mine. Mary is like the child I never had. You are my family."

How different that was from Josef's family, and how it grieved him. Each Sabbath Josef visited his parents and asked if he could bring Mary the next time. No answer; they just showed him to the door. His two brothers, at least, would meet him at the well for a short visit, but never come to visit them at Samuel's house. When he returned, Mary looked for his smile, a gleam in his eye. Each week, her prayer remained unanswered.

When six weeks had passed, Mary and Josef left before dawn to go to the temple for Mary's purification and to redeem her first-born, as custom required. Golden spears reflected off the temple's dome at each rise in the road. "I can't wait to be there," Mary said. "I hope I see her."

"The prophetess, of course." Josef clucked her under the chin. "My sweet wife. You're as fussy as a mother bird today."

"I'm nervous about what she'll say."

"What does it matter?" Josef gazed across the Kidron Valley and handed Mary the water flask.

Her voice trembled. "I don't want to disappoint her."

"How could you do that? She doesn't even know you now. You're a beautiful woman, a considerate wife, a loving mother. No man could ask for more." Josef kissed his fingers and touched her nose. "Here, let me carry the baby for a bit." He reached out for Jesus.

"Are you sure?" At his smile, she unwrapped the cloth sling and helped Josef wrap Jesus across his chest. She giggled. "Let's hope he doesn't get hungry." Josef started down the road.

Mary relished Josef's tenderness. It was the little kindnesses like this that erased her childish concern over his scarred face. She still wasn't comfortable asking him how it happened, but she knew that, though his face was scarred, his heart was clear and beautiful, as beautiful as the dazzling temple rising above them. "Let me take Jesus now." *No need for him to be teased by other men.*

After her purification bath, they joined the group of people at the base of the steps.

"Doesn't it seem like we're in another world?" Josef said, staring at the Golden Gate above them. "Think of all the Feast Days that we climbed to the temple. It never has looked as beautiful, as holy, as it does today."

"Maybe because we are about holy business. Let's purchase our dove offerings here," Mary said. "They will be cheaper than the prices they charge up in the courtyard. If only we could afford more: a pure lamb for my pure little lamb," she said.

"Don't fret, dear wife. Someday we'll have a lamb to sacrifice."

While Josef made the purchase, Mary jiggled Jesus to settle him, her gaze turning from one shop to another. The background of vendors calling out their prices faded as she pondered how her little son would maintain his purity as he grew up. No leprosy, no deformities, no touching the dead. Abruptly, she panicked. The implications of her son's immediate ritual caused her heart to flop: would Josef's scar keep him from presenting their firstborn son? The priests were fanatical about forbidding impurities in the temple. Josef might not be allowed inside to redeem Jesus.

"Mary, look who came here to help." Mary looked behind Josef to see Matthias grinning bashfully. "Matthias, how nice of you to join us."

"It seems like I have a habit of helping my friend in his time of need. Josef told me yesterday that he wasn't sure if the priests would let him inside for the redemption, so I offered to help." He patted Josef on the back.

"I would rather it had been my father or one of my brothers, but Matthias understands." Josef surveyed the row of booths, made the purchase, and grabbed the doves. They climbed up to the courtyard, where Mary handed Jesus to Matthias. She walked with the men to the entrance of the temple and said a silent prayer.

"It was beautiful, Mary. I pulled my headscarf closer, and nobody noticed a thing. Once we were inside, Matthias gave Jesus back to me. I badly wanted to tell the priest about Jesus' royal future, but when he asked why we weren't naming him Josef, I was flustered. Then he named him 'Jesus ben Josef', and I almost dropped Jesus when he handed him back."

Mary laughed. "His time to be honored will come." She smiled widely at Matthias. "Will you come eat with us?"

"I would love to come, but I have some other errands for Susannah. Perhaps back in Bethlehem?"

"We will invite your whole family then."

"I'll see you soon." Matthias and Josef grasped arms.

As their friend left, an elderly man approached them.

"May I hold your son?" he asked, not bothering to introduce himself. He exuded a warm glow, and a soft smile softened the weathered face and deep wrinkles around his eyes. "Yahweh drew me in the spirit into the temple today," he told them. Josef grabbed Jesus from Mary's arms and handed him to the stranger.

"Sing, heavens, and be joyful, earth! Break out into singing, mountains, for Yahweh has comforted his people and will have compassion on his afflicted!" The man rocked Jesus in his arms, gazing at the baby and humming a song. "Comfort, comfort, Jerusalem," he crooned. Then he looked up at the sky and exclaimed, "Lord, now let your servant die in peace, as you have promised, for my eyes have seen your salvation, which you have prepared before the face of all peoples; a light for revelation to the nations, and the glory of your people Israel - right here in my arms.

Josef and Mary hugged each other. She understood Jesus would be a special gift, a king for Israel; she knew that Elizabeth was told that she would be the mother of the Lord. Mere shepherds surprised them with the news that they, too, were told this baby would be a savior. "Christ the Lord", they'd said. *How did this man know? Why was he told?*

"You are so gracious and kind, sir," Josef said. "We are humbly praying that we will raise him up to be the one the Name has called him to be."

The man handed Jesus to Mary. "Forgive me for not introducing myself." He bowed. "My name is Simeon. I have been waiting so eagerly for Messiah to come and rescue our nation. The Spirit of the Lord came upon me and revealed to me that I would see Messiah before I die. I have been waiting for this moment."

The air around them was shimmering. *Was Simeon another angel?* Mary felt a ripple run through her. In her mind she could see all the messages from the dreams, from Aunt Elizabeth and from the shepherds, stacked before her like the temple's brilliant walls. *How can I do this? I wasn't born a queen. I've never lived in a palace. How will I ever teach this child all he needs to know to be our king?* She was supposed to clean the temple courtyards; that was all. She slumped against Josef.

Simeon gently lifted her chin until she could look into his eyes. Their dark brown depths radiated wisdom and confidence.

"My dear, do not fear. The Lord will give you, your husband, and your son everything needed. The Father will not abandon His son." Then this prophet—*yes, he must be a prophet*—laid his time-worn hands on her and she bowed her head as he spoke again. "'Blessed are you, dear woman, and the fruit of your womb. This child is set for the falling and the rising of many in Israel, and for a sign which is spoken against.'" Simeon squeezed his eyes tightly.

Mary turned to Josef, "What does he mean?"

The old man turned her chin back to him. "Yes, a sword will pierce through your own soul, that the thoughts of many hearts may be revealed."

His words sliced her heart. "Josef, did you hear his last words?"

"No, he was whispering those. How could I hear him?"

"A whisper! No, he shouted." Jesus began fretting at her loud voice. She turned back to confront Simeon. He was nowhere in sight. *Was he another angel?*

"What did he say?" said Josef. She couldn't repeat the words; they had already shredded her soul.

As Mary rocked Jesus, a crowd formed around them. A strident voice was praising the Lord beside them, a high-pitched one this time. The tiny, hunched woman making the commotion tugged at Mary's arm.

"It's true, Mary! Didn't I tell you that you were destined to serve the Lord?" Her eyes twinkled as she touched Jesus' cheek. "Praise the Lord, praise His holy name; our redemption is coming," she announced to all those around her. People looked at her and nodded slyly to each other.

Mary grinned. "Dear Anna, I'm confused. Didn't you tell me I would be sweeping the temple with you? I hated leaving Jerusalem because you said I was destined to keep the courtyards clean, that the Holy One had called me to that."

Anna's smile stretched across her face. "I didn't know myself what it meant: 'You will be a caretaker of the Lord's house.' Hee-hee. You are that house; I honor you." She turned to the men and women that had shuffled closer to hear. "Praise the Lord! See this baby? He's our redemption."

People looked at Mary and Josef's simple clothes and back at Anna. "Go back to your sweeping, Anna. That's your job, right?" Laughter sprinkled the crowd. Anna turned to argue, and Josef pulled Mary away.

"She's not crazy, Josef. She was right all this time," Mary said.

"She's not crazy, but no one in our country knows what to do with prophets. They either mock them or kill them. We should leave. I don't think we want extra attention now."

...

Laughing, they entered Samuel's house. "In spite of all the attention, it encourages me to have a reminder of Jesus' triumphant future. How funny that I thought I would be sweeping the temple courts." She went to bed basking in joy.

That night Mary woke from a deep sleep. Simeon's final shattering pronouncement was ringing in her ears. Where was that prediction in the scriptures? A brief memory of Elizabeth's husband Zechariah frowning over his scroll sent shivers through her body. Sleep stole away as she repeated hour after hour, "That shall not happen. That shall not happen. We will take good care of him."

Chapter 12

Josef kept delaying the return to Nazareth, still hopeful his parents would relent. When Mary's parents and Salome came to Jerusalem for Passover, Mary and Josef met them in the city. Mary was elated. They all cooed over Jesus, and praised Uncle Samuel, who had returned in time for the High Holy Days. Mary's father tried to meet with Josef's father, Jacob, and convince him to accept what the angels had said. Jacob crossed his arms and looked away. "You have tricked me and fooled Josef."

When Mary's parents tried to encourage Josef to come back to Nazareth, he protested. "This is my hometown," he told Mary that night. "Work will be better in Bethlehem. I'm building clients, a reputation. Some people give me work, in spite of my father's opinion. I believe he will come around."

"In Nazareth there are loving grandparents to help us raise Jesus and other children we might have. And what about Salome? Did you notice how she carried Jesus everywhere while they were here? She would have fed him, if she could." They argued back and forth. Only Mary's new friendship with Deborah, who had birthed a little boy, not the daughter that was predicted, gave her comfort. In just a few months, the boys would be playing together. If she stayed in Bethlehem, they would grow up together.

Spring blossomed into summer, and summer sweated into autumn. Mary was visiting with Deborah at the well in the center of Bethlehem while their sons crawled at their feet. Suddenly the boys squealed as they spotted a large caravan coming into town. Sheba was the only camel that had been seen before in Bethlehem, and now there were four more and several men. Mary hurried home and set Jesus down to nap. "By their clothes, they must be from a royal family or they're very successful merchants," she told Josef. "I wonder if Samuel knows who they are. Do you think they came to visit him? Do you want to ask?"

"Samuel won't be back for several days. We can't help them with his business."

"Don't you want to talk to them?"

"I'm in the middle of a new table for Matthias. I can make some time to see them tomorrow."

"If they are friends of Samuel, we should show them the same hospitality he would."

"Mary." Josef frowned. "What if they *aren't* friends of Samuel? We'll find out tomorrow when everyone in town will know their story." Mary hoped to scoop up Jesus and slip back to the well, but he had fallen asleep. Let sleeping babies lie, she thought, and reached for her lap loom.

Josef was downing the last of his dinner when the door rattled under pounding fists. "Josef, Mary. Open up."

"Matthias?" Josef hugged his friend. Mary looked past Matthias and her husband to the exotic visitor. Intricate golden threads trimmed the stranger's robe, and a deep red jewel gleamed from the band around his head. She shrank back.

"Josef, I think this gentleman is eager to meet you and Mary," Matthias said. The man stepped around Matthias into the room and bowed low before Mary. Matthias slipped into the room behind him, winking at Mary.

"Respectful greetings, Your Highnesses." A thick accent marked the stranger's words.

At Mary and Josef's frowns, the man continued.

"We come from the East. My masters are scholars of the heavens. The night skies tell them many things: when a king has died and when a new king has been born. We have traveled for months, following the new star that appeared to them. As we traveled west, they pored over the ancient writings of the empires in this region. Their answer aligned with the location of the bright star above. If you are the parents of the young king of Israel, my masters seek an audience with him."

Ignoring Matthias's gasp behind him, Josef took a deep breath and bowed in return. Mary's knees quivered, and she grabbed for her headscarf.

Josef drew her against him. "We would be very honored, but we are just a humble family. We have no place to receive such distinguished visitors."

"Our party has made camp at the edge of Bethlehem." The stranger bowed again. "Our emperor instructed us to find the royal child, which King Herod's ministers indicated would be born in this town." He looked around at Samuel's small home, his eyebrows arching. "Perhaps just a few of our caravan could come at a time," he offered. "We have many gifts for the child."

Mary tugged at Josef's sleeve. While keeping his eyes on the man before them, he bent to hear her whisper. "Josef, I have very little food to feed them and only one flask of wine in the house."

"May I suggest we meet at the inn by the synagogue?" the stranger suggested. *Was the visitor reading her mind?* "My masters would be honored to host a celebration of this significant event."

Mary felt the tension leaving Josef's body, and she breathed freely, too. "Yes, that would be most desirable," he said. "We accept their gracious invitation."

Mary covered her nervous giggles as Josef used the lavish words.

"Would it be convenient if we meet when the sun is at its zenith tomorrow? That would give my esteemed masters an opportunity to refresh themselves," the envoy said.

Josef and Mary nodded and bowed. As the man swept up his robe and turned, they realized that clusters of neighbors had gathered; and as the stranger marched off, the crowd surged toward their door. "Matthias," Josef called, "Help me send them away."

With a chuckle and a gleam in his eyes, Matthias slipped outside to face the noisy throng. Josef closed the door behind him and hugged Mary. They knelt, praying and laughing and praising the Lord. Mary was floating with joy.

By sundown the next day, Mary sat in the middle of a luxurious carpet piled with treasure. Joy bubbled up as her wonder grew. Because of the gifts, they now had money to find a home of their own. Josef didn't have to work; they could even return to Nazareth.

Beautiful gilded tins of frankincense and myrrh, silken sacks of the most aromatic of teas, and delicate jars of spikenard surrounded her. Mary opened one container after another. She ran her hands through sacks of gold coins and let brilliant rubies and emeralds and diamonds sift between her fingers. She stroked the fine linen and silk cloth and, over and over, held up a tiny purple robe embroidered with larks and peacocks and pomegranates.

"I feel like the Queen of Sheba or the Prophet's Bride," she told Josef. "Look at these lovely tunics and scarves and these cubits of fabric. You know how we women are. I can't wait to make clothes from these silks and linens. I can dress my little prince in clothing that befits his status."

She patted the thick red rug beside her. "This weaving is exquisite. We don't want to put it on the floor."

Her joy grew when another traveler arrived the next afternoon while Josef was building furniture in Samuel's cave. There was a brief knock and a jiggling as someone tried to enter. "Open up."

Josef stepped from the cave as Mary opened the front door. "Uncle Samuel! Welcome home."

"Where are they residing? Are they still in our vicinity? I heard about your esteemed visitors while passing through Jerusalem." Samuel latched his arms around Josef and Mary. "I wish I'd been here, Mary. My original plan was to visit to Herodium first, but curiosity overwhelmed me."

"How embarrassing, Uncle; we don't have a bed for you. We've stored all the amazing gifts in your room," Mary said.

"Ahh. I anticipate seeing your inheritance, and we'll solve the bed debacle." He laughed. "Now I want to hold the precious little gentleman who is the instigator of your affluence."

Three nights later, Mary's heart was bursting. "We have the greatest gift now."

"You're right," said Josef. "Because of the astrologers, my parents know that Jesus is who we've said. It touched me deeply that both my father and mother came to see us here. When I opened the door for them," Josef shook his head, "I couldn't breathe. My father shed tears; I've never seen him cry before."

"My heart burst, seeing your reunion with your father. It was a marvel, and for your mother to tell me she believed me, that I hadn't deceived anyone, that I was pure when I married you?" She brushed a hand across her eyes. "The only time I've been more grateful was when our little boy was born."

"My greatest joy was seeing my mother wrap her arms around you. Are you happy that she's coming every day now to entertain Jesus?"

"She has been most kind. I'm grateful for her support." She quickly turned away from Josef.

"What is it? What's wrong, Mary?"

"I miss my mother and my sister. I know they would be just as eager to attend to Jesus and play with him." Her shoulders trembled with sobs.

Mary cried herself to sleep. When she woke, Josef was shaking her hard. "Mary, we have to flee. An angel came to me tonight." In the candlelight, she noticed sweat beading his forehead. "Herod is sending out a murder squad. He told the men from the East to tell him where the new Messiah was born. They didn't do that, but Herod knows they came to Bethlehem, where the scriptures said he would be born."

"We can't leave now. We won't be able to see the road." She rubbed her swollen eyes.

"What's wrong?" Samuel rose from his mat and lit a candle.

"An angel woke me. He said, 'Arise and take the young child and his mother, and flee into Egypt, and stay there until I tell you, for Herod will seek the young child to destroy him.' Herod sees Jesus as a threat. We must escape to Egypt."

"We can't go back there; it's the land of captivity." Mary mumbled, wiping sleep from her eyes.

"When our people were led to Babylon as captives, the remnant in Judah fled there to escape exile," Josef argued.

"Can't we go to Nazareth?"

"Any place near Herod's influence is dangerous. The angel said 'Egypt.'" Josef began collecting large sacks filled with Jesus's gifts.

Her hands flew to her head. "All these gifts, food, clothes: how can we carry them?"

"You can't," Samuel said. "Take some coins and food and blankets." Samuel pointed to the door. "Josef, run to your parents. Tell them you're going. Give them the key and tell them to store everything we leave." At Mary and Josef's startled look, he put his hands on his hips. "Sheba and I will accompany you to get you away from Bethlehem."

"What a relief." Josef's tight shoulders relaxed. "You know the route along the coast well."

Mary grabbed his arm. "Won't Herod expect us to go that way when he doesn't find us here?"

"We need to take the shortest route, Mary."

"The shortest route is straight south through Hebron, but that's just as obvious."

Josef took both her hands in his. "If we leave without delay, we'll be fine. I'll pack the grain."

Mary shook her head to focus. "Do I have time to bake some flatbread?"

"Only if the oven still has coals. We have to be on the road before first daylight: no one must see us leave. That gives us a couple hours at most."

Her hands shook as she stirred flour, salt and oil and thrust the flat lumps at the oven's edge. Fragments of their people's story ran through her head. *Egypt! The land of slavery; the land of false gods.* "What was the angel thinking?" she muttered. As she tied together blankets and stuffed them with clothing and beans, visions of forty years wandering in the desert crippled her spirits. *How could this be the Lord's plan?*

A light tap at the door made her freeze until Samuel slipped in. "The camel is ready. We must leave now."

Josef was pacing. "Mary, we either have to head south through Hebron or take the coastal highway."

A sudden thought gripped Mary. "Josef, if Herod's soldiers don't find Jesus here, they would naturally think we had fled to Egypt. It would take them no time at all to overtake us." She prayed silently, *Dear Lord, we need your wisdom, the wisdom of the ages to protect your son.* Instantly, a picture of the temple flashed in her mind. She turned to Samuel, "What does it mean that I'm seeing the temple?"

Samuel tugged his chin. "Brilliant! Yes, of course. If you go back to Jerusalem and down to Jericho, you can pick up the King's Highway east of the Sea of Salt. I made that trip myself several years ago when there were too many brigands on the Hebron road."

"What could be more dangerous than traveling right under Herod's nose?" Josef fumed. "It's insane to think we could sneak by his fortress at Jericho, and watchmen at Herodium can practically see us shop in the market!"

An image of the nearby fortress, another ominous testament to Herod's power, filled Mary's mind.

"I don't think that's wise, Samuel," Josef frowned. "It would be faster to take the Roman road by the sea. You know the proverb: As a roaring lion or a charging bear, so is a wicked ruler over helpless people."

Mary stood inches from Josef's face, breathing hard. "Then that's why going east is the safer route. No one would expect us to be so brazen."

"Or stupid," Josef added. Flushed with embarrassment, they both looked at Samuel to decide.

"Your wife makes a solid case, Josef." Samuel held out his hands. "Who can argue with a wise woman? She's not only wise, but brave."

Josef threw his hands up and left to tell his parents what was happening. He returned with gifts: extra sandals for both of them. He dashed into the workshop to grab a few tools while Samuel tightened the ropes over the camel load. When they came back in the house for a final check, Jesus whimpered and wiggled in Mary's arms. She jostled him and pulled the blanket lightly over his mouth. One more concern niggled at her. "Uncle Samuel, how will we manage the camel?"

"Mary, be at peace." He gave her a quick hug. "I will teach you; I'll go with you for two or three days to get you started on the journey. Now, why don't you make a honey rag for the baby to suck, so he won't cry while we sneak under the eyes of those malicious guards on the ramparts." His eyes narrowed. "We must protect the child's life at all costs. Let me take him now."

Samuel loaded the sleeping toddler into a cozy pack on his back. The moon had dipped away, and only the belt of stars lit the road. With whispering footsteps, they plodded carefully, stopping when Jesus fussed to be fed.

Mary sat on a boulder and Josef stood in front of her. "One other thing I told my parents: in a few days they are to spread the deception."

"Deception? What do you mean?"

Josef held Mary's face with both hands. "Mary, no one must have any idea we are going all the way to Egypt. After Samuel helps us get to Jericho with Sheba, they will spread the story that we have followed the astrologers all the way to the East."

"Hmm. Very clever, Josef." When Jesus was dozing again, Samuel held out his arms, and Mary slipped him into the pack. "Here you are, 'Grandfather.'" Samuel chortled.

Hazy pearled light edged the eastern horizon, and only two stars remained overhead as they passed the turnoff to the king's Herodium palace. Mary froze when the ground beneath them began trembling. Samuel looked over his shoulder and broke into a run. His baby-laden backpack rocked rhythmically, and a snorting Sheba trotted behind them. In the few moments while Josef and Mary were trying to decide whether they should run after Samuel, a louder pounding announced a mounted regiment from the Herodium galloping from behind. They stumbled to the side to get out of the way.

The horsemen yelled at the trembling pair beside the road, holding only the grain sacks and their straw mat while the cohort passed. The lead troops were advancing on Samuel, Sheba, and their baby, who were now a stadion ahead of them.

A violent shout rang out. Terrified they were about to attack Samuel and Jesus, Mary and Josef prayed desperately. No, Uncle Samuel was still steadily moving forward. The soldiers were not. The captain had turned around and was charging back. Mary clung to Josef, her stomach churning like a wobbly top, her knees rattling.

The dark stallion's spit sprayed her as his head was yanked to the side.

"What's in your packs?" The captain grabbed his sword as he swung from the saddle.

"Only our food," Josef answered softly.

"Throw it down!"

The bags were barely out of their hands when the sword swung before them, ripping the burlap apart. Barley and wheat sprayed around their feet.

"What will we eat? How could you?" Mary's emotions swung between fiery rage and icy fear.

"Nothing here. Move out!" The captain rammed Josef against her, causing them to tumble in the dirt; then he mounted and galloped on.

Wrapped in each other's arms, they thanked the Lord that Jesus wasn't with them, holding their breath until the soldiers dashed past Samuel and Jesus. Then Mary stooped to the ground, trying to scrape together what little grain she could. When they finally caught up with Samuel, his tiny cargo was still sleeping and the three fell to their knees.

Samuel began a song Mary had never heard before. "O Lord, keep me from the hands of the wicked. Preserve me from the violent men who have determined to trip my feet. Yahweh, don't grant the desires of the wicked. Don't let their evil plans succeed, or they will become proud."

At that moment, the sun surged above the horizon, and they raised their hands in praise.

"The path of the righteous is like the dawning light," Samuel sang.

Josef joined him with the next line, "That shines more and more until the perfect day!"

...

Afternoon sun warmed their backs as they rested on the last ridge above Jericho. After two yawns, Mary drifted to sleep. A jangling harness and creaking wheels woke her. A donkey cart pulled off the road ahead of them.

"Ari?" Josef ran down to him. "Ari, it's Josef and Mary." When they embraced each other, he brought Ari back to Mary and Samuel.

"Samuel," Josef said, "This is the generous man who bought us soup in Jericho and gave Mary a ride all the way from Jericho to Jerusalem." Samuel was introduced, and then Mary held up Jesus.

"This is our treasure." She glowed. "You almost saw him born; he was born later that night after we met you."

"May the Holy One be praised. I am honored to be in his presence." Mary cocked her head. She didn't remember them saying anything that night as they climbed up to Jerusalem. Ari held Jesus and stared into his eyes. "Yes. Hallelujah." He handed Jesus back, frowning "You are going through Jericho?"

The others nodded.

"Did you know guards have been stationed on the roads coming into the city?"

Mary's heart raced.

"Surely you heard that Herod is searching for a child that will be a threat to his throne?"

Stepping forward, a hand's breath from Ari's nose, Samuel spoke through gritted teeth. "What are your intentions?"

"I'm going to help these people get past the guards. What are you going to do?"

Samuel grasped Ari's shoulders. "I'll assist you, brother."

Within minutes, Mary was bumping along in Ari's cart, muttering. "This plan is so outrageous it has to work. I pray my mother and father can't see me now."

"Let's pray that the guards can't see Jesus," said Ari.

Mary looked back at Samuel, with Jesus tucked in a basket on top of Sheba. She turned forward to watch Josef trotting down the hill. Her hands reached to weave her hair into a braid, but she dropped them. Then they reached to pull her headscarf up, and she dropped them.

"Samuel was sorry he didn't have any cosmetics to paint your face, Mary." Ari laughed.

"I'm not sorry. This charade you've devised is difficult enough."

"You must know it's just as difficult for me, but not as hard as it will be for Josef." Ari frowned.

"I hope he doesn't hurt you," she said. Mary searched ahead, but Josef was already out of sight. She turned backward again.

"We're getting within sight of the roadblock, Mary. You can't turn around anymore. You're pretending to be my sweetheart, remember?"

She wiped her eyes and took a deep breath. "If the Lord is willing, I can do this."

A line had formed at the city gate where three guards were examining travelers entering Jericho. Mary kept her head turned toward Ari but searched for Josef out of the corner of her eye. "Can you look back? Are Samuel and Sheba and; I mean…."

"Shh. There is one group between us and them. Keep your eyes on me now; we're next."

Chapter 13

An armed soldier blocked Ari's cart. "Halt. What are you carrying in your cart?"

Yelling came from behind the guard. Josef strode to Mary's side. "Sister, get down now. You're shaming our mother." Josef grabbed at Mary's arm.

Ari reached across Mary to push Josef. "Leave her alone. She's a big girl now. She wants to be with me."

"Come home now. Just look at you. No modesty." Josef tugged at Mary. "Can't you at least keep your head covered? You're acting shamefully. And you!" He came around the back of the cart to pull at Ari.

"Stop this." A guard pulled Josef's arms behind his back. "I've got you!"

A second guard came to help hold Josef. "Hey, Sister," he sneered. "That donkey driver's too old for you. I'm available if you want someone younger." The crowd that formed was laughing. Glancing at the travelers behind Ari's cart, the third guard motioned to them to pass and took a few steps closer to hear.

Mary kept her eyes fixed on Ari. "I want to be here right now."

Her voice was a whisper, and Ari muttered between his teeth, "Louder."

Looking at her feet, she took a deep breath. "I'm not going with you now, Brother. I'll come home later," she said.

Josef's arms were still locked behind his back, and Mary's heart was banging. *What if the guards throw him in jail?*

Ari growled. "Leave the lady alone; she's a *woman* now." He turned to Mary. "Aren't you, sweetheart?" At the comment, raucous laughter rippled across the crowd, but other voices yelled. "What's stopping traffic? Take your romancing somewhere else."

By turning into Ari's shoulder, Mary could peek at the line backing up. The third guard looked briefly at Samuel and Sheba and the line of travelers behind them and waved all of them through. Mary quickly squeezed Ari's arm twice.

"Just let the poor fellow go," Ari said. "He can have his sister; I don't need the trouble." As soon as the guard released Josef, Ari pushed Mary toward the edge of the cart. When she jumped down, he threw her headscarf at her. Josef grabbed the scarf and pulled Mary quickly into the city. They ran in the opposite direction from the inn, in case they were followed.

Five blocks away from the guards, Mary stopped to braid her hair and replace her scarf. She was still gasping for breath, but her trembling was slowing. Then she and Josef rushed to the inn where they'd first met Ari. Sheba was tied outside, guarded by a young boy. Samuel, gently rocking Jesus, was even at the same table where they'd eaten.

"We'll get a bite to eat from Hiram, then let's get you out of Jericho as soon as possible," Ari whispered as he slid onto the bench.

...

Mary and Josef thought they knew how to travel, but compared to Uncle Samuel, their knowledge was the size of a mustard seed. Samuel showed them how to chop roots from the broom trees they passed to have a hot campfire at night and keep wild animals away. He taught them how to care for Sheba and get her to kneel ("Pray, Sheba, pray"). He drew maps and went east with them until they crossed the Jordan and reached the King's Highway. None of those tips would make the journey any shorter or less dangerous.

Uncle Samuel made the final arrangements in Rabbah Ammon. Josef and Mary were to join a small group going through Nabatea to Egypt. When the group met together the night before, sharing wine at a small inn, Mary had stayed in the corner to keep Jesus from waking. Back at their camp at the southern edge of town, Samuel reviewed the details. "You will need to rise early because they are assembling here before sunrise."

"We'll be fine, Uncle Samuel. We couldn't have escaped without you," Mary said.

Samuel shook his head. "The Lord would have made another way."

"Even so," said Mary, "He asked you, and you said 'Yes.' One more favor, please? Tell me about the other families, especially Deborah and Isaac. They have the cutest little boy."

"Of course." Samuel embraced Mary and kissed Jesus on top of his head. He grabbed Josef's arms to pull him close. "Take care of them." Josef nodded, and Samuel lifted his arms in prayers for their safety. Wiping his eyes with the back of his hand, he rubbed Sheba's nose one more time and shuffled away, looking over his shoulder several times before he disappeared in the dark.

...

Murmurs became whispers, whispers became words, words became commands. "Here." "Hurry." "Kneel." "Up." Swaying to soothe the baby on her back, Mary stood at the edge of the clutch of travelers, searching in the ashy light to distinguish faces she'd briefly met the night before. A donkey was kicking and braying as two swag-bellied men roped a bundle to its back. A shaggy-haired young man named Elias was watering his camel. *Ah, there they are; the man and wife. Samaritans.* The couple was waiting placidly behind a small cart with wide leather straps lying on the ground before it. Mary wanted to dislike them, but both of them had been gentle and welcoming. For a minute or two, she wrung her hands; then she walked toward them. Their faces wreathed in smiles, reminding her of her parents. She pulled Jesus around in front and held him out.

"Our baby was sleeping last night when we met; I'd like you to meet my son Michael."

Josef, Mary, and Samuel had argued after the attack on the Bethlehem road whether to use Jesus' true name. If they used a different name, would it confuse him? If they didn't, would they jeopardize his life? Caution won. "It would only be for a year or so, maybe less; and doesn't the name mean 'He is like God'?" Josef continued. "We can call him Jesus-Michael for a few days, and finally just Michael."

"I hope the Lord understands," Mary sighed.

They started using only Michael last night. Now was the test. "Michael," she said, holding him out, "here are some new friends."

The woman reached for Jesus, "My name is Sharon; my husband is Yefet. May I hold your son? He certainly has bright eyes, doesn't he?"

Mary looked at Jesus. His face was narrow, making his ears seem large in contrast, but his eyes were bright. Like her father, his hair would eventually grow, but as a baby his ears defined him. A month ago, she overheard her neighbor snicker, "Don't tell any secrets near that one; he'll hear every word." How sweet of Sharon to compliment his eyes. Mary handed Jesus to Sharon, who jiggled his serious face into a grin. The two women chatted lightly about babies until a shout from Josef called them to form a circle.

One of the paunchy men was the designated leader; he and his brother were the only ones who had taken this route before. "I am Boutros; this is my younger brother Faizan," he reminded them. "We are returning to our family in El-Arish, the city the Greeks named Rhinocorura." He spit in the dirt at his feet. "If you've been to El Arish, you remember our beautiful seashore and luxuriant palms, so we invite you to come enjoy them. Some of you may go south to Egypt or up to Rafah and Gaza. No matter. I shall do the best possible to help you stay safe while I am with you."

Mary quivered at the strange names, hoping Josef would remember where Samuel had told them to turn.

Boutros looked over his shoulder. "The sun rises and it's time to cross Moab. Here is our order for travel. This way we hope to keep you moving."

Faizan was ordered to lead with his donkey, and behind him were Elias and his camel. Mary and Josef were assigned to follow him with Sheba. Yefet and Sharon picked up the leather straps making a harness over their shoulders and, side by side, pulled their cart behind Sheba, and Boutros brought up the rear.

In each field along the road, parades of reapers scythed the blond wheat, leading trains of humped gatherers. Snippets of harvester's songs mingled with bird shrieks as their feasting on the grain was abruptly attacked. A song lifted in Mary's heart. They would escape.

It was the fourth hour since dawn. Even though they were travelling south, Mary's earlier relief was fading; her confidence had cracked. Mary moved closer to Josef's shoulder as he led Sheba. "Josef, I'm afraid."

"Of what?"

"Of Boutros and his brother. They're Nabateans."

"Why is that a problem?" Josef looked around to see how close any of the travelers were.

"Herod's mother was a Nabatean princess. Won't the brothers want to support Herod?"

"Didn't you know? Herod's been trying to take control of the country for years. Nabateans want nothing to do with our crazy king."

"Shh."

"Don't worry, Mary. Samuel chose the members of the group carefully. You have a good thought, though. I'd like to step up and visit with Elias and get to become better acquainted. He's the only other Jew in our group."

"That makes sense." Mary glanced back at Sheba's disdainful stare and flicked the lead rope. "Hopefully, he'll have some special tricks for dealing with camels." Sheba had never caused trouble, but it didn't hurt to learn as much as possible. Without his brothers around, Josef would be glad to have a companion. He motioned to Mary to keep her place in line while he trotted ahead to join Elias.

Two hours later, Faizan led them aside to a river to water the animals and refill their water-skins. In the adjoining grain field, laborers gathered stalks. In their wake, a woman and three little children gleaned the leftovers. A frail melody drifted toward Mary, and she was caught in the memory of harvesting grapes with Salome two years ago behind their mother in Taoma's vineyard. She swallowed the pang of homesickness and brought dates and figs to Josef, who was playing with "Michael" on the stream bank.

When they took to the road again, Mary asked what Josef had learned from Elias.

"Elias is very unhappy we have to travel with foreigners."

"Didn't Samuel explain who would be in the group before we started?"

"Yes, of course. Somehow he assumed he would be in command."

"He has never been this way before and he is so young. Why would he be the leader?"

"As a single Jewish male, he feels he deserves the honor."

"Why is he going to Egypt?"

"He wants to start a trading business, and Samuel has given him some leads on goods to trade. I asked how he came to possess his camel, and he said he had just purchased it two nights ago. Samuel was quite surprised, he said."

"He has experience with camels then."

Josef's hand smothered his laugh. "Compared to him, *I* am experienced with camels, and *you* are an expert. It's a wonder the camel started out with him." He pointed to Elias tugging on his camel's rope. Mary and Josef both shouted as Elias began beating his camel with a reed. "Elias! Stop!"

Josef ran to his new friend. "Camels are independent; they're touchy," Mary heard him say. She also wanted to give some advice, but sensed Elias would resent anything a woman said. She would bring an apple to Josef, and Josef would get the hint.

Between the lure of the apple and Mary leading Sheba around in front, Elias got his camel up and on the road. Josef stayed alongside Mary the rest of the day, carrying a delighted Jesus on his shoulders.

The next day they left the waving wheat of the Moab plains and trudged through blowing sand. "Why wouldn't the Moabites let our people cross when they came from Egypt so long ago? Why would they mind anyone crossing through miserable dust storms?" Mary tucked the scarf tighter around her son as a dancing funnel swept towards them. The sky cleared momentarily, and Faizan waved at them to draw up closer. "I suppose that since our heavenly Father led our people into the Promised Land up this route, then He will keep us safe as we travel back this way."

"Don't forget Uncle Samuel's words in Rabbah Ammon. 'The Lord of Hosts is the one who told you to go to Egypt. Your way is known to Him, even though it's new and strange to you.'"

"I shouldn't malign Moabites since our ancestor Ruth was one." Her words were swept away in a blast of sand.

The wind attacked from the south, blasting sand into every crevice of their bodies. Mary fretted the storm would be as blinding as the one they'd had on the trip to Jericho. She couldn't stop Jesus from pulling off the scarf she tied over his face, and his eyes were red from rubbing. "If only we had triple eyelashes like Sheba's," she told Josef as the group left the King's Highway to set up camp in a rocky canyon away from the wind.

"If only we could go days without water." Josef moaned. "There's a little here, at least." He pointed to a cluster of acacia trees.

Mary scanned the ground, searching the rocks and willow bushes for signs of scorpions before spreading out her rug and laying down their pack. She pulled out dried fish and handed the food to Josef and Jesus.

The previous night she lay awake listening to a hyena's chattering laugh, while Jesus lay squeezed between Josef and herself. Now her eyes flitted across the sand for waving snake tracks. A thumping of wings made her look up as a black ibis swooped and landed in one of the acacias. Hungry eyes glimmered from his scarred face. Mary snatched up Jesus and wrapped him tight against her. In Israel, the predators were human; here they came from raw nature. She didn't know which was worse.

At night, the gnarled oaks and spired pines of Nazareth floated through Mary's dreams. Each day she prayed they would reach water by nightfall. Faizan asked every group of travelers they met, "Is there still water ahead?" When they settled to camp at night, Mary tended to Jesus and Sheba, while Josef met with the others in their group.

Elias came to meet with Josef after one of the camp meetings, trying to convince him to separate from the others. As the young man left, Josef turned to Mary's whisper. "Samuel said to go to Nessana. He would look for us there," she said.

"Yes. However, there are two ways to travel there. Is there water in the wadis? Are there Roman soldiers at Obodo? I'm trying to find out. I'm being careful, Mary. I'll listen to Boutros and Faizan; don't fret."

"I don't trust Elias."

"He's harmless, Mary. Didn't you see the ball he gave Jesus to play with?"

"What ball?"

"The green one he had."

"Show me."

"He took it back. I'll show you tomorrow."

"Remember that Samuel put us together with the Nabateans as leaders. There must have been a reason he didn't choose more Jews for our travel partners." Mary thought back to Samuel's instructions. His parting warning had been, "You must protect your child at all costs." Those words haunted her.

Two nights later Josef returned from a stroll with Elias. His brow was wrinkled, and he was scratching his head as he tossed a green ball in the air.

"What's troubling you?" Mary handed him bread and a bowl of beans in return for the ball.

"Elias."

She folded her arms tightly against her chest and pressed her lips together.

"Elias asked me about Jesus today."

"Hasn't he done that before?"

Josef finished his bread. "He was asking different questions this time: where was he born, when was he born." He put down the bowl of beans and wrapped his arms around Mary, then knelt to rub Jesus' back as he slept. "I told him we were from Nazareth. Then he said, 'How do you know Samuel, then? He's from Bethlehem.' I told him the truth: He's your mother's cousin, and you got to know him when you visited your aunt."

Mary lay the ball on her rug and pressed her palms against her head. "Let's think."

"No. Let's pray." Josef took Mary's hands and clenched them between his own. "Holy One of Israel, Lord of Heaven's Armies, give us your wisdom and favor."

"And protection. Protect our baby, *Your* baby."

"So be it," Josef said. "I'll talk to Boutros in the morning. Maybe we can rearrange the order for our travel." He patted Jesus' head and went to hobble Sheba.

As the dawn's black lightened to gray, Josef lashed their belongings on Sheba's back and took Mary and Jesus with him to the brothers. "I'm not comfortable with Elias's glances at my wife," he said after wishing them a good morning. "Do you mind if we walk in front of Boutros?"

The men's eyebrows jumped. Boutros bowed to Mary and grabbed Josef's arm. "For you two, we gladly allow it. Walk behind me, if you desire. You and your wife are good travelers, and you both can handle your animal. I trust you at the rear."

Mary whispered to Josef, and he nodded and turned back to the brothers. "Mary is concerned what Elias will say."

"We'll tell him we like to get to know all the members of a group; it's our decision. Elias may be left behind at the next town if he continues to argue," said Faizan. "If it weren't for your wife's uncle, Boutros wouldn't have accepted him." His eyes narrowed. "Haven't you become his friend?"

Josef blushed. "Knowing Samuel as I do, I believe he was trying to help the young man start a business, as well as provide a fellow countryman as a companion for us. It appears Samuel was mistaken, if not deceived, and I have been as well." Josef pulled Mary closer.

When the group lined up for travel, Elias's whining was heard clear at the back. "I hope he isn't spiteful." Mary frowned as she watched the young man swatting his camel. "Did we just make an enemy?"

"We'll be careful, and our Nabatean friends will watch, too."

At the midday oasis stop, Elias was a fly flitting from Sharon and Yefet to Boutros and Faizan, always glancing over his shoulder at Josef and Mary. Her frown grew deeper. "He's turning the others against us." She threaded the ropes to tighten their pack onto Sheba.

"Don't worry. There's a reason Samuel put us in this group," Josef said.

"He didn't know enough about Elias." She watched Jesus toddle with his new ball to where Sharon was refilling her water skins. "What does Samuel know about the others?" Mary dropped Sheba's lead to follow Jesus.

"Mary." Josef's sharp tone stopped her. "We've prayed about this. Leave the results in the Lord's hands."

"But." As Mary took a deep breath, Sharon scooped Jesus into her arms.

"Ball, ball," Jesus called.

Sharon delivered Jesus to Mary. "I'll get his ball."

"Thank you, Sharon. Michael loves to wander. It makes me nervous sometimes." Mary glanced sideways at Elias, swatting and yelling at his camel again. Suddenly the camel whipped its head, slinging a mushy wad of cud across the young man's face.

Elias's profanities were a magnet; everyone turned to stare. The men covered their mouths to stifle their laughter, and the two women busied themselves talking to Jesus. More ugly words poured from Elias's mouth, and in moments he was spouting fury that Josef and Mary had put a spell on his camel and on everyone else in the group. "She's a witch, that woman, and her husband is a liar. They're traitors who have deceived everyone one of you."

Sharon and Mary, Josef and Yefet, Boutros and Faizan froze, mouths open.

"They were part of a plot to kill King Herod, and now they're trying to escape. Herod's soldiers are looking for them. I heard about them in Jericho." Elias ran to Boutros. "Help me grab them and we can all get the reward."

Boutros turned his back on Elias and waved at the others. "Form a line; we're moving on. Faizan, you're in the lead; Yefet and your wife, follow Faizan; Josef, you and your family after them. I'll take the last position."

"What about me? You need me." Elias stomped to Boutros and grabbed his sleeve. "I'll tell Samuel what you've done. He'll never trust you again." He stared as the others headed away. "You're all making a mistake. Those two murderers will murder you next, take all your money and goods and live like royalty."

Mary ignored his taunts and sang songs to Jesus to drown out the ugly words while she followed in Josef's steps. He looked over his shoulder, flinching at the sight. She stopped her song when she saw Josef's face. "What is it?"

"Elias is seething and emptying his rancor on his closest victim."

Mary chanced a look behind. Holding the rope in one hand, Elias was beating his camel savagely, and the camel was squalling. Mary turned away, distress wrenching her stomach.

"Get down!" Boutros thundered. Mary swung Jesus' sling to her stomach and dropped to a huddle. Tremors shook the ground and Sheba squealed as Elias's camel pounded past them, blood spraying from his muzzle and a scarlet gash on his neck. Elias ran after him, cursing.

When the others relaxed from their tense positions, Sharon came to Mary. "I'm not bringing Jesus his ball. Do you know what it is?"

"What do you mean?"

"It's a fruit called Sodom's Apple. It grows on flowering trees to the east. If you bite into it, the heart will stop." She shuttered her eyes and grimaced. "Jesus would have died."

Chapter 14

What was Egypt like? Hot. Sandy. Lonely. "The sandstorms are unbearable and I'm afraid to make friends. Elias has had time to spread his story and word will get back to Herod," Mary said after two weeks in the Nabatean town of Nessana.

"That's also why we live sparingly. I don't want to call attention to our family. But it's time for me to start carpentry and for us to live a normal life. Your only acquaintance is the woman next door."

"That's true. Other than 'Michael', she is my one joy."

Amali had come to their doorstep, bowing low, the day after they rented the stacked stone house. "Welcome to Nessana." She'd smiled and held out a basket of freshly baked bread. The yeasty aroma captivated Mary, who had been afraid to shop for yeast to make her own dough. A little girl with darker skin and even darker eyes peeked out from Amali's skirts. "This is my daughter Lara."

Mary brought out Jesus, stooping in front of the little girl. "Would you like to meet my son Michael?"

Lara was enchanted with 'Michael' and he with her. Their attraction to each other reminded Mary of her early years with Salome. As for Amali, she was just as sweet and tender as her daughter. They visited each other daily while Josef walked the neighborhood soliciting small carpentry jobs.

"I'm glad you can join me for tea." Amali ushered Mary into her mud brick home.

"The pleasure is mine!" Mary looked around the walls and benches. Rugs and blankets striped in purple, emerald green and indigo covered the walls and floor. "I've stepped into the heart of a rainbow," she said. "These colors make my whole body vibrate. Did you make all of these?"

Amali blushed at the compliments. "You're so kind. Yes, I made most of them."

"Would you teach me?" Mary covered her mouth at her brashness.

"Certainly. Why don't you start with a little tunic for Michael? You can use some of my yarns, and maybe I can show you how I use the dyes."

Amali continued teaching Mary something new each day.

Over evening soup with Josef, Mary sighed deeply. "My friendship with Amali is helping me bear the separation from our family. She adores our 'Michael', too, and she and little Lara always bring some new toy when she comes to teach me or when I go to her home to see how she makes one-piece tunics." Mary giggled. "She says I'm still too restrained in my use of colors. You should see how Amali adds zigzags. I think I'll make a splendid blanket for Sheba. Then everyone will recognize Samuel when he comes to a city." Her smile turned to laughter.

"I wish *you* could see the joy on your face that I'm seeing now," Josef said.

"When Samuel comes to visit, I'm going to ask him to bring the red dye we make from the oaks." Her face glowed with the thought of repaying both Amali and Samuel for their kindness to her.

On his first visit, Uncle Samuel's news wiped out Mary's desire for dyes.

"It was the day after we left. Matthias had gone to Jerusalem for supplies and was returning home when he passed a centurion gathering his regiment in the Kidron Valley below the Holy City. Terrible news. He ran on to Bethlehem, stopping any family along the way that had a little boy with the awful words, 'Take your son and escape! Get out of Bethlehem and run as far as you can go! Herod has released murder troops to kill every boy child under the age of two or three!'

"When Matthias arrived in Bethlehem, he ran first to my house to notify you, panicking when he couldn't raise anyone. Unable to rouse us, he then ran to your parents, Josef. They reassured Matthias, saying you had gone after the wise men so that Jesus could benefit from the wisdom of the East. Your father told them he knew not which strange country you were in. (Of course, he didn't know if you were in Moab or Idumea or already in Egypt.)"

Mary was sobbing, her hands over her face.

"Shall I desist?" Samuel said.

Her reply was muffled. "No; we have to hear it all."

Samuel's voice turned husky and broken. "Though Matthias's main worry was lessened, he didn't abandon his mission. He told the first household at the bottom of each street and impressed on that family to spread the word up the hill, one family at a time. He told me the shrieking and wailing blanketed the town like a pall." Samuel was choking on the words. He lowered his head. "It's still there. I experience it myself it when I'm home."

"Go on, please, Samuel. We need to hear it; we need to know their pain," said Josef. He drew Mary closer and stroked her head.

"Some families acted immediately, and others were frozen in fear. Even of those who tried to depart the area, not all escaped." Samuel took both of Mary's hands. "Mary, it grieves me to tell you. Isaac and Deborah were one of the first families to lose their precious son. A dozen more of Bethlehem's treasured boys were butchered as well."

"The cost is too great!" Mary sobbed. "How can we raise this child with all the bloodshed? Will our friends and neighbors ever speak to us again? They must know the soldiers were after Jesus, just as Matthias knew."

Josef wrapped his arms around her. "Nothing is impossible for the Lord. We will succeed by His grace and protection, dear one."

"Grace and protection." Samuel took a deep breath. "First, as you had directed, I sold some jewels from the stargazers to increase your finances. Here they are. Speaking of protection, there is another great concern. Because of Elias, Herod is sending spies south of the Judean border." He raised his hands at Mary's gasp. "I know, Mary. He has no authority. Nevertheless, necessity requires you to move farther into Egypt. I suggest you go to the coast and south to Matariya."

At Mary's gasp, Josef wrapped his arms around her. She turned again to Samuel. "Uncle, I gather there's something more you want to say."

Samuel looked at the ground. "Yes. Unfortunately, I need to take Sheba back with me."

Grace and protection. That night Mary repeated those words like an anthem. "I feel your protection, Lord of Hosts, but right now it's difficult to receive your favor when others have lost so much."

Samuel was feeding Sheba when Mary woke the next morning. "Your girl missed you, Uncle. I can see she's happy to be returned to you."

"Hah! Her countenance offers no clue, and she is as ornery as she was previously."

"She was a treasure for our travels, but I think she was bored here. By the way, did you hear any more about Elias or his camel?"

"I'm usually an astute judge of character; I regret the arrangement. It was only when his malicious lies filtered into Jericho that I discovered my error."

"Did anyone find the poor camel?" Josef said.

"Ah, that account has a felicitous conclusion: the runaway camel was retrieved by Boutros and Faizan at the waterhole when they came north on their next trip. They were delighted to have some recompense for the troubles they endured with Elias, and they were quick to squash the lies he had spread."

Mary rubbed her hand down Sheba's silky nose. She stepped into the house and quickly came out. "Here's a farewell gift, Sheba." She laid an apple in her hand and Sheba gobbled it.

"Michael, come say goodbye to Sheba." Josef picked Jesus up and they all hugged Sheba and then Samuel.

Mary kept her hand on Samuel's arm. "Will you be back here soon?"

Samuel shook his head. "I must travel north, to Sepphoris." He tilted his head at Mary's frown. "I'll carry all your affection to your parents and sister when I pass through Nazareth." Mary tucked her head into Josef's chest, and Samuel picked up Sheba's lead and walked away.

After a day of planning, Mary told Amali about their departure the next morning.

"You have a frown when I was expecting a smile," Amali said.

"What do you mean?"

"Does Josef know the good news?"

A blush spread across Mary's face. "Is it that easy to tell? Of course another woman would notice a baby is on its way." Mary shook her head. "Josef has been so busy filling orders for people, he's too tired at night to do anything more than fall into bed after supper, and our visit with my uncle brought us other news." She wiped her eyes. "We will be moving on."

"You're going home?" Amali hugged Mary.

"No." As Amali took a breath, Mary leaned into her friend. "We're leaving tomorrow for …. I'll miss you. Yahweh sent you to me because he knew I needed a friend like you."

Questions filled Amali's eyes, but she nodded her head and held Mary tighter.

…

A sandstorm kept the family inside the mud hut they were renting on the Egyptian delta. Mary pulled out the leather ball she'd been hiding. "Would you entertain Michael?" She handed the ball to Josef. "I want to light lamps and finish cooking for Sabbath." With one hand, she poured oil into the lamp on the shelf.

As she stretched the candle in her other hand to relight the lamp, Jesus ran up.

"Me do it. Me do it."

Mary moved to the side, but Jesus had come beside her, pulling on her robe, and she tripped on him. "Wait!" She teetered, and the hands holding the oil and candle wobbled.

"No-o-o-o!!" Josef lunged, trying to grab the oil. His hand caught her wrist, and she was pulled on top of him. The oil jar flew past him, splattering oil and cracking on the stone floor.

The candle dropped to the floor beside Jesus, who stared at the smoldering wick for a moment before breaking into howls.

Josef slowly moved Mary and helped her to her feet. He turned away, shoulders heaving while Jesus hid his sobbing in his mother's robe.

Josef sat down and buried his head between his knees.

Mary finished lighting the candle, prompting Jesus to help with the prayers. She gave the boy his soup and bread, set him on the mattress they all shared, and sang him to sleep.

Her husband was still sitting on the bench. "Josef." Mary was breathing heavily and praying silently, *Holy One, tell me what to say.* "Josef, it's time to tell me about your scar and how you were burned."

She brought their soup and sat beside him. When he said nothing, she started eating.

Josef picked up his bowl for several seconds and put it back down. His head dropped to his chest. "I was a couple years older than Jesus is now when I was burned in almost the same way. I was watching my mother light the oil lamps. She had two placed on the shelf together, and she had left the half-empty oil jar next to them. A cousin who was visiting brought a burning brand from the oven. It was too hot. Sparks flew from it and landed in the oil jar. In the commotion, it spilled on me. My face was deeply blistered, as you know." A deep sigh followed. "I'm still afraid. It's why I usually let you light all the fires in the house."

How that admission of fear must have cost him. Mary set her bowl on the table. As if they had a mind of their own, her hands rose up to stroke Josef's cheeks. And, for the first time, she kissed her husband's scar.

...

The travel had been constant. Fears of Herod's murderous nature kept them moving. They had crossed the delta, then trudged south along the dark Shichor River, and now had returned to the delta. Once again, labor pains struck Mary early.

"It's a girl? I have a daughter?" Mary leaned back against the wall. The local midwife placed the baby on her chest and fetched Josef.

"What a wonderful blessing." Josef kissed Mary and stroked the baby's cheek. "What shall we name her?"

Mary yawned. "You may choose."

"I'm thinking you would want Hannah or Salome."

"My mother or my sister." She yawned and smoothed the baby's damp hair. "There is another person I'd like to honor, if you don't mind."

Josef scratched his head.

"Deborah. It's not only the name of our friend who lost her little boy, but a warrior and judge of our people was named Deborah."

"This tiny child has a lot to live up to then."

"Yes, but so does her brother."

"I like that: Deborah it is."

A month later, Josef woke later than usual. "Josef, are you ill?" Mary sprang to her feet.

"No; why?" A twitch flickered on his mouth.

"What is it? Don't tease me."

"An angel visited me last night," he said, drawing her into his arms. "Herod is dead. It's safe to go home." His eyes widened. "Mary, this is like the prophet Hosea predicted, 'When Israel was a child, I loved him, and out of Egypt I called my son'."

She squeezed his hand. "I don't know that I'm 'trembling like a bird' as the scriptures say, but I'm eager to return home."

They sent a messenger to Samuel, and within a month he arrived with Sheba and a donkey.

"It's wonderful to have your help to pack up this house and our two little ones." Josef said.

"Your company, alone, is wonderful." Mary inserted.

"And your guidance for the quicker route through Hebron."

Jesus tugged Samuel's robe. "I like Sheba." Everyone laughed.

"Yes, and Sheba." Mary said.

On the trip north, Samuel constantly entertained them with stories of his trading trips.

"How was this so easy?" Mary said as she assembled their last campfire outside Hebron. "Even with our tiny baby, I wasn't worried about snakes or scorpions. The only difficulty has been teaching Jesus his true name."

"You have become a daughter of the desert," said Samuel.

"No, Uncle Samuel, my wife is like a donkey headed to its stall."

Mary swatted Josef. "*You* aren't eager to see your family tomorrow?"

"I'm glad we sent a runner ahead yesterday to prepare them."

"Do you have trepidation about being rejected?" Samuel frowned. "You must stay with me."

"On the contrary; we're not worried about my family welcoming us. Much as we would appreciate your hospitality again, I believe my parents want us to stay with them."

"Ah, certainly, but be assured you are always welcome to reside in my home."

"We owe you so much, Uncle. I wish we could repay you." Mary wrapped her arms around his thick body.

"The only recompense I desire is for you to instruct that boy in the ways of the Holy One."

Deborah squeaked as morning light seeped through the trees. She nestled in her mother's arms to nurse, while Mary wiped sleep from her eyes. The sun appeared to wipe sleep away too, as the leaden dawn brightened to a rosy blush. Two figures were silhouetted against the morning light. Who would be approaching so early? Were they soldiers from Herodium? Had Herod's son heard? Mary's stomach cramped, and she twisted to see where she could hide Jesus.

"Josef!" Mary's sudden shout frightened Deborah, and she began wailing. Samuel, dagger in hand, rushed in front of Mary while Josef grabbed Jesus and slipped behind the tent.

The figures stopped. "Mary? Is that you? Where's Josef?" Josef's brothers moved forward slowly.

"Here. He's here." Mary's heart was still pounding, her breath coming in gasps. Samuel stepped aside, keeping the dagger in his hand.

Josef came from behind the tent, holding Jesus. "All praise to the Holy One, we've come home safely. My prayers are answered." He set the boy down and wrapped his arms around Jacob and then Cleopas. "What a wonderful welcome. Cleopas, you've grown so much. Jacob, you have, too." Josef patted his older brother's belly. The brothers laughed and swatted each other on the back.

"We couldn't wait to see you," said Jacob. "The Holy One even gave us a full moon, so we started at midnight. I told my wife to prepare a feast for you."

"It's safe to come to Bethlehem?"

"Why not?"

"We've heard Herod's son Archelaus is as evil as his father, and Samuel hasn't reassured me."

"I'm sure you'll be fine as long as no curious astrologers come around. Besides, Mother and Father will have my head if Cleopas and I don't come back with those two grandchildren, especially this beautiful girl they've never seen. With three boys of their own and my two sons, entertaining a daughter-in-law and grand-daughter are their greatest desire."

"What? You're not married yet, Cleopas?"

"I only have fifteen years, Josef. I've plenty of time."

As they broke camp, Josef's brothers took turns holding the baby and swinging Jesus in circles. "I'm sorry we're not helping with the packing," Cleopas said.

Mary grinned. "You are more help than you realize." Within the hour, they'd eaten, folded the tent, and loaded Sheba. The road was smooth and few travelers were up so early. The traveled quickly, and Sheba snorted at the fast pace.

Josef's parents were waiting outside the gate as the travelers climbed the hill to their house. At the welcome shout, Jacob's wife and children joined them. Jesus and Deborah were passed back and forth while Sheba was unloaded.

"It's time to celebrate." Josef's father held out a flask of wine and passed wine to everyone, even Jesus. Neighbors who walked by were invited to share as well, but each one declined.

When Mary and Josef lay down to sleep that night, he held her close. She could feel his quick breaths on her cheek. "What's wrong?"

"I'm worried. There's something different; the air is heavy."

"You've been in Egypt too long. You're used to the drier air there."

"I don't think that's it, but we'll see. My mother is ecstatic. She'd be devastated if we didn't stay." Josef rubbed Mary's back until she relaxed and slept.

The next morning when Mary joined Josef's mother to buy groceries, conversations stopped at her approach. None of the women met her eyes. The barley merchant refused to barter with her. "One price, or I can make it higher." He glared until she paid the price he'd stated.

In the afternoon Mary visited with her friend Deborah. Her friend's dimples appeared when Mary held out the baby named after her, but she wouldn't look Mary in the eye. Mary left her the rug she'd woven for her in Egypt, and returned to Josef's family, staying inside the rest of the day, helping her mother-in-law and playing with Deborah and Jesus.

"Deborah was touched that we named our little girl after her, but it didn't take away the desolate look in her eyes," she told Josef. "She still hasn't conceived again."

"We must pray for her consolation." Josef pulled at his beard. His tossing and twisting during the night kept her awake.

"It's best that we move to Nazareth," Josef told his parents the next morning. "There is some risk in Galilee of Herod's son Antipas hearing of Jesus, but in Bethlehem we are reminding these dear people of their awful loss."

"Also, I wouldn't want Jesus to be treated unfairly," Mary said.

"Surely you don't have to leave right away. We've barely spent time with the babies. What if you stay inside more, out of sight?"

"We'll think about it, Mother. I know the children have hardly had a chance to be spoiled by you." He grinned and pulled her close. "We'll pray about it and let you know in a few days. Jacob needs help with the new room he's adding. For now, you can cuddle that baby girl and make toys and dollies for her."

In the middle of the night, Josef stood over Mary and shook her awake. "We have to leave right away." He pulled her up and held out her cloak.

"Why? We just arrived."

"Sh." He grabbed her arm and guided her to the lower floor. "The angel spoke to me again. We are in danger here, as we guessed. We must leave immediately."

Chapter 15

Mary rubbed her eyes, yawned, and shook her head to wake herself. "Do we have to go back to Egypt? Samuel has gone to the coast with Sheba; we don't have a guide."

"We don't need them. We're going to Nazareth and traveling light. We're leaving now."

"Wait! The children." Her voice squeaked with panic.

"Mother is already bundling them, and my father is gathering supplies for the trip. We wanted to let you sleep as long as we could."

Josef's mother glided into the yard, holding Deborah, and his father followed her with Jesus. Jesus stirred as he was passed into Josef's arms, and Deborah in her sling was slipped onto Mary's shoulder.

"I'm sure your mother will be delighted to have you home again. I hope you have forgiven me for not believing, for everything," Josef's mother said. "Go with the Holy One. We'll come to see you when we can."

"Of course; thank you for all you've done." Mary gave her mother-in-law a tight squeeze.

Josef's father pushed the front door slowly, half lifting it to prevent any scraping. "We'll be sending up the rest of your treasures when we can."

"Treasures?"

"From the men, the stargazers."

"We hadn't even thought about that. It's mostly just spices and fabrics left now, isn't it? Keep what you want. Tell Jacob and Cleopas goodbye, and come visit us." Josef adjusted Jesus' body and grabbed the sack of food lying at his feet.

"Wait, wait." His father ran back into the house.

"We have to go. Now." Josef kissed his mother and motioned to Mary to follow him down the narrow street. Slapping sandals prompted him to turn around.

"The other coins. I had forgotten." His father tucked a small pouch into his sack. "We still had some we were going to send down with Samuel. We'll bring the remaining gifts later."

Josef nodded. He tried to move Jesus so he could grab his father's arm, but the little boy stirred. "Be well, Father." He took Mary's hand and led her into the blackness.

...

"You're home at last!" Mama was shrieking. "Such a big boy he is now." She clucked as Jesus stared at her. With so much that happened since the child had seen her two years before, Jesus didn't even remember her mother.

"I'm going to be four," he told her solemnly.

Her mother responded gently, "Much as I desire to wrap you in my lonely arms, let me hold Deborah while you help your parents unload." Before long, though, Hannah was holding one child and then the other, beaming as she prompted both of them, "Say 'I love you, Grandma'."

And Mary's father! He was dancing first with Jesus, then with Hannah, even with Josef and Mary, then with both children in his arms while they shrieked with fear at this crazy stranger.

Heli continually thumped Josef on the back. "I knew you'd return. With the help of another builder here, I added two more rooms to our home for you and enlarged the courtyard. As you've already noticed, the workshop is bursting with projects." He turned to Mary. "Broken stools, splintered rakes, and half-sawn boards: that little room is cluttered, and I didn't even have you to sweep the sawdust."

Josef shook his head slowly when they went to bed that night. "Your father seems to have lost interest in building anything new. It appears he's lapsed into simple repairs. I'll ask around. Hopefully I can get us new clients."

Salome was glowing too, with having two little children to entertain. "I'm your Aunt Sali." She tickled them, bounced them on her knee, and completely captivated them. All they wanted the next few days was to play with Aunt Sali, much to her parents' disappointment. As Mary watched Salome the next few weeks, she realized it wouldn't be more than two or three years before her sister would marry and have children of her own.

...

"I can't believe how many more people have settled in Nazareth in the four years we've been away." My little village has grown into a town," Mary said after a trip to the market.

Josef patted Mary's stomach. "If I'm finally learning to notice these things, I'd say a person around here is growing, too."

"I hope we can raise the children all in one place now." Mary grinned. "I don't want to move, especially in the middle of the night. I finally feel safe."

"In spite of the tensions with the Romans? Sepphoris is now a capital for Herod's son, and more and more people are complaining about the taxes. Will it come to fighting?"

"There will always be taxes, and there will never be a safe place." She shook her head as she set out the cheese and figs she'd bought.

Josef tipped his head to study her. "You know better than to say that. The Lord is our refuge."

...

Hannah was helping Mary feed Jesus and Deborah. "You know how it is. Everyone is happy and healthy and so more children come." She laughed. "Children are the heritage of the Lord. Our heavenly Father always sends a loaf of bread with each child."

Mary's new baby, Huldah, cooed from the sling on her back as she scooped lentils into bowls and handed them around. "It seems like the perfumed air of Nazareth sweetens her temperament," she said. Seven-year-old Jesus was like a mother hen corralling her chicks. He fussed over his sisters when they wandered too far from Mary, and at bedtime, he scooped up Huldah and grabbed Deborah's hand to set them on the mat for a bedtime story before his mother tucked them into their blankets. Mostly, though, he stayed at Josef's side, which naturally pleased his Grandpa.

Mary's parents adored Jesus. "No one ever calls Jesus handsome, but he always has a soft smile on his face," Hannah said.

"And his eyes! So bright; it's as though he can see right inside you," her father added.

"He's such a quiet boy; he doesn't use many words, does he?" Abigail said when she visited Mary. Abigail had moved to Capernaum but came back to help her father and brothers with the grape harvest.

"It's because of his two chatty sisters dogging his footsteps."

"I can see the resemblance to your father, too."

She gritted her teeth at Abigail's smirk. Why couldn't people forget? Most people beyond Nazareth remarked that Jesus looked like Josef, even though Mary did agree with Abigail that her son resembled her father. Would her pre-wedding pregnancy always be on the minds of everyone in Nazareth?

...

Mary had assaulted heaven with her prayers when they had to flee to Egypt. She prayed even more when they returned, as she and Josef rose especially early each morning to ask the Lord for wisdom in raising Jesus. The first time Jesus fell and cut his knee, she feared an angel would strike her for not being more protective. Josef heard her crying and came into the house.

"Mary, are you hurt?"

"No, Jesus is." She sniffled, wrapping a cloth around her little boy's left leg.

"Jesus," he then asked, "are you hurt?"

"It only stings a little, Papa." Jesus said, and Mary sensed he understood the humor of his mother crying while he was the brave one.

She asked Josef, "Do we let him run outside with other boys?"

"Ask the Holy One," he replied.

"How will I know His answer?"

"See what Jesus does when the boys run."

"Should we encourage Jesus to pray more?"

"Ask the Holy One," Josef replied.

"How will we know the answer?"

"See if Jesus starts praying longer," he said. A smile teased his cheeks. "Mary, we are setting the example for him, but he will build his own relationship with the Holy One."

Ah, such wisdom. She knew Josef was praying for the answers he would give her. Much as she tried to smother Jesus, her husband pulled her back to let her child grow.

"Josef, I'm so proud of his quick intelligence. Blessed be the Lord who provided that. He's been reciting his morning and evening prayers since he was two. Now, with Papa's help, he's memorizing passages of the Torah."

"Your father tells me you had been precocious."

"Not like Jesus."

"Your father says the same: not like Jesus."

...

Mary hardly noticed how quickly Jesus was maturing, especially after Jacob was born. What stood out was that Jesus was an example. Her mother was the first to remark.

"Of course, Mother; he's the oldest."

"Not just for them. Haven't you noticed? He's an example even for the boys in the neighborhood who are older than him. They all know they can depend on him. They ask for his opinion because they know he is thoughtful and true."

Pride puffed Mary until a week later when she overheard Jacob talking to Deborah.

"I'm trying to be good for Mama today, so I'll get a special hug like she gives Jesus every night," he said.

"You may as well stop trying, Jacob. You can't be that good."

Mary peeked through the curtain into the sleeping alcove and saw Jacob's face pucker.

His voice wavered. "Why not?"

"Jesus never does anything wrong," Deborah said. "He never fusses or whines; he never argues with anyone in the family. He never tries to snitch an extra piece of sweets, either." She sighed, and her face glistened with tears. "I've tried, but I don't know how to be that good."

Then it was Mary's turn to weep. A memory from childhood teased her. Hadn't the same situation occurred with Salome and herself? She was the studious "good" daughter, and Sali was constantly being told to sit still, to be "more like your sister."

When Mary went to bed that night, she brought her concerns to Josef. "I want to think that it will all work out, like it has with Sali." She pulled the blanket around their shoulders as she considered what had transpired in Salome's life.

Just as she and Abigail had discussed years before, parents wanted to choose just the right man for a girl's husband. Mary had told her mother, "Papa likes to think he was the one who chose Sali's husband, but it was she herself. And Abigail thought she would be the one to marry an older man, but instead it's Sali."

Mama had nodded. "You're right; it wasn't Papa who decided, but Salome who picked him out."

Mary relaxed against Josef as she remembered her sister's maneuverings.

When their friend Abigail married a man in Capernaum, Sali was invited to be a bridesmaid at the wedding there. One of the guests was a handsome man with a fishing fleet on Galilee Sea. His wife had died, leaving him with two adolescent boys. Zebedee wanted still more children and a mother's influence on the two he had, so he was looking for a wife. To his delight, Sali was looking for him to be her husband.

"Do you remember, Josef, how she plagued my mother with questions? 'Wouldn't you like to go see relatives in Capernaum? You must have relatives there!' 'Wouldn't you like to ride on the sea?' Then she pestered my father every night after work. 'Wouldn't you like to go meet this man, Papa? Maybe you could get some more business there building fishing boats.'"

Josef snickered. "Your mother never discovered how Salome arranged for Abigail and her new husband to bring Zebedee and Noah and Avner to visit us here in Nazareth."

"I was surprised, too, at the thought of Sali being domestic, but Papa knew she would love those boys even though they were only two or three years younger than she was. Now she's as protective with them as she was with me."

"That girl will never outgrow her fierce determination. That's why your father approved the betrothal."

"I've always thought that the boys had such a solemn life the last five years, they were desperate for Sali's laughter and enthusiasm," Mary said. "But Salome's family isn't our family, and now we have a problem."

"Hmm." Josef tugged his beard. "We must encourage and complement each one, especially in front of the others, and …."

Mary twisted her hands and waited.

"I believe we should be more discreet in commending Jesus. Wouldn't you say so?"

She blew out the breath she was holding and nodded.

"I'll tell your parents in the morning. We need their agreement, too."

Jacob remained a challenge. He would swing from tears to joy from one minute to the next, and from agreeable to angry within seconds. When Jesus was helping in the wood shop, Jacob insisted on being there, too, usually wanting to do everything his big brother was doing. Jacob ruined pieces of wood by his impatience and when he swept the floor, he spread more sawdust around than he collected. Jesus remained patient.

A few weeks later, Hannah and Heli left early to go to nearby Sepphoris for supplies. Mary was rocking Judah to sleep, when someone called from the courtyard. She sent Deborah to the gate.

Deborah returned. "Papa has a visitor."

"He doesn't want to go around to the workshop?"

"He wants you, too."

Mary handed Judah to Huldah and went to the gate. The man looked vaguely familiar. "Yes?"

"Shalom, dear woman. I'd like to speak with you and your husband, if I may."

As Mary led the man around to the workshop, she recollected where she'd seen him. He was president of the synagogue in Capernaum; he had come to talk with her parents before Salome was married.

Josef put down his adze when they came in the shop. The man greeted him with a big smile. "Josef, you may remember me. I'm Eleazar Bar Ananais, the president of the synagogue in Capernaum." As he grasped Josef's wrist, his eyes darted around the room and his forehead tightened in wrinkles.

"Blessed be the Lord," Josef responded. "It is with pleasure that we welcome you. Please come back to the house for refreshment," he added, taking off his apron.

"And your other son, is he here also?" the president added, nodding to Jacob.

Josef grinned. "Jesus is delivering some casks to a customer this morning. He should be home within the hour. Please come and have some wine." Josef took Mary's arm as he led the man back to the house. "This is my wife Mary, the devoted mother of Jesus as well as our other beautiful children."

The men settled on benches in the courtyard, and Eleazar chatted about the grapes swelling on the vines and the coming wheat harvest while Mary brought dates and cheese and poured wine. Finally, he cleared his throat.

"I asked about your son Jesus because we would very much like to have him come and speak for the Sabbath."

Mary caught her breath. She knew Jesus was causing favorable comments with the small group of men who gathered on Sabbath in Nazareth. They had even met at their house. Her father also continued to help Jesus memorize portions of the Torah and the words of the prophets, just as his own father had done with him.

"What an honor," Josef exclaimed, echoing her thoughts. "But that is such a long way to go for one day and he's so young."

Mary's heart began pounding when Eleazar cleared his voice. "We would like him to stay four weeks." Surprised by her white face, he quickly added, "There is a lovely family who would feed and lodge Jesus. They have a son his age." He spoke more quickly as she reached for Josef's hand. "And he would get the benefit of listening to some other teachers and the visiting rabbis."

The jug of wine began to slip from Mary's hands. *Would Josef be so flattered by this grand offer that he would accept precipitously? Was she already losing her son to serve their people? Wasn't this too early for Jesus to become well known? He hadn't even been presented at the temple.* She held her breath, fighting the compulsion to shout, "No, he's my son, and you can't have him!" A sudden idea struck her: *Isn't he also Someone else's son?* She shoved the question aside.

Josef took the jug from her, contemplated Mary's frown, and refilled their guest's cup. "Your offer is very kind. It is also very flattering and worthy of our serious prayer and consideration. You will forgive us if we take some time to seek the will of the Holy One."

"Of course, of course," Eleazar replied. "May I expect to receive your answer within the week?"

Without even looking in Mary's direction, Josef answered, "We will inform you when we have reached a decision. Then we will discuss the arrangements."

Mary could hardly wait to tell him farewell, but Josef had just refilled the man's wine cup. The small talk continued while she quietly tapped her feet. Eleazar finally emptied his mug.

Mary moved toward the gate, but stopped when Josef stayed where he was.

"Won't you stay the night with us?" Josef reached for Mary's hand.

She quickly pasted a smile. "Yes, please do. It's a long journey, and I'm sure you'll want to be rested." Her stomach twisted as hospitality fought with privacy.

"It's very kind of you, but I have an appointment back near Magdala."

Josef grasped his arm, and they politely wished Eleazar the Lord's blessings on his trip back to Capernaum.

Whispered conversation inside the front door alerted Mary that they had eavesdroppers. "Deborah, Huldah, come out here."

"All of you, come here," Josef said firmly.

Even Jacob was there, holding onto Huldah's hand.

"To snoop on your parent's business is not permitted in this family," Josef began.

"But Papa, you didn't tell us not to listen," Deborah whined.

"Enough," Josef said. "You are to forget what was discussed."

Mary's groan interrupted him. When he turned to her, she leaned over to him and whispered. "Josef, one never tells anyone, child or adult, to forget what they've heard. The words just lodge more securely."

"What, then?"

"Children, why don't we plan a special dinner tonight to celebrate all the grapes that are ready for picking?"

"Oh, Mama, can we make sweets?" Huldah asked.

"Yes, of course! Jacob, would you see if there is still honey in the honey jar, and Deborah, would you start grinding us some more meal? Huldah, why don't you go see if there is another egg or two that our chickens have given us?"

One more child stared at them.

Josef scratched his head. "Jesus." He sighed. "Did you receive payment from the wine merchant?"

"Yes, here it is, Father." Jesus handed the coins to Josef.

"We'll stop working for today. Would you help me clean the workshop?" His hand on Jesus' shoulder, they left.

The festive dinner with the sweet cakes was a success at taking the children's mind off the visitor's request only too well. The children wanted one story after another at bedtime, and once in bed, jumped up several times to tell their Mama or Papa "one more thing".

Mary and Josef were both yawning as they sat on their mats. "Oh, how we need prayer over Eleazar's request," Josef said. "You know how we've tried to attract a teacher here, but most rabbis stay closer to the larger cities. They gain more support as well as a room in which to live."

"You and my father have been trying to build a meeting house here, but no one will donate the land."

"Mary, we can't wait for other rabbis to come here. Jesus will grow in knowledge as he converses with other wise men. Don't we want what is best for Jesus?"

Did this request come from Yahweh? Was it right for them to refuse it? Was it right for them to accept it? What would this mean for Jesus? Mary and Josef got on their knees and raised their arms. "O Holy One, give us wisdom." Suddenly Josef's eyes widened. "I believe the Lord spoke to me, either he or an angel did."

"I may have an answer, too. Why don't we pray more?"

"Why? What message did you hear, Mary?"

"The voice said, 'This is good training. Allow Jesus to go for one month.' Josef, I can't let him stay with strangers like that." She bowed her head and covered her face.

"That's matches what was given to me. What if Jesus stays with Salome and Zebedee? Sali would love that."

"Shouldn't we ask Jesus what he desires?"

"Yes, of course, we will listen to him," Josef said. "I'll go get him."

"Is he still awake?"

"Yes, and I believe he has been praying too."

With Jesus standing before them, Josef placed his hands on his shoulders. "You heard that the synagogue of Capernaum wants you to speak there?"

"Yes, Papa." Jesus' eyes glistened and his mouth twitched.

"What are your thoughts?"

Jesus took a deep breath. "Papa, I mean no disrespect, but you know how when we start a fire, you always hand the kindling and the wood to Mama or to one of us children?" His parents looked at each other, wrinkling their brows.

"Yes; go on."

"I feel the reason for your scar is that fire harmed you long ago." Mary eyed Josef carefully, noting his face softening.

Jesus must have seen the same softness she did. He continued, "For you, fire is… a threat. It seems you have made an uneasy peace with it. For me, fire is joy because it's like the Lord's word in my heart. His words burn in me like fuel, and when I talk about them, saying the words over and over, I become overjoyed. I love to watch a fire burn, because the songs of King David leap and tremble in me the same way."

Jesus' foot tapped as though he was dancing with the flames he described.

"We are praying still, and we shall discuss this with your grandparents. However, we propose that you might go for the month, but you would stay with your Aunt Salome." Josef patted Jesus on his back. "We must wait for the consent of Zebedee and your aunt."

Mary pulled Jesus close and hugged him. "We will send a message to my sister in the morning."

His face bright, Jesus glided from the room.

Ribbons of clouds lightened the sky the next morning while Josef sipped at the broth Hannah set before him. "Will Salome welcome Jesus right now? She has a new baby," said Josef. "Jacob."

Heli put his hand on Josef's shoulder. "This is the nephew she coddled when she was a girl of ten. Who wouldn't want a sweet, considerate boy of twelve years in their home? He will be a blessing to them."

Hannah sat down next to him. "He can help keep her house clean."

The others chuckled. "Mother," Josef said, "Jesus will study the Torah and the Prophets constantly. I hope she doesn't expect him to be her servant."

"Maybe he'll be a good influence on those big stepsons of hers," Mary said. "Sali would welcome Jesus's company, and he can help around the house if she needs anything heavy to be lifted."

Heli folded his hands across his chest. "It doesn't matter what Salome would say. The question is, 'What will Zebedee say?'"

The word came back: Zebedee would be delighted. Now there was someone who could stay with his wife so he could spend more time with his fishing business.

For Mary, it seemed Jesus was gone four months, not four weeks. For Jesus, it seemed like four days. "The rabbis who speak on Sabbath have such thoughtful insights, Mama. They even shared their scrolls with me." His eyes shimmered and his hands waved as he paced behind Mary while she kneaded dough. "The histories of the kings! How could they dishonor the Holy One? Why didn't they listen to the prophets?"

"Did I tell you I have a friend in Capernaum now? President Eleazar's son, Jairus. I hope I can visit him again. I've already asked Aunt Sali, and she said Yes."

"Your grandfather and father are as pleased with your new learning as you are, son. Already they are discussing introducing you to the priests at the temple."

"I can't wait for Passover."

"Yes. Your father has made arrangements for Grandma's cousin Elizabeth to bring her son John to join us. It will be a wonderful way to celebrate Passover."

"Have I met him?"

"Yes, about four years ago."

"I don't remember him."

Mary turned around, watching Jesus walk back and forth before she explained. "John used to be a very noisy little boy. His father, Zechariah, constantly was telling him to be quiet, to listen to his elders. Zechariah is a priest, and it was embarrassing to him that his son was so outspoken."

"Was Zechariah the one who doubted an angel and couldn't talk until his son was born?" At Mary's nod, Jesus' face turned serious. "Wasn't John the boy who tried to climb the stairs where the priests go?" Mary nodded. "I promise I won't embarrass you and Papa."

"I know you won't, Jesus." Mary rolled the dough into a loaf and set it near the hearth to rise.

"Did I tell you I went fishing one day with Zebedee and his boys?" He stopped pacing and cleared his throat. "They thought I'd be seasick, but I wasn't, and I was just a little scared."

Mary looked over her shoulder as she scraped away the loose flour. "Why would you be seasick or afraid?"

"From the freezing storm. It came on us like runaway horses and we couldn't get out of the way. The wind blasted us with hail, and the boat was swirling like a giant top. That's when water came in the boat."

Mary whipped around on the stool. Blanched, she tried to stand, and stumbled over her stool. Her shriek was half-strangled. "You almost drowned!"

Chapter 16

Passover in Jerusalem. Mary's heart raced as the family bumped and pushed their way through the crowds. So many people, even from other lands: dark skins, sallow complexions, giants of men, slaves in roped-together lines. The children's eyes were as big as platters, and their necks swiveled, trying to absorb everything around them as they neared the temple. The noise rose, swelled, erupted. Plaintive chants with familiar rhythms pulsed above them from the temple mount, punctuated by bleating sheep and squalling calves. Vendors and money changers shouted and haggled, waving their arms in outrage if anyone squabbled over the going price. Ach, calling them names too.

After the men and Jesus completed their cleansing, Heli led the family up the wide steps to the Court of the Women. Josef and Zebedee helped Salome and Mary keep the children contained, but they were scattering like frightened sheep. There were several years when Mary stayed home with a baby or sick child. This year, though, everyone came; Mary refused to stay home with her and Josef's newest son, little Josey. Yesterday, she and Josef and their children celebrated in Bethlehem with Josef's family, and last night Mary's parents and Salome and her family had arrived in Jerusalem. Now, Mary was trying to see the festival and her birthplace through the eyes and ears of their gaggle of children.

"Can you gather here?" Josef pleaded. "We'll wait for Zechariah and his family." Josef motioned to Jesus and Zebedee to step to the side with him and Heli. Mary watched as he handed Jesus the two coins she'd dug out of the old chest in the workshop.

"He's handsome, Mary."

Mary turned to Salome. "Jesus or Josef?" Mary had woven a new whole-cloth tunic for Josef, adding bright yellow and blue zigzags as Amari had taught her. She studied Jesus and Josef standing face-to-face and blushed with pride, not just of her firstborn, but of the father Josef was to Jesus, and to the girls and boys of his own seed.

Huldah tugged her mother's sleeve. "Why do the men need to wait for Zechariah?"

"He's a priest himself, although I don't know if he's still able to make the sacrifices. He knows the High Priest, though. Not every young man gets to meet them. Zechariah's son John is being presented along with Jesus. John is just three months older than your brother."

"Is that John and his parents?" Deborah pointed across the square.

John marched ahead of his parents through the Beautiful Gate, while Elizabeth and Zechariah inched forward, their canes clicking on the multicolored squares. Mary's heart pinched at her aunt's frailty, and she hurried to their side. "Come join us. We've been waiting for you so the men and boys can go in together."

Heli bowed and then motioned to Zechariah and John to join him, Josef, Jesus, and Zebedee with his sons.

Deborah clung to Mary. "Mama, who's that other man?"

The man heading toward them waving his arms was sturdy and grizzled. Gray strands striped his long black locks. "Wait for me!"

"Deborah, guess who's here!" Deborah slipped behind her mother's back.

"Don't you remember him?" Deborah shook her head.

"I guess you were too little." Mary handed Josey to Deborah and ran to wrap her arms around the man who had helped her many times over the years. "Uncle Samuel! Good Passover. We haven't seen you for such a long time. I didn't dream you'd be able to come." She pulled him over to the family group. "Josef, Samuel came. Would you bring everyone here?" Mary was bubbling. "Samuel, which of my children haven't you met? There's Jesus coming this way with the men, and here's Deborah, Huldah, Jacob, Judah, and Josey. Sali's husband Zebedee and his boys are coming over, and Salome has a boy of her own, Jacob. Yes, another Jacob." Mary touched her forehead. "I'm getting light-headed at having so many of our family here. Let's all have a meal together after we leave the temple."

Samuel embraced his sister- and brother-in-law, grasped Josef and Zebedee's arms, then greeted Hannah, Sali, and each of Mary's and Sali's children with Passover blessings.

Josef touched Mary's shoulder. "Now that Zechariah and Samuel are here, we're going in." Mary slipped over to Jesus, straightened his tunic, and kissed his forehead. Josef took Jesus' hand, and they moved toward the tall temple doors.

Elizabeth was frail and tremulous, her face creased with age. She kissed her squirming son and squeezed him to her chest. Her eyes flooded as she let him go. John ran past his father to catch up with Jesus.

"Zebedee, where are you going?" Sali grabbed her husband's arm as he moved to join the men and older boys. "We need you. We can't keep track of these skittery youngsters by ourselves. They're harder to round up than a herd of sheep, and just as noisy."

"*All* the men of this family are going in." Zebedee snickered. "I know you, little miss. If you can't go in, you don't want me to go either. I'm not worried about any children escaping. You'll line them all up in even rows and have them marching two-by-two before we come out of the temple."

"Husbands!" She smiled and shook her head as Zebedee trotted to join his sons, her father and Josef, Samuel and Zechariah, Jesus and John.

"I'm so jealous. I want to disguise myself in long robes and a hood and sneak in," Mary told Sali.

Sali's eyes twinkled with mischief. "Why don't you? I would!" Her gaze fastened on three-year-old Jacob. "Maybe when it's his turn then," she sighed.

"Yes, I'm guessing you will," Mary smiled. "But for now, we'll watch the children and keep Mama and Elizabeth company."

Mary turned at Elizabeth's wispy words.

"The joy of raising my miraculous gift has ended," the elderly woman said. She clutched Mary's arm. "The knowledge we are following the leading of the Lord of Hosts sustains us. Do you know that our lively John will not come back out with his father?"

"How can that be?" Hannah gently placed her arm around her cousin.

"He is joining a select group of men in the desert; he needs their discipline and teaching. Zechariah and I," Elizabeth paused and took a deep breath, "we believe we have reached the number of our days."

"No." Mary touched Elizabeth's thin shoulder. "If he's too much work, too much energy, *we'll* take him."

"Or Zebedee and I will," Sali said. "Ask my mother here; she will not forgive me if he doesn't come home with us."

When Elizabeth shook her head, Hannah faced her cousin. "Does John know this?"

Elizabeth forced a smile. "Yes, and I think he's excited about the challenge ahead of him. Zechariah and I are quite dull people, and this last year John has had frequent dreams about living in the desert." She looked over Hannah's shoulder at Salome and Mary. "You're both very generous to offer to take him, but we believe this is Yahweh's plan for John's life.

"Have you heard of the Essenes? Two elders from their desert community are already inside. They will escort John away through another door." She hiccupped and her voice faltered. "We will not see him again." With this last whisper, Elizabeth pulled her headscarf over her face, and Hannah embraced her tenderly.

Salome scanned the group to see if Mary's girls were keeping all the little ones contained, then pulled Mary a few steps away. "Who are the Essenes? Is this a good thing?"

"They are like the Pharisees, but they live in an old mansion against the hills by the Sea of Salt. Samuel told me about them one time. They can be mystical, but they are very devout."

Sali shook her head. "I hope John will be happy there."

...

A stooped and solemn Zechariah came out alone, blinking in the midday light. He stumbled to his weeping wife. "Our feisty little boy who loved to bound from rock to rock like a goat allowed the priests to say a solemn prayer over him. He stood straight as a Roman spear, Elizabeth: jaw tight, and eyes burning like an oven full of flickering coals." Zechariah himself straightened as he spoke, and his eyes glistened. "The men have collected him. We've done our duty to the Lord."

He took Elizabeth's hands, and his voice boomed. "John will prepare a path for the Messiah; I know he will not fail. The Lord of Heaven's Armies remembers; my life is complete." Suddenly his face drooped as the full import of his words surrounded them.

Mary's eyes were darting from Huldah to Jacob to Judah, and she barely caught her aunt as Elizabeth collapsed against her, sobbing with deep gulps. Josey was still in Mary's arms, so she stumbled under the weight, slight as it was, almost losing sight of Jacob running behind a column.

"Deborah, fetch Jacob. He's as obstinate as my ram Moses was. If we lose him in this throng, it will delay our trek home for hours." She shifted Josey's weight.

Elizabeth reached for Mary's cheek. "I know this was the Lord's plan, Mary," she stuttered. "I truly want to celebrate the special assignment of my darling, but."

"Sh, sh; it will get better." Hannah patted her shoulder.

Elizabeth gulped and coughed, then resumed speaking. "I just saw John through the crowd. Two men were leading him away. John was dancing and twirling around them." A thin smile creased her face in spite of her tears.

Josef, Jesus, and the other men huddled beside the temple doors, and Mary frantically waved for her husband and son to join her. She gave Jesus a quick embrace. "I want to hear what you did in the temple, but you and your father will have to tell me later. It's so late in the day and the inns are so crowded here; we can't have a meal now. We need to care for these two." She gestured toward Elizabeth and Zechariah.

Mary held Jesus back when the others escorted the elderly couple to where the rest of the family congregated.

Jesus' eyes were glassy. Mary stroked his arm, but he stared over her head. "Some of us need to escort Zechariah and Elizabeth back to Ein Karem; they're so distraught," Mary said. "I'm worried their grief over John will make the walk home even more difficult. Wait while we decide who will take them home."

A flicker touched Jesus's eyes, and he nodded.

The tug on her sleeve turned Mary around. "Abigail. What a joy. Good Passover. I didn't know if I'd get to see you here, especially in all this crowd." Mary hugged her former neighbor. "Are your parents here today? Who is this sweet baby you're carrying?"

Josef's shout turned her back. "Mary, we need to start home." As Josef came closer, he recognized Abigail. "Peace to you and joyous holiday."

"Peace and good Passover, Josef."

"Thank you. It has been very good. Excuse me, Abigail, but we're ready to return home. Greet your parents for me."

"Yes, naturally, but we'll probably see you on the way home."

Josef put his hand on Mary's arm. "Your mother shared your concerns, and we all agree. We decided Samuel and you will take Elizabeth and Zechariah back to Ein Karem. I know you'll want to keep Josey with you. The rest of us will start for Nazareth. You should catch up in a couple days."

"Doesn't Samuel have business?"

"It's Passover, Mary."

"May I have a few moments alone with Jesus?" Jesus had moved several cubits away, staring at the temple.

"We need to start home, and Zechariah and Elizabeth's strength is ebbing. They should start home as soon as possible."

When Josef walked away, Mary waved Jesus over. "Uncle Samuel and I are taking Zechariah and his wife home. When Samuel and I catch up in a day or two, then you can tell me all about what the priests said. I can't wait to hear. We're very proud of you." She drew Jesus against her and squeezed him tightly.

His eyes met hers briefly; then he pulled away and began walking toward the others. Mary called to his back. "Your father needs you. You'll help him, won't you?" Jesus nodded again, and she turned back to say goodbye to Abigail.

Mary hurried to join the tangle of family. Zebedee was already gathering the children into a line, and Sali was rearranging them in her whirlwind fashion. "Deborah and Huldah, help Papa with Jacob and Judah. I'll see you soon." Mary wished she'd had longer to talk with Jesus, but they'd have their conversation the next night.

...

They walked four abreast down the temple steps. With Josey sleeping on Mary's back, she could hold Elizabeth, who grasped Samuel while his other arm supported Zechariah. "May we hire a donkey for my wife?" said the old priest.

Samuel quickly made the transaction and lifted Elizabeth onto the donkey, and Mary tied Elizabeth's scarf under her chin.

"Zechariah, you can support Elizabeth on this side and Mary will keep her seated on the other." Samuel caught Mary's eyes, and she nodded, understanding that Zechariah would gain stability by holding his wife.

Samuel took the lead, and pushed past thronging pilgrims, bleating lambs, and scowling soldiers like an ox plowing a field. Mary's shoulders tightened, trying to keep Elizabeth upright. The elderly woman weighed little more than a leather cloak. Mary feared she would collapse before arriving home. In the sling on his mother's back, Josey chattered happily, enthralled with the exotic sights and smells.

Shadows from the mulberry trees formed dusky pools as they padded along the narrow track in Ein Karem. Exhausted, Zechariah fumbled with the latch. Samuel lifted his sister from the donkey and carried her to bed. Within minutes, Mary and Samuel had the donkey stabled and the fire lit.

Elizabeth fell asleep instantly. Mary filled a platter with dried fruit and cheese for the men, then sat in the corner to feed her toddler while the two men ate. Not much later, the old priest lay snoring beside his wife.

Yawning, Mary jostled Josey to sleep. She looked over at the sleeping couple. "I'm afraid we must stay with them tomorrow. Elizabeth is too fragile to be left alone."

"I'm willing to stay with them any length of time, but I've obligated myself to escort you to your family." He patted his knees. "While we sleep, we shall ponder how to restore you to your family in a timely manner. The Lord will provide." He pointed at Mary. "You, out of all the Lord's people, have evidence of that."

Mary shook her head. "Josef is the one who hears the angel in his dreams."

"Ah, remember: you were the receptacle for all our dreams."

...

Three days since they'd first parted from the family in Jerusalem, Samuel and Mary recognized neighbors from Nazareth on the hill below them. Her pace quickened, and she searched through the group of travelers for Josef and her children. Her eyes flitted over Josef, her children, and her parents. Puzzled, she recounted and caught her breath. Jesus wasn't with them. Why wouldn't he stay to help Josef? Was he farther ahead with Salome's family?

Her mother and children were sitting in the shade while Joseph and Heli helped a neighbor redistribute the load on his donkey, and Mary, the baby bouncing on her back, ran toward her husband. "Josef, where is Jesus?" A cramp had set in and she held her side while four children wrapped their arms around her legs. "Mama, Mama, you're back." Mary hugged and kissed each one, then called to her husband.

Josef left Heli to finish retying the bundles. "What are you talking about? I thought he went with you and Samuel. He was standing nearby when you were talking to Abigail; remember?"

A deep crease wrinkled Josef's forehead, and his jaw was tight. "When was the last time you saw him, Mary?"

Chapter 17

"Before Samuel and I left, I gave him a big hug and told him how proud we were. I saw you gathering the children and my parents and told him, 'Your father needs you.'" Mary's eyes widened and fear paralyzed her. "Josef, do you think he followed John, and that he thought his heavenly father requires him to study with the Essenes? Jesus is so committed to Yahweh, he may have followed John's example and ran after those desert people." A torrent of tears streamed down her cheeks, and her body trembled.

"Peace, Mary, he wouldn't have done that." Doubt was creeping across Josef's face. "I will go back for him. Now that you're here, it's best you travel to the inn where the family is staying tonight."

"No, I have to find him. I have to come with you."

Josef looked at her pressed lips and nodded.

"We want you to stay with us, Mama." Deborah held Jacob by the hand and Huldah carried Judah. Her mother came up behind the children.

"Yes, but there's a problem, Huldah. Jesus didn't join Samuel and me, and I thought he was with you." She blinked rapidly.

"Your mother and I...." Josef began, then looked at Samuel, who nodded gravely. "And Samuel will find him."

"We'll bring the other children home," said Heli. "Don't worry. The Lord knows where he is."

Hannah slipped her arm in Mary's. "Do you want me to take the baby? Will he make do without you?"

Mary rubbed her eyes and yawned. "Yes, I think so. I've hardly nursed him the last two days, and he drank some of Samuel's broth this morning. He's chewing on fruits easily, too."

Hannah pulled Josey and his sling from Mary's back and twirled him in a circle until he laughed. "Here, children. Come stay with Grandma. You'll see Mama later."

"Be good for Grandma." Mary kissed and hugged her children once more before joining Samuel and Josef on the climb to Jerusalem.

"You're exhausted. You should have stayed with the rest of the family." The two men waited beside the road for Mary to catch up.

"Don't start going now that I've reached you." She wrinkled her mouth at the whine in her voice.

"Would you like to refresh yourself?" Samuel asked her before turning to Josef. "It would be a minimal delay."

"While I'm getting my breath back, let's think. Did either of you men see him going in a particular direction?"

Samuel shook his head. "Would he have exited through the Beautiful Gate or the Shushan? He knew you were descending to Jericho."

Mary's shoulders were heaving. "Maybe he was trying to catch up with us, Samuel, but what if he followed John or was abducted by a slave trader? How can we tell someone else what he looks like? I barely remember what color tunic he wore. Raising and keeping him safe until he establishes his kingdom is too heavy a burden for me. I've failed my Lord and my child."

Josef's voice was firm. "Where is your trust? Do you remember those words the old prophet Simon spoke, that the Lord would not abandon His son?" He pulled her close and ran a hand over her head. "I know you're tired, but the Holy One is faithful." After she stopped quivering, he took her arm and continued up the road.

...

Iron gray clouds boiled overhead as they crossed the Court of the Gentiles. The sun had set; how would they find Jesus now? Was there anyone who would even remember seeing him? A contingent of soldiers from the fortress marched across the courtyard, and Mary shrank against Josef, fears from her long ago demoralizing visit to Jerusalem with Piltai and Yael churning her stomach. Inside the temple square, Mary's eyes swept the black corners. The flickering lamps on the towers above them cast menacing shadows, squeezing her spirit. No one was here.

A single man entered, and Josef rushed over to him. "Praise the Lord!" Josef's voice carried across the square, and he brought the man to Mary.

"Matthias? Jesus is at your house?" Mary's face fell at Matthias's frown.

"Mary, I wish that were so, but I'm happy to help you look. I just left my brother and a friend at the inn below here. I'll get them to help you search. Jesus must be twelve years old now, right?" At Josef's nod, he turned and ran.

As they walked out to the Gentiles' courtyard, fear and fatigue shattered Mary's heart. A piercing wail broke from her throat and she crumpled to the pavement. In seconds, two Roman guards grabbed Josef and Samuel. "What have you done to this woman?"

"No. Don't arrest them." Mary grabbed Josef's leg to pull herself up, gasping to pull air into her lungs. Samuel's suave words calmed the soldiers and explained the situation. One soldier left to assemble a search party, while Josef placated Mary.

"Can't you give me more information than 'thin, twelve-year-old Jew'?"

She cringed at the way the soldier said "Jew," and focused on picturing Jesus. "Yes, yes. He was wearing, I mean, he *is* wearing a gray wool tunic with a dark blue sash. And he had his little pack."

Along with three more soldiers, Samuel and Matthias and his friends divided Jerusalem into sections to scour every corner, while Josef took Mary to an inn. She slept fitfully, and each time she woke, thunder rumbled overhead.

Josef had already left the next morning when Mary's eyes flickered. Despair crushed her, and she struggled to rise. She dragged herself to the front of the inn, and peered out at rain-slicked streets. Back in the room, Mary knelt on her sleeping mat, crying to the heavens, the Lord, the angels, Moses, Abraham—anyone she could imagine would influence the outcome of their search.

Another day of thunder and rain passed, and the men came to the inn by ones and twos, reporting they'd had no success. Mary could not eat supper. *What had become of her son? Didn't the Holy One still have a plan for him to be their King?* Josef and Mary avoided each other's eyes and tried to squash the accusing thoughts that snaked through their minds.

At daybreak, Josef prepared to go to Bethlehem and bring his brothers to help.

"What will you tell them, Josef?" she cried. "That we lost the son of the King of Heaven?"

"Mary, I am distraught too, but our Heavenly Father knows exactly where Jesus is. Don't be afraid. What if he went to my parents' house?"

"What if he followed John and those men to the desert?" she whispered.

"We will find Jesus." His words bounced around her mind.

Josef brought Jacob along with Cleopas and his young wife, another Mary, to keep his Mary company. The men spread throughout the poorer parts of the city and returned as the setting sun slid through the strips of gray in the west. Their shoulders sank, and they wouldn't look Mary in the eye. The soldiers that day had been checking at each gate, and no one resembling Jesus had gone out or come in. Everyone gave the same answer: there had been too many pilgrims for anyone to remember one boy in gray with a small pack on his back.

Her young sister-in-law coaxed Mary to eat, but she wasn't hungry. *How could she eat when her son could be stolen or lying sick in a corner?* Her head felt as though a boulder was sitting on top, her stomach like ropes were pulling it apart. Josef gently urged her to gain some strength, but how could she? As the light faded, Josef's brothers and his sister-in-law, along with Matthias and Uncle Samuel, returned to Bethlehem. Josef and Mary knelt on the little mat they shared, determined to pray all night, clinging to the thought that their heavenly Father knew where his son was.

Her head cradled in Josef's lap, a slice of sun woke Mary the next morning. She had a single picture in her mind: the temple. "It must mean we need to pray at the temple! God will hear us more clearly there."

"Then we'll look there, Mary. Why didn't we think of that first? We looked around the steps and the portico. We asked the merchants selling the pigeons and lambs in the Gentiles courtyard, but we never asked inside."

"We should bring some doves as an offering."

"The Lord will understand, Mary. Besides, we can't afford even to buy doves now, what with paying for this room and feeding our helpers." Josef picked up her shawl and headscarf, and she wrapped their warmth around her as they left the inn. They walked soundlessly across the square, Mary drawing the scarf across her face.

When Josef entered the temple, Mary peered over his shoulder. Two rows of candles released flickering light and the faint scents of incense and beeswax. The pervading silence was barely disturbed by a small knot of priests in the far corner.

"Josef." She whispered, putting her hand to her cheek. He saw her, covered the side of his face with his hand and backed out. His scar was hardly noticeable anymore. Not a single priest had mentioned it three days before, but now all attention would be on him as the sole intruder. He slipped the shawl off Mary's shoulders, quickly draped it around his face, and walked back firmly toward the circle of scholars. Halfway there he shouted. "Jesus!"

Seven priestly heads swiveled at once toward the man running toward them. As they changed position, Mary could see the slight figure in the center. Josef turned to Mary and waved. Knowing how badly she wished she could enter, Josef herded the group out to the Court of the Women.

Sputtering with relief, Mary enveloped Jesus. "How could you have done this? Didn't you know we've been looking for you? Why didn't you tell me?" The priests looked at her, eyebrows raised. She hoped they were embarrassed. They should have known a twelve-year-old youth had parents who would be worried about him.

Jesus' innocent face fueled Mary's tirade. "We've spent three days looking for you! The rest of the family had to go on without us. Your uncles from Bethlehem, Samuel–everyone has been scouring the city, even Roman guards!" Mary stopped, realizing her fuming at Jesus was covering her own guilt.

"Shalom, Mother. Why were you looking for me? Didn't you know that I must be here? This is my Father's house, and I'm taking care of His affairs. I want to help Him."

His father's house. Help his father. *That* Father? She shook her head, remembering she had asked him to help his "father". *What did the priests think of it?*

Josef slipped behind two of the priests and gently pulled Jesus to him. "Let's go home now; we'll talk some more on the way. Sirs," he addressed the priests, "we thank you for teaching this bright young man."

"No, no," said the oldest, "You don't understand. He was teaching us. Please bring him again."

Silently Mary prayed, "It's not time. You didn't tell me I had to give him up yet." Immediately words exploded in her mind: *"This is my beloved Son, with whom I am well pleased."* She ran sobbing out of the courtyard. How quickly she had forgotten whose child he was. She wondered, was he really her son, in any way? *What had she done? What would she do now?*

Jesus and Josef's chatter carried them to Jericho. Silently, Mary stumbled along behind them. Streaks of tears continued to mark her dusty face. Her confidence was badly shaken. Questions paraded through her mind: *Should they not have had other children? Should they have a guard for Jesus wherever they go? How could they afford that? What were the scholars learning from him? Was she supposed to be learning from him? That desert community claimed they were making a path for the Messiah; were they supposed to send Jesus to the desert with John?*

Where was the song of praise that would instruct her now? "My soul magnifies the Lord. My spirit has rejoiced in God my Savior, for he has looked at the humble state of his servant," she had told her aunt all those years ago, before Jesus was born. And how could she have forgotten the angel's shining visit? "I want to be the Lord's servant," she had said. Now Mary tried to make old Anna's prophecy fit into what had just happened. "A caretaker of the house of the Lord" still didn't make sense to her, especially if Jesus was going to be a king instead of a priest, but Anna had been convinced the prophecy was fulfilled.

The weather warmed, and they continued until the last rays of the sun sucked all light from the sky, camping beside a gurgling creek. Josef and Mary rolled up close in their cloaks on each side of Jesus. His slender body, almost as tall as Josef's now, reminded Mary that his childhood was gone.

Once home, they settled into the usual routine, with the exception that Jesus was allowed to go to the newly built synagogue whenever he wished. Each night, before she fell asleep, Mary prayed about the assignment the Lord entrusted to Josef and herself. For his part, Josef began to teach Jesus more difficult carpentry skills.

Heli protested. "If Jesus becomes a carpenter, he will lose his zeal for the Lord. How will he learn to be a ruler? Just let him carve a little, if he must be in the workshop." They couldn't convince Heli that, Messiah or no, the young man would need to make a living until he was crowned. Even the beloved King David started out with a trade, simple as it was, one that most of the boys in their region learned when they took turns with the flocks.

Several weeks later, Mary held Josef back as he started for the shop. "It's not enough to train Jesus to work with wood and stone," she said. "My father has a point. When will we teach him to be a king? Doesn't he also need to know how to lead soldiers? Who will help us?"

"Mary, you worry too much," Josef grinned. "Did King David know all those things? He knew the Lord Almighty was with him."

"David had brothers who were soldiers for King Saul, and David played the harp in Saul's house." She set her hands on her hips.

"Be at peace, my love. Hasn't the Commander of Heaven's Armies enough experience? Think of other tales from our people's history: Deborah was a judge, and the Holy One didn't wait for her to be trained before she led our army into battle. What about Gideon? He was hiding from the enemy inside a wine press when the Lord designated him as a mighty warrior." With Josef's reassurance, Mary stopped fretting. In prayer each night, she asked the Lord's forgiveness. Surely, He who gave her this son would faithfully prepare and protect him.

After a few months, Jacob and Judah began their lessons. Mary was grateful for her father's presence, aging as he was. He gathered all the young ones around him and, just as he had with Mary, taught them the wonderful stories of their people. They giggled, as she and Sali had, with quizzes about their Jewish heroes. Soon, he was directing Jesus on how to test the younger ones on the Torah.

With six children, Hannah's help lightened Mary's work by teaching the girls cooking and weaving. Praise the Lord for the children! What a blessing it was to have such a large family, and another son came, Simon, who sweetened their days. Her father loved teaching them all.

One month after Feast of Booths, weather that should have produced clear autumn days enshrouded the hills in winter's chill. Sunlight failed to pierce the thick cloud blanket. Before long, their clothes stank of mildew. All over the Galilee region, people searched for firewood until no branches remained. Even animal dung was quickly collected and used before someone else found it. They sent the children to scour for olive and fruit pits to burn. Then heavy rain came.

"I'm dreading bringing those cart wheels to Magdala," Josef said, sipping morning broth with Jesus and Jacob. "If I move off the road for the soldiers to pass through, my cart will sink in the mud."

Mary refilled his bowl. "If only you didn't have to go on to Scythopolis for the saw blades. Can't you make do until spring?"

"It will rain then, too, and the roads will be in a worse mess."

"Can Jesus and Jacob go with you to bring the cart back?"

"I'll bring Jacob. Jesus, I want you to stay here and help your grandfather." Josef whispered, "Grandpa isn't as steady as before, and he won't admit it." He gave Mary a crooked smile, waited for Jacob to grab warm clothes, and waved goodbye.

Just before midday, a young boy came to their door, his tunic so wet it stuck to his skin. "I'm Uriah, son of Davon." His voice trembled. "My father's cart has broken an axle. Can the carpenter come fix it?" Deborah went to the shop to bring her grandfather, and Jesus followed him into the room.

"You shouldn't go in this weather." Hannah shook her finger at her husband.

"You don't understand," Heli said. "Without an axle, the man can't collect wood or bring produce to market."

"You need to eat before you go. We'll feed you both," Mary said. Uriah wiped his soggy hair aside and his eyes lit up.

"Just give us some bread and cheese," Heli answered. "We'll take it with us. This boy's papa isn't going to get anything to eat until we fix his wagon." He pulled a tanned goatskin over his shoulders and stuffed a hunk of bread in his jaw while handing some to Uriah.

"I'll go too," Jesus offered.

Heli shook his head no, but as he started out the door after the shivering child, he paused. "Jesus, grab some bread and a warm cloak. Let's put those manly muscles of yours to work." Despite the foul weather, Jesus beamed.

Mary watched the boys trail behind her father, slogging down the road. It was midnight and still raining when Heli and Jesus returned. Mud caked their legs and clothes. Drops fell from Jesus' matted head.

"Those wretched Romans," Heli sputtered. "Two of them watched us, just watched with no offer to help, while we repaired the axle. One of them even laughed while we slipped around in the mud to lift the cart onto the new axle." He shook his head. "That poor child. Did you know his mother had just passed away? And that farmer was reeking of wine. He must have been drinking all the time his son came to fetch us."

"Shh, Father." Mary and her mother handed rags to Heli and Jesus.

"That wasn't the worst of it. We finished and were halfway home when a chariot came racing toward us. We moved to opposite sides of the road so it could pass. Then, just abreast of us, the driver swerved the horse toward Jesus and made him fall into a puddle."

"Jesus! A Roman did this to you?"

"Probably a Roman, but we couldn't tell," Heli said. "He was all in black."

Mary felt every nerve in her body tingle. She pulled Jesus to her chest. "I'm sorry; I'm so sorry."

"Mama, it's not your fault," Jesus said.

"Yes, it is. I shouldn't have let you go. I've neglected my responsibility." She cringed, wiping his hair and face and rubbing him with a towel to warm him while her mother laid out dry clothes.

Her father shook his head. "Then I'm to blame. I should have left him at home, but I couldn't have repaired the axle without his help. With the state he was in, that Davon didn't know his arm from his leg."

Heli's coughing began the next day. Two days later, he was bedridden. During the night, a rustle disturbed her prayers. A shadow shifted in her father's room. Jesus was standing over Heli's shivering body, hands lifted to heaven and tears slipping down his face.

Despite Jesus doing as many tasks as he could, Josef returned to a workshop full of unfinished projects and a father-in-law who had been in bed for a week.

A sharp chill had seeped into Heli's lungs. He could barely sit to sip the soup Hannah made. "How can he keep shivering when his forehead is burning?" Mary asked her mother as they ground mustard seed and thyme for salves.

The grandchildren huddled at the door to his room, but Mary and her mother wouldn't let them in. They could see the yearning in Heli's eyes, but his voice was barely a whisper.

As light seeped through the shuttered window, Mary studied her father.

Josef placed his hand on her shoulder. "We'll ask Jesus to bring Salome home."

Mary swiveled. "No, Josef; not Jesus. It's not safe for him to be on the roads."

"What are you talking about? Some fool ran him off the road. Travelers are always at the mercy of crazy Romans."

"We have to protect him. We can't send him out alone." She shook her fists.

"Mary." Josef pulled down her arms and drew her tightly to his chest. "Jesus is a young man now; let's trust that the Lord has assigned angels to cover him."

"But I'm afraid for him." Trembling started at her shoulders and reached her knees.

Josef stroked her head, straightening her hair with his fingers. "You have other children. *We* have other children. You can't be with Jesus everywhere he goes. Don't you think the Holy One of Israel can handle every danger?"

Mary's "Yes" was muffled against his chest.

"Will Jesus' own faith grow if you're holding his hand all the time? Hiding him at home?"

Jesus left for Capernaum. The family gathered around the fire and beseeched the Lord for Heli's healing. "Lord of Heaven, our house is so quiet without his songs," said Deborah.

Jacob knelt beside his sister. "O Holy One, who will quiz us about your mighty prophets? Give us our Grandpa back."

"Don't take my Papa before Salome arrives," Mary pleaded. "She'll want to say goodbye."

Her mother had no words, just tears.

A day and a night passed with constant prayers. Mary was kneeling beside her father when he gave a shudder. Gray dawn slid over Heli's skin, stealing its color. She placed a hand on his lifeless chest and then grabbed her hair and began keening as she rose to get her mother. Thin light streaked through the window while they anointed Heli and wrapped him in burial cloths.

That evening, Jesus returned with Salome and her toddler Jacob. As Sali grieved beside her father's body, Mary brought her food and patted her sister's belly. "Are you with child again?" Sali nodded.

Hannah enfolded her. "You are a spark of joy to see us through our dark days. I'm truly blessed; both my daughters are here."

Confident Heli would recover, the family hadn't considered the need for a burial site. In honor of Heli's passing, Josef and Jesus removed their sandals before being sent out to search. A third man, holding his sandals too, came through the door with them when they returned: Samuel.

"I must burden you with additional sorrow," Samuel said as he embraced Hannah. "My dear sister Elizabeth and her revered husband also passed away this month. This vile weather and my travels to Egypt prevented me from bringing you word. We interred them at Ein Karem."

Josef caught Hannah as she collapsed, picked her up, and laid her on the couch. Sali and Mary's wailing joined their mother's feeble sobs as they pounded their thighs. Josef and Jesus left Samuel to rest and mourn with the women while they prepared the cave they'd found.

As soon as they sent the news around the community, the family began the sorrowful walk north to Sepphoris. Josef carefully led the donkey bearing Heli. Samuel supported Hannah, and Mary carried Simon. Jesus, carrying little Jacob on his shoulders, followed Sali and the older children.

When the man who had been the best carpenter within a two days' journey dies, everyone knows. Neighbors and clients, crying and throwing ashes, joined the trek to the gaping hole in the hillside. Josef and Jesus placed Heli on the shelf inside. Mary pulled out a gold flask of frankincense. The sweet aroma drifted around them as she and Sali rubbed their father's body and wrapped him in more cloths.

As the men rolled the stone across the cave, Huldah held out her rain-soaked hand. "Look, Mama. Even the heavens are crying."

Chapter 18

Hannah closed the door behind the messenger and spread out her hands before Mary. "I have to go. I helped you with all your children but two. You have your girls to help you, and Salome has no one."

The message that Salome was in labor had come sooner than expected, more than a month early. Mary's mother didn't return for three months, needing to nurse Sali back to health and coddle tiny John until he began putting on weight, too.

"Oh, if you had seen him, it would have broken your heart; he was so tiny and blue," Hannah said to the family when she returned. "What he needed was to bake a little more." Their grandmother's rescue mission fascinated Mary's children.

"Did you put him in the oven, Grandma?" Judah's eyes opened wider.

"He was no bigger than a loaf of bread," Hannah said, her face smiling at the drama she was creating. "Spring brought cold weather; the wind coming off the sea chilled us even more."

"Then how did you cook your food if the baby was in the oven?" Huldah wrinkled her forehead.

"Mama," Mary warned.

Hannah relented. "I'm saying the baby would be stronger if your Aunt Salome hadn't delivered so early. Little John is formed perfectly, but he had some trouble breathing the first week. Your Aunt Sali was exhausted, too, but she'll be up clapping her hands to get all her boys moving before you know it."

The children laughed, reminded of their aunt's favorite attention-getting method.

At dinner that night, Hannah shared more news from Galilee. "Zebedee's business is expanding. Noah and Avner each take a boat out on their own, so now all they eat is fish. I'm glad to be back, looking forward to more chicken at my Sabbath meal and less fish."

...

Two years later, Sali's stepson Avner was at the door, and little John was peeking out from his robe. Avner's voice wavered. "My father requests that Salome's esteemed mother come and see her through her time while she's with child."

"What? She's due already?" Mary turned to her mother. "She can't be."

"No, dear woman." Avner shuffled and his face turned red. "But she has to stay lying down all the time. My father respectfully asks if you will consider taking care of John until my stepmother is back on her feet."

"What about little Jacob?" Mary looked around her crowded home, trying to figure where to lay another sleeping mat.

"My father says he's old enough to go out on the boats with him."

Hannah waved Avner and John inside. "Come in and eat something while I gather a few clothes." Hannah scooped nuts and dates in front of the two and disappeared. Mary picked up John, called to Judah and Simon to find him some toys, and went to the workshop to tell Josef. Within an hour, Hannah left for Capernaum with Avner.

...

Deborah hung up a dishtowel. "Mama, I'm worried about little John; he's not at all like Zebedee's older sons. He's so small and frail."

"I believe Salome protected him because of his early breathing difficulties, or perhaps he's quiet by nature."

Deborah nodded to Jesus coming in. "We're talking about John. He won't play with the younger boys and their friends. I think he's afraid their energy will knock him down."

Jesus cleared his throat. "Let's see what happens if I bring him into the workshop to help me."

A week later, Mary whispered to Jesus. "What did you do?"

"First, I set him on my shoulders while I worked. Then I put him on the end of the workbench and gave him simple tasks. You know, sanding a little bowl or handle, just as Grandpa did with you, and Papa did with me when I was John's age." Within two weeks, Jesus was teaching him psalms to sing. By the end of the month, John was running around with the other children.

Only one lamp flickered as Mary packed bread and cheese for Josef before he left for another pre-dawn delivery. "I'm wondering why Jesus is closer to John than he is to his own brothers."

"What do you mean?"

"It saddens me. Those two are so affectionate. Our other sons respect Jesus, but I don't believe they love him like John does."

"Mary, they're boys. They won't fawn over him."

"I have the impression Deborah and Huldah feel the same. They admire his intelligence, but they aren't close to Jesus."

"Have you heard Jesus complain? Did he ever play tricks on them or hurt their feelings? The Holy One has a call on his life, and I assume they sense that." Josef swung his pack to his shoulder. "I'll be back before sunset."

Mary sat at her loom, putting the yarns in order. She sorted through the skeins in the basket beside her, picking up a dark blue ball and caressing her cheek with its softness. Why hadn't she told Josef she was expecting another child? Was that why she was despondent over Jesus' relationship with his brothers and sisters? She must speak soon, before her mother guessed the cause of her lethargy and blurted out the news.

Josef returned early, bringing a parcel of fish as his payment. "Let's cook these while they're fresh," he said.

Mary bit her tongue. "You don't want to save them for midday tomorrow?"

"After I've been smelling them all the way home? No, let's have them now. The boys can clean them. Jacob and Judah, take care of these for your mother."

Judah pinched his nose. "Phew. Why us all the time? You never ask Jesus to gut fish."

Josef glared at Judah, and Mary sucked in her breath while the pressure built in her chest. Her words caught in her throat before tumbling out. "In a few months, you will have a new brother or sister." There was cheering all around her.

...

Jesus was repairing blocks on a customer's wall; Jacob was apprenticed to the fuller, so he wasn't home. Josef had sent Judah with other boys from Nazareth to herd the flocks with old Nahor until the lambs were born. That left Josey to work with his father at the quarry.

"He challenges me over every task," Josef had groused to Mary as he dressed that morning. "That boy doesn't like supervision, much as he loves building." He stomped to his shop to get his chisels.

Mary was lying down with her new daughter Esther, listening to Huldah humming while she washed clothes. Her mother had taken Deborah to the town well. Mother is lining up eligible husbands, Mary thought.

"Help! Mama!" Josey bolted into the house, dirty tears striping his cheeks. "Papa's hurt; it's a boulder; I can't lift it off. Help!" He bent over, panting.

"Huldah, run to Taoma's, then get Jesus. Wait, take Esther." Mary leapt from the mat and dropped the startled baby in Huldah's arms.

Josey dashed ahead of her up the hill where his father was face down, groaning. Beside him, a monstrous stone pinned his left arm. Blood was seeping from the side of his head. As Josey tried to push the boulder away, Josef moaned louder.

Taoma and his youngest son Gideon came up behind Mary.

"Look for a big branch," Taoma directed. His eyes scanned the trees near the quarry. "There's one." Gasping, he rushed over and snatched it. In a blur, Taoma and Gideon leveraged the stone away, and Josef's groans slowed.

"Help him sit up," Mary cried, but Gideon restrained her. "Don't move him! His ribs may be broken!"

When Gideon rolled Josef over, Mary sagged against Taoma. The chisel Josef had been using protruded from his chest. Blood leaked out with each labored gasp, spreading its bright stain across his tunic.

Just as Jesus arrived, the gasping stopped. He fell to his knees beside Josef, slinging the chisel aside and pressing on the wound, begging life into the body, begging the Holy One to help. Wine-red, the blood oozed around his hands, mingling with tears flowing from his face.

Again, the keening, the ashes, the trek to the tomb. Mary stumbled through the days and weeks. The burial, preparing meals, washing clothes, feeding the baby were like snatches of dreams flitting through her mind. Her prayers changed from adoration to accusation. Family members swirled around her like shadows. When she sat at the loom, every bundle of wool looked dingy, and her fingers fumbled as she separated weft and warp.

"Dear woman."

Mary raised her eyes to Jesus'.

"We need you."

She stared at the thin young man before her. *Isn't this the little child she was called to care for and protect? When did he grow up?*

"Mama, we are all grieving over Papa. Grandma does everything possible to help the girls, and I'm doing what I can to encourage the boys."

"But?"

"We still need you." Jesus sat beside her and wrapped her hands in his.

Mary examined Jesus' hands. They were large and sinewy and warm. A man's hands, like Josef's. She looked up at her son's face. "Will you pray for me?"

...

Mary picked up the distaff and tied the strands of flax before looking at Hannah. "Mother, how you've managed without my help? Forgive me for deserting the family. I wish you'd said something to me."

"I tried; your heart wasn't open."

"I'm sorry."

"I know you are, and I am too, but now that's behind us. Have you noticed how well Deborah and Huldah are weaving? They have even been selling blankets at the market."

A blush crept across Mary's face. "I didn't know."

"Deborah is past ready to wed, Mary, and we need to find a husband for Huldah, too."

How had she let that responsibility slip? Mary caught her breath. How would she start the process?

"Have you noticed how handsome and industrious Abigail's younger brother is?"

"Taoma's son Daniel?" Mary titled her head. "Yes, I suppose so. He's over here frequently helping, isn't he? I Imagine Orli asked him to look after us."

Her mother chuckled. "I don't think Orli had anything to do with Daniel's willingness to help Deborah with her chores. Why don't you see if Jesus wants to meet with Taoma."

"Jesus? I'll approach him tonight."

Less than two weeks later, Taoma asked Jesus if Daniel and Deborah could wed. He and Orli offered to host the ceremony overlooking his vineyards. Mary's approval set both Deborah and Huldah busy weaving wool, leaving Mary and her mother to embroider flax. Laughter and singing looped through the house like elegant lace.

When the wedding came, even the boys went to Taoma and Orli's to drape flowers around the tent poles. As Daniel and Deborah said their vows, a balm of peace seeped into Mary's soul. *Praise your Name, Holy One. Yes, I am still blessed.* She gazed across the courtyard at Jesus, catching his eye, and he beamed at her. *You will yet be king. I must wait for the Lord of Hosts' timing.* As if Jesus had heard her, he nodded.

...

"Mama," Mary said only a few months later, "I notice you've developed a close friendship with the wife of our new synagogue president, Levi. I hadn't noticed before what a handsome son they have."

"Yes. Tirtzah and I are dear friends."

"I'll speak to Jesus." Mary walked back to the workshop and stopped in the doorway to inhale the woody aromas. Joy burst from her soul and transfused her body. With a pang, she realized how long it had been since she had entered the shop. She closed her eyes and took a deep breath.

When she opened her eyes and stepped forward, Jesus spoke. "It *is* like a temple in here, isn't it?"

"This room holds precious memories of my father and my husband. The fragrances of almond and cedar and resin restore my hope and peace. They've done so since I was a child." She looked across the room at the row of tools. Chisels, saws, planes: instruments for building as well as cutting and gouging. "The Lord was with your father... with Josef that day, wasn't he? He didn't suffer long."

Jesus nodded. "Yes, He was here then, too." Her son set down his mallet. "What brings you to the shop today?"

"Mama thinks President Levi's son would be a desirable husband for Huldah."

"Micah, she means?" He put his mallet away and straightened a few other tools. The sun's last rays flashed briefly, and the room became shadowed.

"Yes. Grandma has become remarkably friendly with Micah's mother. You must know the family well, having spent so many hours at the synagogue." She waited for a response. "He is a handsome young man," she added. Still, Jesus said nothing. "What is your hesitation, son?"

"Huldah is tender. The Word of the Lord advises a young man to leave his father and mother and cling to his wife. I believe that would be very hard for Micah to do."

"You are saying no?"

"Micah is immature. I don't believe he has a mind of his own."

"We will wait, then. I'll ask Grandma to show more restraint around Tirtzah."

Two days after Mary asked her mother not to encourage a match between Micah and Huldah, Hannah was in bed with chills. She choked and coughed with each shallow breath. Mary tried to keep water boiling over the fire. Hope flared when she remembered the myrrh that stored with the remnants of gifts from the star-gazers. Neither the myrrh nor her regular salves brought relief.

All the family fasted and prayed, but Mary was perplexed by Jesus' agony over his grandmother's sinking health. Even from the workshop, she could hear his groaning pleas. Yet, her mother died. As Jesus plodded beside her on the familiar trek to the cave at Sepphoris, she heard his whispered plea, "What more could I have done?"

Mary had her own question: *Now who will help me put him on the throne?*

The mourning period was over, and Huldah dragged into the kitchen, her hands over her face. "I miss Grandma. She knew Micah is the right man for me. Why didn't you listen to her? I'm going to be alone like Widow Rachel, but I'll be the auntie who never weds. Why can't Jesus see what a sweet boy Micah is?" She whined all day while she swept or carded wool.

When Jesus came from the workshop that night, Huldah stopped him at the door. "What is wrong with Micah? What could be a better family than one where the synagogue leader is the head? Aren't we called to take our religion seriously?"

"There's a difference between religion and faith, Huldah," Jesus said.

"Micah's father knows all the laws, Jesus." Huldah put her hands on her hips. Then she lowered her head to mutter. "Some people think he knows them better than you."

"His legalism is the primary reason I disapprove of your marrying into that family, Huldah."

"Mother." She stretched the word. "Jesus just doesn't want me married. Am I supposed to wait on him and you all my life?"

"Huldah!" Mary's gasp bounced around the walls.

"If you don't show more respect to your mother than that, you may not be mature enough to marry." Jesus glared, his face hard.

Mary was alone carding wool when Jesus came in a fortnight later. "What is it?"

"Some very devout scholars have invited me to study with them."

"That's wonderful. You're studying in Jerusalem, or is it Capernaum again?" Seeing his demeanor, she lay down her paddles. "Where, then?"

"With the Essenes, by the Sea of Salt."

"Isn't that where Elizabeth's son studied?" She began chewing her thumbnail.

"He's still there, and I'd like to visit with him. I'll be away for a few months, maybe more."

Mary looked around the room, as if a reason to keep him was sitting on a stool or lurking behind the water jugs. She raised her eyes back to Jesus. "You realize what that means, don't you?"

"Yes. I'm going to turn the decision about Huldah over to Jacob. He's aware of my thoughts, and Huldah knows them, too."

"You've talked to them?" She lowered her head, covered her face, and mumbled. "It means we'll have a wedding soon." Silence. She looked up quickly, fearing a travel bag was already on his back. "When are you leaving?"

"The first day of the week."

The day after Jesus left, Jacob gave permission for Huldah to marry Micah. The betrothal was short; they married within six weeks, and then Huldah was gone. The rest of the family was under Mary's roof or a courtyard or a few streets away, but a shroud of loneliness hung on her shoulders. She wandered from room to room, expecting to see her parents or Josef or Jesus. When Deborah came on the Sabbath, Mary commented, "It was a lovely wedding, but they both still act like such children."

President Levi didn't allow Huldah to visit her mother's home; Mary only saw her in the marketplace or at the well, and Tirtzah always accompanied Huldah. After her weekly shopping at the market, Mary remarked to Deborah, "Micah doesn't seem to have a mind of his own. His father has added a few of his own rules to Torah."

Torah. Guidance. Her thoughts turned to Jesus. *What is he learning? Does he know when his reign will begin? How will our people defeat Herod Archelaus? Will we move to Jerusalem? What will the Romans do?* The suspense of autumn was upon her, each brisk wind robbing more gold from the trees. Mary kept her door open in the morning to capture the twirling dance of leaves. Afternoons, she stood at the door looking beyond Taoma's grape-laden vines for each figure climbing to Nazareth. She was daydreaming about Jesus when Jacob came in from work.

"What do you suggest I do about Judah?"

She stared at her son. "What's wrong?"

"Do you know where he is now?"

"Isn't he in the workshop?" She cocked her head to listen for him. "He must be at the quarry, just late getting home."

"He's at the wine shop, drinking with the Zealots."

She sunk to the bench and covered her eyes. "Are you positive? He's only fifteen."

"I wouldn't say it if it weren't true, Mama. Gideon thought I should know, since Jesus isn't here. I stuck my head in the wine shop on my way home." He crossed his arms.

Mary put her face in her hands. "Did he see you? Did you ask him to come with you?"

"His friends saw me and told him. He turned to look at me, and then took another drink and laughed."

The courtyard gate squeaked, and Mary whispered to Jacob. "What do I do now? What would Jesus do?"

"What do you mean, 'What would Jesus do?'" Jesus said as he walked through the doorway and lay down his pack.

"Good of you to come home." Jacob grasped Jesus's arms. "Your brother needs you."

"Which one?" Jesus looked squarely at Jacob, then walked over and helped Mary to her feet. "Are you well?"

She held Jesus at arm's length and a smile broke across her face. "I am now."

With a sniff, Jacob grabbed a bottle of wine and poured himself a drink, then offered the bottle to Jesus. "You want some?"

"Thank you, yes; and Mother probably would take some now."

Mary took the cup from Jesus. "Judah is in trouble. Jacob says he's associating with the Zealots."

"He's also heavy-handed with the bottle, and Gideon says he gets into fights." Jacob lay bread and cheese on the table. "I just realized that story he gave us about a board slipping and knocking his jaw probably isn't the truth."

"No! Lying to us?" Mary grasped Jesus' sleeve. "Please don't leave again."

"For now, I'm here."

Chapter 19

Pounding resounded from the workshop when Mary woke the next morning. She rose, threw wood on the fire, and slipped out to the shop. Jesus was supporting a board for Judah, who was driving a spike into a frame.

"Ow!" Judah sucked his thumb, then turned and glared at Mary. "You're distracting me. You made me miss."

"Your mother wasn't the one holding the mallet. It wasn't her responsibility to keep her eyes on the spike. Try again, Judah. I've seen the excellent work you can do." Jesus waved his hand toward his mother. "After we finish the sides of this cart, we'll be making some deliveries and soliciting more work. We won't be back for the midday meal."

Mary nodded. "I'll pack food for you."

Except for Sabbath, Mary rarely saw Judah in the next few weeks. He shoveled beans and leeks in his mouth at the evening meal, then went right to bed. Jesus dawdled over his meal, asking Simon and Esther about their day and helping them learn scriptures.

"I'm enjoying watching the children learn their lessons," Jacob said one night after Judah had gone to sleep. "It brings back wonderful memories of Papa."

"This week I noticed Judah wasn't leaving the table as quickly. Did you see him mouthing the words along with Simon?" Mary rinsed the platters. "I wish Josey wasn't fishing with Zebedee. He's so far away; I enjoy having all my family around me." Her eyes rested on Jesus, and he looked up.

"Judah's just as enchanted with the Zealots, but he's too tired after work to spend time at the wine shop with them."

Esther tugged Jesus' sleeve. "What's a Zealot?"

Jesus smiled. "That's a good question. We remember King David for his zeal, his powerful feelings, and devotion to the Lord. But people can be impassioned about other things, and now there are men who are zealous to rid our people of the Romans and their heavy taxation of us."

Simon's eyes darted around the family. "Wouldn't that be a good thing?"

"It would be if we could convince them without using knives and clubs. Those who rule have a right to get paid for their services, but the Romans have doubled the taxes year after year. Not everyone can pay, and some men take out their helplessness and fury by killing and stealing. They formed a group so they could work together."

"So they have zeal to kill others? That goes against the laws of the Holy One." Esther's eyes grew wide. "Judah hasn't killed anyone, has he?"

"You're not being fair, Jesus." Jacob's face turned red. "The Zealots are also scrupulous about keeping the dietary laws and the rules about cleansings and the temple." He was sputtering. "You've seen all those money changers in the courtyard yourself. You've complain about those Pharisees, also. Don't be a hypocrite."

"You speak well, Jacob." Jesus' shoulders relaxed. "It's not enough to speak the Law; we must be doers of it, and some of those in the Pharisee sect have forgotten that." He pulled Esther into a hug. "I don't think Judah will kill anyone. Your brother is a ardent young man. We'll see if we can keep him passionate about his work and his family and the Holy One."

Over the next few weeks, Mary noticed three things about Judah: his ruddy complexion, his bulging muscles, and his respectful attitude. Jesus had the answer: give him enough work to keep him busy, and pride in his work to keep him focused.

Days glided by with laughter at the midday meal. Nights passed when she slept through to dawn. Then one night she woke, startled, from a dream. It was a dream she'd had before, many years before. No, it wasn't a dream: the angel, her duty, her son's assignment. Jesus had a calling, a throne to fill. *What am I doing, keeping him here? He needs to be in Jerusalem.*

"A word with you, please." Mary stopped Jesus when he was following Judah to the workshop. Her hand touched her cheek, and she searched his face for a sign of… she didn't know what. She cleared her throat. "What are you doing here?"

A slight smile twitched his mouth. "I'm helping my mother raise our family. Simon is only thirteen, Esther ten."

"You're staying because of me?" She sat down quickly. "But you have an assignment, a responsibility to the Holy One."

"That time has not yet come. There is still much I can learn in Galilee." He nodded toward the shop. "And some still need my attention at home."

Jesus stroked her cheek, and Mary leaned into his touch. "Thank you."

Josey was fishing on Zebedee's boats, but Esther and all her other sons lived with her. Some mornings Mary woke to Jesus singing King David's songs in the workshop, and her heart swelled. Other mornings he left early to build, sometimes in Nazareth, sometimes in Sepphoris. The other boys grabbed their share of rye bread and left for the day. Mary sat at her loom, marveling that she had raised such a large family. Her father's instructions from the holy writings, her husband's comfort and wisdom, her mother's steadiness with the children, and Jesus' sense of duty: all were part of her life's tapestry. How she wished Josef could have seen Jesus as he tried to assume duties as the head of the household, corralling seven younger brothers and sisters.

...

Esther was now marrying age. How did the years fly so quickly? Her youngest daughter's wedding was occurring next week. Joy and fear tumbled in Mary's mind. The girls were provided for. How wonderful that Esther was betrothed to Benjamin, a local farmer. Deborah came almost every day to visit, bringing her Naomi and little Danny. Once or twice when Mary was ill, Huldah, poor, childless Huldah, could visit. After much begging, Levi gave Huldah permission to come with Deborah to help Mary prepare for Esther's wedding. She sighed as she rose. *It's time.*

As if he'd heard her, Jesus stood in the open doorway.

"You're leaving again." Mary touched his sleeve, stifling a sudden urge to grab him and pull him close.

"A few days after the wedding, I'm going to the wilderness for a season of reflection." Even though his gaze fixed on Mary, he seemed to be seeing other people, other places.

As if Judah had been the room to hear, his arguing with Jesus began that day. The rising voices carried from the shop.

At sundown, Judah followed Jesus to the house but stood in the doorway, hands leaning on each side. "I won't be back." Judah's eyes narrowed to slits.

"Tonight, you mean?" Mary's voice quavered. Esther was wide-eyed.

"I have other places to stay. I need not live here and do all this work by myself." Silence vibrated around him.

"What about Esther's wedding?" Mary pulled the girl to her side.

Judah lowered his arms and glared at his mother. He took a deep breath and mumbled. "I'll be there."

"Promise you will stay close to Mama and your sisters and brothers." Jesus moved beside Mary. "They care about you."

"Their only concern is themselves. They don't even care about Mama." Judah's words stung Mary.

"That's not true." Jesus sighed. "They watch out for her all the time. They collect the firewood. Josey brings fish when he comes. Jacob dyes Mama's yarns and bleaches her cloth. Simon even picks up grain after the threshers have been through."

"They're here to eat your bread. Jacob stays so you can fix his broken bleaching table."

Mary's face flushed at the bickering.

"Jacob mends his own tables," Jesus countered gently. "Won't you continue to assist Mama?" His words came out slowly, and Mary guessed Jesus hated to ask that.

Judah stammered. "I'm no help to her." His eyes lowered, then he flicked a quick look at Mary. "I'm sorry." He stomped across the room to grab his sack, then reached for bread on the table. He stopped and turned; everyone was staring at him. He dropped the roll and left, bumping against Simon and Jacob, who were coming through the door.

It was a week since Esther's wedding. Mary was carding wool, planning what she would prepare for the noon meal, when Jesus entered. "It's been so quiet, I thought you were at the quarry," she said. "Or that you slipped away without saying good bye."

Dust motes glistened around his silhouette in the doorway. "I'm leaving in the morning. There are some unsettled affairs concerning the house we need to discuss first."

"What do you mean?"

"The inheritance."

"You inherit this property; all my children do. It's what your father wanted." Silence. "It's what my husband wanted–for the girls, too, just as Sali and I had it."

"I want no part of it. It means nothing to me."

She stood to face him. "How can you say that?"

"I'm leaving. Jacob is the new head of the family."

"Did you discuss this with him? Is he strong enough, temperate enough?" She pulled at the wool to keep her hands from shaking. *How can I help Jesus if he keeps leaving?*

His "Yes" was the only answer he gave.

A new intensity tightened Jesus' shoulders the next morning. His farewell embrace was a swift, light squeeze.

"You're going to the Jordan?" He nodded. "Travelers tell me that Elizabeth's son is immersing people there; they even call John 'the Baptizer'." Mary wondered if Jesus wanted to join John's ministry. Her son's face was clear and his eyes gleamed. He stood in the doorway looking south past Gideon and his brothers harvesting grapes. With a last glance over his shoulder, he walked away, leaving her wondering when she would see him again.

...

Mary ticked the children off her fingers: Jacob and Simon resided in Sepphoris for their work; Josey was still fishing for Zebedee; Judah had disappeared; Esther was helping her husband on his farm. With no midday meal to prepare, her days were empty, and the house was quiet. No hammering or pounding, no visiting with customers needing stools repaired or window frames fashioned enlivened her days. Jesus was somewhere near the Jordan, but no one had seen him lately. If it weren't for Deborah with her youngsters and lonely Huldah coming to visit for a few hours on Sabbath, Mary would wither from loneliness. They all forgot no one was in the workshop anymore to keep her company the rest of the week. As if she lived alone in an abandoned beehive, their lives buzzed along without her.

A month later, Deborah brought the stories from the town well. Jacob and Simon heard them at the synagogue. Every Sabbath, a new rumor.

Mary tried to piece together what had happened at the Jordan River. One weekend, Josey came home from Capernaum to say his cousins, Salome's boys, had been there, getting baptized themselves and learning from Elizabeth's son. *Could Josey have understood the story right?* Jacob and John had rushed back to Capernaum to tell all the relatives: Elizabeth's John wanted Jesus to immerse *him*, and he bowed to Jesus. The rest of the accounts, clouds shimmering with golden sunlight and people hearing thunder, were too fanciful to have credence. Jesus, they said, had swiftly left the crowds and headed south into the crags and crevices of the wilderness.

Mary shivered with excitement. She knew what this meant. Jesus' destiny, the purpose for which he was born, was beginning. *Was he going to collect Mighty Men as King David had done? Would he take a wife?* She caught herself wondering what it would be like to be the "Queen Mother".

Will I move to a palace in Jerusalem? If I stay here, will Jesus come see me. Would he share his dreams and hopes, his plans and struggles? Mary wished she could talk to Salome, confide in her.

Three Sabbaths had passed; Mary was kneading dough for the evening meal when a shadow sliced across the table. "Jesus! You're back!" She rushed to wrap him in her arms, but he held her off.

"Stay."

Up close, she could see how gaunt he was, emaciated. His skin was dry and burned by the sun. The eyes that had glittered on his departure had a dark depth. There was still a gleam, but it was steadier, focused.

"Would you like something to eat? Are you thirsty?" She wasn't sure how to act toward him.

"Yes, anything, please." Jesus dropped onto the closest bench as she poured water into a goblet. "I didn't know it would be so hard." He looked away. "I thought I was ready. I only pray that I truly am."

No one else was around, and Mary beamed at being alone with Jesus. As she handed the filled cup to him, he held her wrist. "I want to share with you what my Father accorded me."

"What Josef had for you?"

"What the Father, my Father, presented me." He groaned. "It was my first test. I pray I did not disappoint." Another groan while he covered his face with his forearms. "I need to speak this aloud to remind myself what is at stake."

"I keep secrets."

What happened to him? Why is he so agonized? Mary set the dough to rise, closed the door firmly so visitors would know anyone was home, and pulled up a stool close enough to rest her hands on his knees. He flinched as she did, but then relaxed and covered hers with his own.

"I went to the desert, west of En Gedi."

"Ahh, King David's territory, all wadis and rocky cliffs."

"Yes, but no one was chasing me, other than the Evil One."

"I'll wish I hadn't heard, but I want to know." She grimaced.

"I thought the testing would be the lack of food and the loneliness. Strangely, though, I never felt alone; the Lord's Spirit was always there; in fact, he compelled me to go. The fasting was only the beginning."

Anguished, Mary closed her eyes as Jesus described the hunger pangs that gripped him after the first two weeks of his fast. *To survive forty days?* Only Moses and Elijah had ever before lasted so long. Exhausted, starving, alone.

"It surprised me when Satan taunted me to put the Lord of Hosts to the test." Jesus gulped. "The devil demanded I throw myself from the temple pinnacle in Jerusalem that overlooks the Kidron." He shrugged his shoulders. "That was part of my ordeal."

Her hands flew to her face. She couldn't conceive of such a being, conniving and cruel. "Where did you find the fortitude, let alone the answers for the enemy's attacks?" Jesus raised his eyebrows. "Ah, yes," she whispered. "Growing up, you were the one walking around with a scroll in your belt, telling the younger ones how the Lord of Heaven's Armies always rescued His people and would again save them from bondage."

Jesus formed a half-smile. She grasped his hands and brought them to her lips and then to her heart. She moaned, but he quickly covered her mouth. A sudden question landed in her mind. She gasped and stared wide-eyed at him.

"He was handsome," Jesus said. "You were wondering what he looked like."

"How did you know?"

He shrugged his shoulders. "The Father is revealing much. I'm discerning situations I didn't understand before. I can tell you this: do not let appearances deceive you. The Accuser was dressed in rich robes and wore fine jewels, but many who dress in rags or goat hair will receive more honor in heaven."

He glanced around until he spotted the jar of water she had used, then poured more into the goblet. It splashed on his tunic, causing a dark stain to spread.

"What's that? What happened to the water?"

His eyes dropped to his lap. "No, it's just the wine."

"That was water!"

Jesus scrutinized her and looked back at the jar. He inhaled, and a frisson shook him. "It is not yet complete. I have much to learn, but the Kingdom is at hand. There are many people to teach; some are even waiting for me now. My cousins will join us soon."

"Where have you seen Jacob and John? Aren't they helping their father?" Mary frowned. "Are they coming here? And your kingdom?" Her mind was spinning and her heart pounding. "At last!"

"Not yet." Jesus swiped his forehead. "There is much preparation ahead. I have work to do. I will add your prayers and love to the Holy One's presence, but the time is so short. The sheep need so considerable care."

Mary's brow wrinkled. "Are you becoming a shepherd? I don't understand."

Jesus stood abruptly. "I need some rest before I travel again. Would you prepare food while I sleep?" He touched her cheek and, without waiting for an answer, slipped off his sandals, passed through the curtain, and lay down.

There was so much she longed to ask him. How was Elizabeth's son? Was it true the Pharisees wished to be rid of him and were considering violence? Did John really subsist on locusts? Did people come to the river from Jerusalem? In recent months news worked its way up to Galilee that Elizabeth's John was prophesying in the desert. Not only that, but he also was denouncing the Pharisees!

Mary looked at the tattered goatskin cloak Jesus had dropped on the bench. The garment he wore was a rag, with as little substance as a dusting cloth. Burrs stuck to the tassels on the corners. She remembered there were garments in her chest in the workshop. She doubted Jesus would stay long enough for her to make another tunic.

The heavy door squeaked against the stone. She used the room mostly for storage now. Judah, Jacob, and Simon no longer worked here. She was the only one who went inside, and that was rare.

A sweet memory greeted her: her father and Josef teaching little Jesus how to hold and use a saw or a mallet. Her precious son was so intent on getting everything just right. He was such a good listener too; they rarely had to tell him more than once. Not like the other four. Their primary interest in the workshop was as a place to hide during games or from chores. *Did they still resent Jesus for attracting more attention?* But their personalities were so different! Jesus, even as a boy, was so studious, whereas Jacob, Judah, Simon, and Josey could have fit in better in Salome's home; they were so full of energy.

"My soul magnifies the Lord. My spirit has rejoiced in God my Savior, for he has looked at the humble state of his servant." The familiar psalm unexpectedly swept over her. Now, knowing Jesus was following the call on his life, she sang the hymn that came out of her heart at Elizabeth's doorstep. "Behold, from now on, all generations will call me blessed. For he who is mighty has done great things for me. Holy is his name."

The experience Jesus described to her from the dark angel's testing released more of her song: "He has scattered the proud in the imagination of their hearts. He has put down princes from their thrones and has exalted the lowly. He has filled the hungry with good things." Yes, the Holy One of Israel surely furnished her eager son with desirable things.

She had moved old baskets and a row of chisels off the chest and pried up the lid. The long-suppressed scents of myrrh and frankincense tickled her nostrils, triggering memories of the wise star gazers and the escape to Egypt that followed.

Gently pulling away two scarlet scarves the visitors from the East had given her, Mary lifted out a favorite tunic that had been Josef's. She had made it for her husband to wear for Jesus's special visit at the temple. After that, he only wore it on a few feast days. How difficult it had been to weave after years without practice; it had taken her days on the round loom to make the robe all in one piece, trying to remember the directions her friend Amali taught her for adding the colorful zigzags. This would be just the thing to replace Jesus's rag of a covering. A heavy wool cloak of Josef's, lay there as well. It had two or three moth holes, but it wouldn't take her long to repair them. Frowning, she remembered Josef's requests to mend them; it was the day of his accident. His sudden death had wiped all thought of moth holes from her mind. The mourning, the burial, the sadness had been overwhelming. Now, perhaps her simple repair could supplant the somber memory. It would have blessed Josef for her to pass these clothes on to this "almost" son of his.

Before closing the lid, she tucked her hand down to the bottom right corner. Her fingers touched doe-skin; the sack was still there, mostly depleted of the original glimmering coins. Josef passed away so quickly, she hadn't been able to call a doctor. She'd had no need for the coins then. Mary grabbed the soft bundle. Jesus's years as a carpenter were over now, and he would require food and lodging. She wondered, "Will he ever build anything again?"

The cloak was ready for Jesus when he awoke, along with boiled eggs and bread for his journey. While he ate a bowl of lentils, he eyed the tunic. "Are you sure you want to part with that, Mother? Doesn't Jacob deserve it?"

"I don't think Jacob even remembers it; it's a joy to me that you do. It would have made Josef happy." Her smile slipped slightly as she laid the tunic over the cloak. "The large water jug is in back for you to bathe before you go." She reached out and laid a hand on his shoulder. His new seriousness, his restraint, caused her to hesitate embracing him. It wasn't as though he were a guest, but she felt a transformation, as if an invisible dust devil swept through and rearranged their relationship.

While he was bathing, she assembled dry fish and figs to go with boiled eggs and flatbread. When he'd finished, dressed in Josef's tunic, she brushed away tears: she had called the tunic Josef's own "coat of many colors."

She held out the soft sack. "You will need this for your journey. I still have some gold coins; they're yours, anyway."

Jesus gave her a puzzled look. "Mine? I have no gold."

"But you do! They were gifts to you when the princes came. Have you forgotten?" She tried to recall when they had told him about the astrologers. "Do you remember the elegant purple tunic you wore as a baby in Egypt? I wouldn't let you wear it outside our home."

Looking at the pouch in her hand, Mary sighed. Her thoughts swirled over the thirty years of his life, trying to think if or when she or Josef had told him about his birth and destiny. In the south, it had been dangerous to reveal the truth. When they returned to Nazareth, they remained quiet about their previous history, so people would believe they lived in Bethlehem for all Jesus' infancy.

Mary's demeanor brightened over another memory. "You had two of the coins the star-gazers brought to you in Bethlehem. We gave them to you when you met the priests in the temple, the time we left without you. We worried you would lose the coins in the crowds." A twisted grin crossed her face. "Instead, we lost our son, but with the coins you could buy food." Sighing, she pushed the sack at him. "If you are traveling, you will still need to eat and pay for lodging."

Gently, Jesus stroked her head. "And who will care for you?" There was a pause, and he smiled. "The Lord of Hosts provides for the birds of the air, and He has provided you with many sons and daughters. You will be well-cared for." He took a deep breath and looked away. With a sigh, Jesus slung his bag on his shoulder. He snatched the cloak and slipped out before she could wrap her arms around him.

Mary stood in the doorway and watched him glide swiftly to the south. She had learned nothing of what she intended to ask and too much of what she didn't want to know: *Would he be safe? Had his destiny truly found him? Was her duty complete?* She was afraid of the answer for the first question, and very sure of the answer to the last two.

Chapter 20

"What has Jesus done to my John and Jacob?" Salome shouted as she pushed through the door one week later. Since she still lived in Capernaum, Mary only met her at festivals or weddings. A relative of theirs was marrying in Cana, to Taoma's grandson, and Salome would remain with her for a few days.

Sali dropped her pack on the table and grabbed a jug to pour some water. Mary watched her sister. She wondered if wine would come out. Only water, this time.

"Jesus is like a rabbi now, collecting students to follow him." Salome took a quick breath. "All my boys talked about after they returned was 'Jesus said this and Jesus said that.' Zebedee needed them to man the fishing boats, but he told the Jacob and John, 'You may as well go; you're no use to me with your mind on Jesus.' Jacob told me Jesus sounds like the Baptizer; they both are calling on people to repent of their sins."

Bringing food and wine to Sali, Mary smiled over her own memory of Sali's youngest. "Your John was like a little lamb following its mama, and Jesus was so gentle with this child who didn't understand why his mother had sent him away." She sat and motioned her sister to do the same. "Tell me more about Elizabeth's son; how did this all start? I've only heard snippets here and there."

"People are calling Elizabeth's John the 'Baptizer'. As I remember, John was a handsome boy, but you wouldn't believe it now. He wears goatskins and eats locusts and honey. He has let his hair grow like a Nazirite; I didn't realize anyone did that anymore. My boys wanted to see what he was doing, since they always loved their Torah studies and heard John was preaching about the Messiah coming." Salome was rattling as fast as ever.

"Salome, slow down; I don't understand. Where did your boys find John?"

"At Bethabara, across the Jordan from Jericho. Jacob and John were the only two of our sons who went, and it's a good thing for them. I'm grateful it was those two instead of Noah and Abner, or Zebedee would have gone down to drag them home!"

"Did your boys become followers of Elizabeth's son?"

"They told me they only wanted to ask some questions, or I wouldn't have let them go. I didn't tell their father; he never would have allowed it. Elizabeth's son wants to immerse people to show their repentance from sin, like using a mikveh. He says righteousness will prepare a way in the wilderness for the Messiah to come."

Is Jesus to be the Messiah, not a new king? Was there are difference? Phrases of scripture tickled Mary's mind until it settled on the prophet Isaiah's proclamation, "Prepare the way of Yahweh in the wilderness! Make a level highway in the desert for our God" and something about Yahweh's glory being revealed. *The Baptizer must be that voice. Does that mean the Holy One's glory will protect Jesus when he is their king?* Her breath caught as the rest of the verse came: "all flesh shall see it together!" *Would all their people accept Jesus as king? No battles to put him on the throne? No bloodshed?* Mary trembled, but she didn't want Salome asking what was on her mind; she had to divert her. Jesus had told her the time had not yet come.

"Salome, come help me prepare the chicken, and then you can tell me more while we eat."

"Better a chicken than a lamb!" Sali retorted, a lopsided smile crossing her face.

Mary's head snapped. "What did you say?"

A smirk blossomed on Sali's face. "The Baptizer referred to Jesus as the Lamb of God."

"What is that supposed to mean?"

Salome's face turned red. "I'm sorry; I don't understand what he meant. I think it's funny to think of Jesus as a sweet, little lamb," she stammered. "John must have meant that Jesus is so obedient to the Lord."

"You mustn't disparage someone who follows the Lord as devotedly as Jesus does, Salome."

Her sister frowned and flipped her hair off her neck. "Anyway, now that Jacob and John are chasing after Jesus, Zebedee has to hire additional men to take out the boats, and they cost more than we paid our boys. It's difficult for Zebedee to get good men these days." Sali took a deep breath and grinned at Mary. "Except for Josey."

Over their supper, Salome and Mary discussed the wedding they would attend. "Did you hear Jesus and his group will be there? My boys said they're staying at the home of one of his followers, Nathaniel."

Mary's eyes widened.

"Yes, they're all invited. And did anyone tell you that Jesus has taken them all fishing?"

"That can't be! He only mentioned shepherding to me." A frown etched her face.

"I may have misunderstood; you know me: I never stop long enough to get all the details." Salome stood to rinse their plates. "Did you hear about the amazing catch of fish?"

"The boys and Zebedee were rinsing and mending nets, when Jesus told them to launch their boats again. They had been fishing all night without success, not even a minnow. Jesus insisted, so they gave in. When they dropped their nets, they struggled to haul the catch on board. Zebedee bounded after Jesus, wanting to hire him! Instead, your son walked away, with the young men following him."

Sali chattered on, Mary listening for every morsel about her son. *Was Jesus satisfied? What more did he learn about his future?* And the one question she couldn't share with her sister: *How had he turned the water in her jug into wine?*

...

Family groups of three and four lined up at the courtyard gate, laughing and squealing. Mary's eyes glimmered as she and Salome squeezed inside. Sali shrieked, waving her arms at friends across the square. In one corner, young men surrounded Jesus like pieces of iron around a magnet.

The sisters pushed their way over to congratulate the bride's parents, then turned to greet Taoma and Orli, whose grandson was the groom.

"Why aren't you smiling, Taoma?" Mary said. "I thought you and Gideon were happy about the match.

"Can't you see the crowd we have here? We didn't dream there would be so many guests. I tried to tell Solomon, the bride's father, to order more wine, that we had lots of friends coming." He gestured toward Jesus. "And I hadn't heard the family is related to Jesus, and you. I could have warned them your son has more disciples now." Taoma wiped sweat from his forehead.

"This sultry air is begging for a breeze, and these people are drinking more than usual. It makes both Solomon and me look foolish, that I didn't advise him well."

Mary scanned the crowd for Jesus. When she spotted him among his students, she slipped around the clots of relatives to his side. "Jesus." She tugged on his tunic, her voice soft. "They have no wine."

Jesus' eyes pierced her, and all his young men were glaring too.

"Woman, what does that have to do with you and me?" His words pushed her back a step. He pulled in a deep breath, and she wondered if he might turn away. Was he surprised that she saw he had turned the water in her jug into wine? Was this a secret?

Mary clutched her hands to keep them from trembling and returned his stare. "People have told me you've been helping the poor, those in need, and besides, Solomon needs more wine."

Her words made little sense, and a flush swept her face. *Would he dismiss her in front of his men? Was this necessary for him to become king–to reject his mother, the one who suffered ridicule and shame as a newly betrothed girl, the one who bore him, who had to escape across the desert to Egypt, far from family and friends?* Her knees shook.

Jesus let out the breath he'd been holding, and his features softened. "You meant well." He shrugged, but for an instant, before he turned back to the group of young men, he became still as a Roman statue, his eyes blank. Then, when she turned to slink back to the group of women like a whipped puppy, he reached out and tugged her sleeve. "I'll be there in a moment," he whispered.

Rather than heading back to Taoma, Mary glided to the courtyard wall and slid back to the servants. Their chatter caught her attention.

"How can we empty the water in these jugs and take them to other homes to fill with wine?" one said.

Another shook his head. "Nobody is home, anyway; they're all here."

The men hushed as Mary came close, and then she looked over her shoulder at the person coming behind her. She turned. Jesus lay his hand softly on her arm and gave a light squeeze. With a shaky voice, she told the servants, "Whatever he says to you, do it." She slipped away to where Sali and other women were standing.

Within a quarter hour, the guests were congratulating Taoma on his fine wine. "Did Gideon make this from his new vineyard to the west or your old Sumer grapes? How would you compare the Abraham vines at the top of the field with the Lot field in the valley?"

Taoma smiled faintly. "I always thought the Sumer Lot grapes produced the best wines, but it's all in the winemaker's hands."

...

Gnawing churned Mary's soul. *"Lord, I don't understand. I'm willing to let go of my son; I believe I have completed my task, but is there more for me to do?"* She received no answer, except a desire to hear Jesus preach persisted.

From the market to the well, and on to the synagogue and back, gossip about Jesus circulated around Nazareth. Every time Mary went to the well, a few women would ask if she'd been to visit Jesus or if he was coming to Nazareth soon. Few seemed to know about the water becoming wine, but other stories of healings were rampant. Now every Sabbath, Taoma asked if Jesus was teaching in their synagogue.

In contrast, little clusters of men or women also whispered behind their hands when she walked by. Her other sons and the girls dismissed the stories when she asked them what they had heard. The more the neighbors talked, the less Deborah or Esther mentioned Jesus' name. They assured everyone within speaking distance that their brother wasn't who people thought he was. Saddest of all, once again, Huldah was not allowed to visit her mother.

Mary sat before her empty loom. She struggled with her dilemma: when was the right time to tell them what the angel had told her? Was it too late? Would her children believe her if she told them now, or would they decide she had become demented?

Gideon faced her in the market. "Mary, what news do you have from Jesus? Will he be coming back to Nazareth soon?" She shrugged her shoulders, and he kept talking. "We understand there are some unusual stories about his preaching. Did he ever talk to you about a kingdom? I know you wouldn't want him in trouble with the Romans. That could be bad for all of us."

Her face turned red. "Gideon, how could you say such a thing! You've known Jesus since he was a child. A kinder, gentler man you'll never meet!" Her stomach tightened. "It will all be fine; don't worry." *He is bringing hope to many Galileeans.*

Jesus had made Capernaum his headquarters. "The best thing is to bring all of you there to listen to your brother preach," Mary told Deborah and Esther. "If you hear him yourselves, you'll understand his popularity and his plans for Israel's glorious future. People have been telling us, too, about those Jesus has healed of diseases. Maybe we'll see him heal someone."

Esther's eyes widened. "If he prayed for Huldah, could she have a baby?"

"Why not?"

Esther's eyes swung to her older sister.

"Mother, I'm sorry to say this, but you won't get my brothers to come," Deborah said. "According to them, Jesus isn't quite right in his head."

"No; you all misunderstand him. Hear him for yourself."

Trying to convince her children to go to Capernaum was like corralling goats, Finally, she wrote to enlist Salome's support, and a family gathering was planned in honor of Zebedee's acquiring a new fishing boat.

"It's a wonderful idea, even if I came up with it myself." Salome preened in her letter to Mary. "This will flatter Zebedee. He complains that Jacob and John are following Jesus instead of fishing for him, but he is truly proud they were two of the first students Jesus chose. I wouldn't be surprised if my young sons don't convince your boys to learn from Jesus as they did."

Mary's eyebrows jumped. It never occurred to her that her own boys might follow Jesus. From what Deborah said, they'd rather bring him home and lock him up before he got them in trouble with the religious leaders. *I want to show them they're wrong about him,* she thought.

Mary's children agreed to go to Capernaum for Aunt Sali and Zebedee's sake. Levi even gave Huldah permission.

Mary pulled the gate shut and locked it, handing the key to Simon. Brown and gold leaves swirled around the autumn trees. Overhead, charcoal clouds threatened rain. For an hour, puffs of dust blew around their feet.

Mary and Simon joined the rest of the family waiting at the junction for Capernaum. "Did you bring your leather cloaks?" She looked around. Yes, everyone bundled for the rough weather. Their eyes looked down, and the boys were shuffling their feet. "There might be rain before the day is over," she said. "How can we keep in good spirits? We have a full day's travel just to reach Magdala."

They all stared blankly.

"I know: story games! Children, are you ready to guess the heroes?"

"I will, I will," Deborah's children yelled.

"I taught them all Grandpa's stories," Esther said.

"We'll see!" Mary laughed, rummaging through her mind. "Tell me, who defeated Sisera?"

"Grandma, that's not fair." Deborah's daughter Naomi pulled on her hand. "When we say, 'Barak', you say 'Sorry, it was Yael,' and if we say 'Yael,' you come back, 'No, it was Deborah, because it was her plan.'" Everyone laughed at the joke Mary learned from her father.

"Well," she chuckled, "what about the hero of the Battle of Michmash?"

"Jonathan, son of King Saul!" came the chorus.

"Jonathan, Jonathan." Little Danny repeated the name for another furlong, and the stories and psalms kept them going that day, aided by a reprieve from the storm.

Mary rose in the dark and tiptoed from the inn as light spread over the Golan Heights on the far side of the sea. The sun lost the battle for its rights in the sky, and clouds rolled up from the south. She stood in the brush overlooking Galilee and raised her hands. "Lord Almighty," she declared, "Prepare the way for my children to comprehend Jesus, for all of us to see him as the teacher he is."

By the time the family gathered to leave the inn, a low ceiling of gray and wisps of fog surrounded them. When a squall swept through, everyone's clothes clung to them. To cheer the others, Simon and Esther reverted to childhood and made a game of jumping over mud puddles with Naomi and Danny until brown stains covered their robes. Simon lost a sandal in a mudhole and they stopped to rescue and clean it. An hour from Capernaum, a lone figure emerged from the heavy mist.

Cheering erupted; Josey had arrived to escort them the rest of the way.

"Zebedee gave us the morning off because of the weather. It's not safe to be in the boats when those crazy winds arise." By the time he had hugs from everyone, he was as muddy as they.

"Look." Simon pointed to the east. "The sun's breaking through."

"A rainbow!," Esther shouted.

Mary raised her arms. "Praise the Lord." She took a deep breath. *Coming to Capernaum was a sensible idea. All will be well.*

Josey opened the gate and the family shuffled inside. Salome skipped from one to another. "Wait here in the courtyard while I grab dry tunics for you; I've already collected them. Josey, bring them the bread and soup. Here, eat. Hurry."

"Sali, why are you rushing us?"

"There is a mass of farmers and other people from the countryside, and you'll want to be up close. I listened to Jesus speak yesterday. He's teaching at Simon's mother-in-law's home. I'll stay with Deborah's little ones and any of yours that don't want to go."

"Thank you. Naomi and Danny may stay. I insist all my children come," Mary said, setting her jaw. Judah and Jacob frowned; Josey turned his head away.

Salome pointed. "Walk up the third street on the right; it's the house in front of the synagogue. You won't miss the crowd. Josey, you take them."

It wasn't hard to find the home; it was getting close enough to hear Jesus speak that was the problem. Josey tried to make a way for all of them, but he, Simon and Esther were pushed back out the doorway. Judah and Jacob forged through the congestion, and Deborah dragged Mary and Huldah behind them. As they slipped in by the door, Sali's son John spotted them and waved.

Jesus was in the middle of a teaching, something about the kingdom, when John sidled up and whispered to him. Jesus surveyed the crowd, then focused on his brothers and sisters and Mary in the doorway. He looked down at the audience at his feet and at the woman who had delivered him a pitcher of water. He poured himself a drink, handed the pitcher to another, and grinned at a child sitting on her mother's lap.

Jesus pointed first to Mary and her family, before sweeping his arm across the crowd, at the disciples seated at his feet, and the serving women on the side. His authoritative voice rang across the throng, "Who is my mother? Who are my brothers?" He stretched out his hand toward his disciples and the crowd below him, and pronounced, "Behold, my mother and my brothers! For whoever does the will of my Father who is in heaven, he is my brother, and sister, and mother."

Mary's face colored and her shoulders slumped as the people in the room all turned to those he had first identified. *Why did he reject her and his family? Did he believe she had disobeyed his heavenly Father's will when she said* yes *to the angel?* Her heart fluttered. *Did he imagine she and Josef scorned the Lord's will when they fled through the desert and hid him in Egypt?*

Chapter 21

"Let's leave, Mama," Deborah whispered. The five of them pushed their way back outside, past the crowd still surging in.

"I'm confused," Mary said, shaking her head. Her tight throat made breathing ragged.

Jesus' words rattled in her mind. They piled into an avalanche that struck her very being. Her heart was shattering like a heavy water jug that had slipped through clumsy hands. "I don't understand." She looked up, only to meet the basket merchant from Nazareth.

She wrapped her shawl over her face to hide the flush of embarrassment and stumbled past stragglers still pushing forward to hear Jesus.

Josey, standing at the outer edge of the crowd, pulled on her elbow. "Mama," he whispered, "What happened? Did he do something to you? What's wrong?" Simon leaned in closer, tugging her robe.

"Never mind. We're going." Her voice was raspy. She broke free of his grip and stumbled. She winced at the ugly words that threatened to spill from her lips and dropped Esther's hand to cover her mouth. "We don't belong here." Like soot sticking to an oven, despair clung to her rejection. *We don't matter. Why would he say that? What a disrespectful son. That wasn't how we raised him.* Her stomach churned as she lurched up the hill. Tears dribbled down her cheeks. Lunging toward a fig tree, she grabbed a bare branch, waiting for Esther to catch up.

The leafless tree reached black claws to the sky. Its bark was thin and knotted. *Old and worn out, like me.* She took a deep breath, shaking her head as she tried to make sense of Jesus' words. *He couldn't really have said what it sounded like.* Jacob wrapped his arm around her, and she whispered into his chest. "Did you hear what your brother said?"

Esther tugged Mary's sleeve. "What did he do? What's wrong, Mama?" Esther turned to Jacob, whispering. "How did Jesus hurt Mama? Did he call her a bad name?"

Stepping forward and pulling Mary to her chest, Deborah raised her voice. "He dismissed her, and all of us, too. He's rejecting his kin." She waited for her brothers' and sisters' attention. "Jesus doesn't consider us his family anymore. It appears he doesn't want to associate with us. He's only happy if someone waits on him hand and foot. I'm glad we left before he embarrassed us further. I tried to tell you we don't belong with his crowd."

Judah grimaced while he scrutinized his brothers and sisters. "I told you before; we're better off staying away from him. He'll just get us into trouble. There are other ways to fight Rome than rejecting your own family."

A low groan escaped from Mary's throat as she shook her head. "If only your father were still alive."

The setting sun was sucking all the pink, leaving an icy gray, and Mary rubbed her arms to stop shivering. *Had she and Josef made a mistake not telling the other children that Jesus had a heavenly Father? Is that why Jesus didn't consider them his family? But why say other people were his family? How could she influence the children now?*

Her heart felt pinched, and a wave of sorrow swept over her. She had hoped by visiting Jesus in the midst of his followers, his brothers and sisters would be caught in his excitement and filled with the same purpose of restoring Israel's kingdom. Her thoughts tumbled and twisted. *How had she misunderstood Jesus' destiny? Salome's sons had already joined as Jesus' students; why couldn't her own children, too? Was there any hope, or had Jesus put an end to that today?*

Jesus had pulled away from them. She couldn't imagine why he dismissed them outright. He rejected them all just when Jacob and Judah had an opportunity to gain something profound from his teaching!

Salome opened the door to them. Her smug grin faded before their gloomy faces. "What happened? Wasn't he there? What's wrong?"

"We will not talk about it, so don't bother asking questions. We'll leave first thing in the morning." Mary's glare and her children's stern faces confirmed her intentions.

"Zebedee's party is tomorrow. You're staying for that, aren't you?"

Mary studied the stony faces of her sons and daughters. She wanted to concede, knowing her sister usually had her way, regardless, but another notion crept in. "Salome, are Jesus, John, and the rest of his disciples coming to the party?"

"Yes. Why?"

"Mother," Jacob stepped in between them. "I know you wanted to visit Aunt Sali and Noah and Abner and celebrate with Uncle Zebedee. What would you say if the rest of the family left in the morning? Then maybe you could talk to *him*." A frown cut across his face. "Possibly he can explain to you what he meant. I already know." Jacob crossed his arms over his chest.

"Explain what? Who are you discussing?" Zebedee entered, his thick gray eyebrows a shaggy line across his forehead.

"It's the weather; it's better we should start home before the roads get any muddier," Mary said.

Scratching his beard, Zebedee pierced Mary. "Forgive me for saying so, sister, but that's the first time you've ever told a lie."

Everyone turned to Mary as she ducked her head. Even with her gaze lowered, she saw Esther's wide-eyed shock. For a moment, she closed her eyes and squeezed her lips. Then she threw her head back. "You're right, Zebedee. That was a lie; I regret I told it, and I'm sorry because of what prompted me to give it." She looked around the room at her children and turned back to Salome. "We've abused your hospitality. If you'll still have me, I'd be delighted to stay and celebrate your good fortune." A deep breath shuddered through her, and she raised her chin. "We disagree with Jesus, or, truthfully, it's *about* Jesus. We don't want to settle it in your home."

Zebedee gave Sali a questioning look until she moved to him and whispered in his ear. Then he nodded his head a few times. When he cleared his throat, every glance was on him.

"As happy as I am to celebrate my new fishing boat, I can't pretend this would be a very joyous gathering. I'm canceling the festivities for tomorrow evening. If you want to leave in the morning or choose to stay, it's your decision."

Before Mary formed an answer, Jacob stepped forward. "I apologize for our behavior, Uncle. We'll all be going home in the morning." He glanced at Josey. "Except for Josey, of course. I realize he has responsibilities here."

At the prospect of excluding Josey from any family discussion, Mary clutched Zebedee's arm. "May Josey come with us for a week?" She couldn't conceive what she would say to her children or even how to open the conversation, but she desperately needed to talk to them all at once.

Zebedee studied Mary; then he gave a quick nod. "As you wish." One by one, her sons and daughters shook Zebedee's hand, gave Aunt Sali a hug and went to bed.

While Esther's breathing beside her was deep and even, Mary tossed until her blanket was tangled. Her eyes stared at the blackness, and her thoughts whirled. Her sons were primed to argue with her, and the girls sided with them. Her stomach lurched and tightened. *How might she convey to her children why their older brother was different? Was it too late to explain? Could Jesus help her with that?* Perhaps that wasn't a good idea right now.

Her mind kept repeating what Jesus had said: "Who is my mother? Who are my brothers? Here are my mother and my brothers." Then he had pointed to his followers "For whoever does the will of my Father in heaven is my brother and sister and mother." *Hadn't she done the Lord's will? What did her children make of that? Did they think Jesus was referring to their father, Josef?* "Lord of Lords, I need your wisdom! My children need your mercy, and so do I."

The next morning, Salome, without a word, passed around bread and cheese to Mary and her family. She sorted the cloaks draped around the oven, handed Mary the knapsack filled with nuts and dried fruit, and gave each of the children, big and small, a hug when they went out the gate.

A weak sun barely wore a hole in the gray blanket above as Mary stood with Zebedee and Sali at the courtyard gate. All her children and grandchildren, except for Jesus, were adjusting their packs and rubbing their hands to warm them. "I'm dreading the trip back to Nazareth. How I wish Jesus would suddenly arrive," she whispered to Sali. "I expect he would straighten us out and explain himself."

"My John came home last night after you were in bed. From what he said, you have good reason to be nervous about talking to your children." She gave Mary a last squeeze. "I'll be praying for you."

Like a stray dog, misery nipped at them all the way home. Deborah's children whined because no one would tell them stories or jokes. Danny sat in the road four times. The others barely spoke. Mary searched her mind for ways to begin the explanation she wanted to give, but the older boys marched quickly ahead of her, and Huldah and Esther took turns helping Deborah with the little ones. Simon scooted from the front of the line to the back. Even at the night's stop in Magdala, Mary's expression was so glum, they avoided being next to her for more than a few minutes. Every hour, Josey begged to return to Capernaum.

Chapter 22

"Mama, we're all tired, and Naomi and Danny are whining."

"Your children are half asleep." Mary stepped in front of the door and set her hands on her hips. "Deborah, they aren't expecting you until tomorrow. Put Danny and Naomi on my bed and sit down with your brothers and sisters. Esther and Simon, spread this blanket on the floor for yourselves. Huldah, would you pass those sweet cakes to everyone?" The murmuring collapsed into silence as her children glanced from one to another.

"It's time—or well pastime—that you understood the story about Jesus."

"Mama, there's no need...," Jacob waved his hand at the others. "We all know."

Her sons and daughters shifted their eyes around the room. Anxiety clutched Mary's throat like a boulder damming a swollen river.

The buzzing began. "Stop. You have speculated enough. Now you're going to hear what is behind all the ugly rumors and name-calling you endured growing up and why people called me names." At her first word, tension eased its grip and the words spilled out, a few at first until the pressure released and the story splashed over them.

Her children looked at their laps. "You thought I wasn't aware, but your father shared with me how other children taunted you. I'm sorry now that we never found the right time or the right way to explain."

Mary pushed her voice louder as she related the angel's announcement, Josef's unbelief, Aunt Elizabeth's pregnancy, and her unborn baby's response. "He's the baby they now call John the Baptizer." She recounted the crowded, smelly floor in Bethlehem where Jesus was born, the sheepherders' visit, the gifts from the stargazers, and the escape to Egypt.

All the things she had pondered through long days and sleepless nights poured out. Mary even included Josef's parents and brothers' disbelief, so these children would understand why her father Heli adopted their father. Yes, all that, and why she believed Jesus could turn water into wine at the wedding.

She dropped her head, took a deep breath, straightened her shoulders back, and pierced each one with the expression she had used when they misbehaved as children. "I'm convinced Jesus is our promised Messiah. You can believe what you want. Aunt Sali's boys have faith in him, or they wouldn't be his disciples." Deborah opened her mouth and Mary held up her hand. "In Capernaum, when Jesus said those other people are his mother and brothers and sisters, my mind rebelled. Yes, it stung me. However, I haven't understood every verse of the law or the prophets either. There are doubtless some things I'll never know." A curtain of silence hovered around her.

"I beg your pardon, Mother," Josey whispered, "Israel has had messiahs before this. Papa taught us about King Koresh of Paras, remember? The prophet Isaiah called him a messiah."

Jacob planted his hands on his hips. "Wasn't there a revolt here in Galilee by a man named Judas years ago? I heard that people called him a messiah? The Romans lock up his followers as murderers now."

All eyes pivoted to Judah, and Mary gasped. "Jacob!"

Judah's face turned purple. "Jesus may have the gift of the prophet Elijah, but he's no different from any other man," Judah said. "He puts on his sandals one foot at a time like we all do."

The silence lowered, covering the room like a thick straw mat, the kind that made people itch and twitch. Then came the coughs, the hm-hms, and the sidelong glances.

Looking at the floor, Deborah rose and gave Mary a hug. "I need to bring my children home." She pulled Naomi to her feet and took Danny in her arms. Still avoiding Mary's eyes, she shuffled out. The older ones paraded past in a similar manner, muttering about going somewhere else to spend the night. Their eyes swept the floor or the walls. Not one of her children looked her in the face. Even Simon slipped away with the others.

Every wrinkle of her mattress provoked her; the blanket twisted right and left. She pleaded with the Holy One, the One whose invitation she'd answered while barely more than a child. When she wasn't praying, she tried to sing, but the words of the psalms floated away like thistles. A gray light filled her tiny window. Mary stumbled to her feet and gripped the sill. Heavy as a stone slab, a cloud layer stretched across the sky. She stoked the fire methodically. As the coals leaned against each other and the deep red of one fired the lump of charcoal beside it, Mary once more pictured Jesus standing before the crowd, arms outstretched. *He was inviting them all, inviting her also to belong to something bigger. Was she ready to join his new family? How would she fit in?*

She poured a handful of water, splashing it on her face. Wiping it away, her eyes fell on her loom, the loom her father had made for her mother after they'd moved from Jerusalem. Its sturdy familiarity drew her closer. Her fingers opened and closed with anticipation. How many days had it been? Had she left this weaving or was this Esther's work? The sun had broken through the clouds. Ah, Esther started this. Only five balls of wool remained in the basket, but the rug begged her to finish it.

Mary settled before the loom. As if the yarn was coming from her heart, the familiar shuttling unraveled her tension. Knots of fear separated and unwound until she saw in her hands what she had released: her will. In a flush of warmth, fragments of the song she sang at Aunt Elizabeth's doorway spilled with her tears. "My soul magnifies the Lord. My spirit has rejoiced in God, my Savior, for he has looked at the humble state of his servant. All generations will call me blessed for he who is mighty has done great things for me. Holy is his name. He has scattered the proud in the imagination of their hearts. He has put down princes from their thrones and has exalted the lowly. *Yes. I want to hear the word of the Lord and do it.*

...

Jacob had come home at noon to get some other tools from the workshop. By the time he sorted through what remained, it was too late for him to return to Sepphoris before sunset. Sabbath was about to begin, and Mary was in the back room searching for candles.

Low grumbling from outside alerted her, and she called out. "Jacob, who's there? What are you doing?" Mary picked up a taper, lit the Sabbath candles, and went to the front. Arms out-stretched, Jacob was blocking Jesus in the courtyard.

Mary's voice squeaked. "Until I die, this is still my house. Let Jesus come in. The sun is about to set."

With a quick glower at her, Jacob elbowed past Jesus.

Mary looked beyond Jesus to see Simon following Jacob down to Deborah and Daniel's house at the vineyard. No one else was in sight. "Where are Jacob and John and your other students?"

She turned back to Jesus, who wrapped her in a rare hug. "There are other homes open to them," he whispered. "I didn't expect I would need to sleep elsewhere with them."

"You are always welcome in my home. You are my much-loved son. Come in; I need for you to stay with me." She placed Jesus at the table. "Please eat." Mary piled lentils and apricots in his bowl. "Since the others aren't here, there's plenty." She stood next to her son, ready to pour more wine.

"You've misunderstood me, dear woman," Jesus said, taking her hand.

"That's not so." Mary blushed.

"I thought you, surely, would understand that the Father, the Lord of Lords, wants us to be one family, one family of all people, loving Him by serving others."

"You don't realize how confused your brothers and sisters are. Your father and I, I mean Josef and I, we never revealed you have another father. The explanation was preposterous."

"Sharing the prophecies in the Holy One's word would have helped them understand. Did you try Isaiah or Micah?" Jesus smiled. "And Zechariah, naturally."

Mary opened her mouth to protest, but he calmly spread out his hands. The silence became a hollow canyon as his smile dissipated. Jesus' cocked his head. "Are you coming to the Sabbath service tomorrow?"

"Naturally. Will you stay here tomorrow night? You won't be sleeping outside, I hope."

He shook his head. "One of my men has a home here. No need for the rest of the family to find other beds." He picked up her hand and kissed it.

The next morning, Jesus left the house before daybreak. Twisting her hands, Mary repeated her prayers, hoping that Jesus would speak gently to his family and neighbors at the synagogue. Mary wrapped herself in an extra cloak and pasted a smile on her face. Closing the gate, she slipped on a loose stone and fell to the ground. Needlelike pain shot up her leg when she tried to stand. She had waited to be the last one at the synagogue, and now no one else was around to help her up. If only Jesus had stayed. Not only would he have helped her up; he would have healed her. She hobbled into the house to bandage her ankle.

As if a wildfire had swept through the town, within two days, the whole town was inflamed because of Jesus' behavior in the synagogue.

"Such an uproar! Mama, I wish you had been there." Deborah set the bread and vegetables she'd brought on the low table. Jacob, Simon, and Esther trailed after her.

"Then I'm glad I slipped and my sore foot kept me home. I heard some shouting at the gate yesterday. Was it something Jesus said?"

"Jesus read the scriptures from Isaiah about the Messiah healing the afflicted and opening the eyes of the blind," Simon said. "People say Jesus has been doing that."

"Yes, I know. Is that why they complain? I think that would be a good thing."

"Mama!" Deborah's hands flew in the air. "That's crazy. Yes, some people were healed here in Galilee. But calling my brother the savior of Israel?"

"He is, Deborah." Mary's intensity stunned her children.

Jacob's short cough swung her around. "You can't be serious, Mama. Jesus is bringing ridicule on our entire family. They ask, 'Why didn't he heal anyone before?' I ask *you*, if he's who you think he is, why didn't he bring Papa back to life?"

When someone rapped on the door the next morning, Mary expected a curious neighbor. She steadied herself to answer it. It was Jesus. "You're still in town? You don't have to knock," she said, reaching to embrace him.

"I'm saying goodbye." A faraway look flickered across his face. He caught her gaze and added, "I will see you again."

Mary remained at the gate and watched him stride toward the main square. As he approached the second alley, three men shouted rude terms. One of them bent for a stone, one who looked too much like her son Judah. "No!" Her holler surprised her. "Stop!"

The men quickly slipped into an alley. Mary lingered until her breathing slowed, glaring at the spot where they had stood.

Chapter 23

There was a price on Jesus' head! Would Caiaphas, the Jewish High Priest, convince the ruling council to lock Jesus up - or worse? With Passover less than three weeks away, the rumor-makers were in a frenzy, and fear battered Mary's heart. Who could help her? Her Uncle Josef, her mother's brother, was on the Sanhedrin Council now. Could he help, or did he oppose her son's mission? Perhaps Uncle Samuel, old as he was, still had some influence.

At daybreak, she pulled the headscarf tighter around her face and scurried to the market, hoping to encounter the scribe Uriah alone.

"Ah, dear woman, how can I serve you now? His eyes darted above her shoulder, then pierced her. His mouth widened in a sneer. He picked at a sore on his chin as he eyed the pouch Mary held.

She clasped her trembling hands to still them. "A letter, please, Uriah."

"To your eldest son?" His upper lip curled. "He may be difficult to contact."

Mary studied the ground. "No, not to him. To my uncle." She straightened her shoulders. "To Samuel, the trader in Bethlehem."

"We haven't seen him for a few months. Is he still living?"

"Advise him I'm coming." Mary focused on the man's forehead rather than his reddened nose. "How much do I owe you?" She placed the usual shekel amount on his table.

"It's double that." At her pause, he added, "Samuel may not be home and the courier would have to search for him. There's a rumor Jesus has disappeared, and maybe Samuel is with him."

"Uriah, why so high?" With a shake of her head, Mary pulled out the additional coins.

The pudgy hands snatched the money, dropped it into a pocket, and slapped the table.

"Aren't you going to compose my note?" Her words came out softly, but fire smoldered inside. As Mary raised her eyes to Uriah's, she noticed more merchants and customers inching closer. *All those people watching, watching Uriah humble her. How did Uriah become so horrid?*

"Ah, do you want your missive written today? You must wish it sent out today, too." His low chuckle caused her hands to clench. She inhaled slowly while she studied his face. Releasing her breath, she relaxed.

"Mary? I haven't seen you since the last festival." Mary turned at the voice, and Gideon walked over. "Have you been well?"

"Yes, until a few moments ago." She glanced at the scribe, took another deep breath and smiled. "Uriah hasn't been to visit me for several years now. I remember once when he came to our house. That's been many years ago." She turned back to the scribe. "When your father's cart wheel broke, wasn't it, Uriah? I recall thinking what an honor for a boy to carry the name of King David's general."

Gideon's eyes widened. "I had never considered that. I usually only see Uriah when he orders his wine from us."

A gentle smile softened Mary's face. "Years ago, Uriah was so protective and gentle with his little sister after their father died. I reminded him of that."

Uriah opened his mouth to speak, and his glance ricocheted off Mary. He scooped a handful of coins to the table and slid them toward her, eyes on the table. "I was informing this dear woman how I'd like to contribute to her son's cause. Excuse us, Gideon, while I write a letter for her."

Gideon looked from one to the other, his forehead puckered. "Weren't you going to talk to me this morning about another purchase, Uriah?"

The scribe fumbled with his reed. "Yes, but first I must take care of this correspondence and send my runner off with it." He pushed the coins closer to Mary, and she brushed them into her pouch.

With a long look at Uriah, Gideon put his hand under Mary's elbow. "I'll be back right away to get your order, Uriah. Since we're leaving tomorrow for Jerusalem, I'm going to walk my friend home."

Gideon opened Mary's gate and waited for her to enter. "Uriah was acting strangely," he said. "Was there a problem with your message?"

Her eyes glistened. "I'm learning a lesson, Gideon, a lesson Jesus taught. That man Uriah is like a son to me; Uriah is family, just as you are, Gideon." Her face held the same tenderness she'd shown Uriah.

"You're my sister-in-law's mother, Mary. How generous to deem Uriah part of the family." He bowed to her. "I'll send my wife over with some of our latest vintage."

A voice called her from the road to the south, and a man was trotting toward them.

"Josey." Mary ran down to meet him. "What's wrong? Is Salome in good health?"

"Yes." He took deep gasps, holding his side. "She wants… come; she wants you to come with her to Jerusalem. Hurry; we have to hurry."

"Gideon, thank you." Mary put an arm under her son's elbow and led him past her wide-eyed neighbor.

"Sit down, Josey. I just sent a letter to Uncle Samuel that I would like to stay with him for Passover. Why do I need to leave now?"

"Aunt Sali learned Jesus is planning a special gathering. She wants me to bring you there, too. We have to leave now."

"You'd better run down to Daniel and Deborah's while I'm pulling clothes and food together and tell them what we're doing. I expect we'll see them at Passover, anyway."

Mary scurried around the room, throwing a cloak and rolls and nuts into her pack. She dipped in her pouch to count the coins Uriah returned, and her eyes widened. There was more money than she had given him. She raised her arms in thanks and began laughing.

Josey was back in minutes." Are you ready?

"I think so." Mary put her hands beside her forehead. "Wait. A robe. He needs a special robe."

"Jesus? Why?"

"In the chest." Mary skirted Josey, rounded the house, and pushed against the door to the shop. Speckles of dust wavered in the stale air. The lid to the storage chest creaked, and she struggled to push the lid against the wall. Scents of oak and myrrh, wool and frankincense hovered around her head. She slipped her hands to the bottom, gently extracting her husband's whole-cloth tunic with the zigzagged trims.

Josey stood in the doorway watching his mother. "That was Papa's; his Passover tunic," he said.

"Exactly." Mary folded the garment and gave it to him. "Put this in my pack," she said. "I'll be with you in a flash."

"You always yearn to stay in here, but we don't have time, Mama. Aunt Sali will be waiting for us at Scythopolis."

"I need a moment to myself." The door closed, and Mary plunged her hands to the back corner of the chest and wrapped her fingers around three pouches. They were lighter than she thought until she remembered using the powders, trying to heal her father and mother. She grabbed the sacks and hurried to the house.

Mary's eyes swept the home, flitting over the oven, the loom, the mats on the floor. What would a palace be like inside?

"Mama, you're wasting time. We don't want to be late meeting Aunt Sali. I'm not sure she will wait."

Mary tugged the gate shut, locked it, and they scurried down the hill.

After a brief night's rest at Magdala, they rose before daybreak.

Gusts swept the mountain passes, bringing in a warm spell which welcomed them. The Jordan's waters winked at them from between oak and mulberry trees. Clumps of fluffy clouds mirrored the shepherds spreading their flocks on the hills, and blossoms from lemon trees perfumed the air as they approached Scythopolis.

The road was filling with more and more travelers. Passover was over two weeks away, but already the crowds were raucous. Mary clung to Josey's sleeve as they pushed through the throng surging past the coliseum. "Hold tight to your pack, Mama. Pickpockets are everywhere these days."

Mary slung her pack around to her belly, where it pressed against the coin pouch inside her robe. She wrinkled her nose and stepped carefully around the piles of excrement lining the street.

"Look. There's Salome in front of the inn."

At that moment, Salome saw them and began jumping up and down and waving both arms. Mary returned the greeting. "She still has twice the energy I have."

"Mary, I have a wonderful plan." Salome pulled Mary and Josey into the inn. "We have to find where Jesus and the disciples are."

"Aren't they in Jerusalem?"

"They've disappeared; they're hiding in the hills somewhere. I've asked all around, and no one knows. I expect they'll be back in time for Passover." Salome set her on a bench. "I've already ordered our meal, and we have to eat quickly. We want to be in Jerusalem when the men get there, before they go up to Bethany."

"Why Bethany?" Mary set her pack beneath her knees.

"You haven't heard, then? He raised a man in Bethany from the dead. Jesus is a friend of the man's family."

"Jesus has already done a miracle like that, for Jairus's daughter." Mary said. "You probably don't remember that Jairus was his friend when he was a boy."

"Mary, this was different: the man was already in the tomb three or four days, stone in front and everything."

Josey shook his head. "I can't believe that, Aunt Sali."

"It's true, and that's why the Pharisees want Jesus arrested. They say demons are making him do that." She pushed a plate in front of Mary. "Here. Eat, so we can get on the road. I want to talk to Jesus before he gets to Jerusalem."

"Why would the Pharisees think demons are controlling Jesus, Aunt Sali?"

"I don't think the Pharisees know anything about how to cast out demons. Maybe they're jealous that Jesus can set people free. Jesus set that man Lazarus free from death." Sali popped a cabbage roll in her mouth and grabbed a handful of dates. "Hurry and eat or take it with you. I'll tell you my plan when we're back on the road."

"Can't we rest a little? We just sat." Mary grabbed Josey and pulled him back beside her, glaring at her sister. "If Jesus is ready to come into his kingdom, there will be time for everything he wants to do."

Salome shrieked. "Mary. You know." She beamed.

"What are you to talking about? Jesus? Kingdom?" Josey shushed them and his eyes darted around the inn. "You'll both get us jailed. I don't want any part of this. What would Jacob and Judah say?"

"You'll see, Josey." Salome smirked. "Put the rest of the food in your mouth, and let's take to the road." She rose and put on her pack. "I'm leaving; you are too, aren't you, sister?"

Josey was standing with his arms crossed, glaring at them. Her hope tumbled that he would follow them once she and Sali left the inn. Mary straightened her shoulders. "Do what you want, Josey. There are only a few more days on the road; I'll be fine; the Lord of Heaven's Armies is with us."

Chapter 24

"Slow down, Salome. I can't keep this pace another day." Mary stepped to the side of the road and readjusted her pack.

"The junction is just ahead, and I don't want to miss him. Where we stayed last night, people said Jesus and his disciples have been in Ephraim, but they'll be leaving soon for Jerusalem. Once they approach Jericho, the crowds will be so big, we might not get close unless we say we're family."

"That word doesn't mean the same to Jesus. I've already learned that."

"You're right, and my boys are even like brothers to him."

At the crest of the hill, Mary clutched her side and lowered herself to a boulder. She slipped the pack to the ground. "Go ahead without me. I'll catch up with you at the inn in Jericho."

"I can't do that. And it's downhill from here."

"There has to be someone from Nazareth in that stream of people." She glanced back. "Oh, isn't that Simeon and Judith?"

"Who are they? I haven't met them."

"Don't worry, Sali. Go on. I'll meet you at Hiram's."

Sali bent to give her a quick kiss. "Be careful."

Mary yawned and looked back at the travelers climbing the hill. There was no familiar face; there hadn't been. She leaned her head to view a procession of wispy clouds. Those must be angel's wings covering her, protecting all of them. And Jesus. She kneaded her shoulders. If she didn't get up, she'd fall asleep by the road. A verse came to mind. "Those who wait for Yahweh will renew their strength. They will mount up with wings like eagles. They will run and not be weary. They will walk and not faint." The words refreshed her.

She whirled at the tap on her shoulder. "Josey! You didn't turn around."

"I couldn't desert you, Mama. How could I let my mother travel this highway by herself? What would my brothers say? I've been tailing you and Salome since Scythopolis. She was foolish to leave you unaccompanied and foolhardy to turn off the road to find John and Jacob."

"Thank you. You won't be sorry you came with me. Wait till you see how everyone loves Jesus."

By the time they reached Jericho's central boulevard, she stumbled with fatigue. Tremors slid down Mary's spine as memories assaulted her. "We aren't staying in Jericho any longer than necessary, Josey." She led him away from the central avenue and veered into the sheltered labyrinth of alleys.

Under the rainbow-hued canopies in the market quarter, merchants hollered, extolling their wares. The scents of fish and meat, spice and slop assailed them. At last, they entered the familiar inn, and Mary leaned against a table while her eyes became accustomed to the dark.

"I'm Reuben, son of Hiram; may I help you?"

"Is there a room available for my sister and myself and space to spare for my son? It's only for one night. Hiram knows me."

Reuben spread out his hands and shook his head. "I'm sorry to bring you sad news. We buried my father two months ago."

"What a terrible loss for you." Mary tore at her scarf and wailed. "He was a man of integrity. I am so distressed. He was always very gracious to us."

"We haven't been letting rooms lately because we've had a special request for use of all our accommodations."

"Mary's face turned from dark to light. Is it for Jesus?"

Reuben took a step back and looked around. His voice hushed. "Why do you want to know?"

"I'm his mother; Josey here is his brother. His aunt, John and Jacob's mother, is my sister. I've known your father since before Jesus was born."

"Ah, Josef of Nazareth's family? Then we'll make room for you with the other women and children. I can't guarantee you a pallet, though perhaps they can decide that."

"I'll wait here for my sister, if I may."

"Of course, dear woman."

Stars already studded the sky when Salome rushed in, slamming the front door. "Mary, I did it!" She squatted at Mary's knees. "I'll tell you, but you can't let anyone else know. Josey, you stay quiet, too."

"Can't tell what?"

Sali looked around and lowered her voice. "I've guaranteed a place for John and Jacob on each side of Jesus' throne when he becomes king."

"That's wonderful, Sali. Did Jesus say when that would be?"

"Soon, I'm sure. They'll stay here tonight and go up to their friends in Bethany tomorrow." She stood and twirled. "Can you believe this crowd, all for Jesus?"

"No, we imagined they came for Passover."

"John said they were coming here, but Jesus stopped to visit with a fellow stuck in a tree. I talked to John just before Jesus and the disciples turned and followed the man to his house."

Sali plopped next to Mary, pulled the breadbasket over, and stuffed a roll in her mouth. "I'm famished. Can we order some food?"

As they ate, a cluster of women and children entered. Two little girls ran over to Salome, and she wrapped them in hugs. "Mary, these families that follow Jesus are wonderful. Everyone shares with each other."

"I give to the poor, Sali. You've seen me give away clothes Simon and Esther have outgrown."

"This is different." She handed their bread basket to the children, who ran back to their mother.

"We're still eating from that loaf; we'll need it to sop up our soup, Sali."

"And you were teaching *me* about family? Everyone shares in Jesus' kingdom, Mary. You'll see."

When Mary woke the next morning, sun splashed through the tiny window, and she was alone. Salome stuck her head in the door. "Finally. I wanted to wake you an hour ago when the others left, but they convinced me to let you sleep. Hurry now. We want to meet Jesus when he comes into Jerusalem tomorrow." Salome scooped Mary's blanket and stuffed it in her pack.

"You should have wakened me," Mary said. *But I'm glad you didn't.* She shook her cloak, slung it over her shoulder, and adjusted the money pouch around her neck. "Josey will be here in a moment. We still need to pay Reuben."

"It's all been done. That other Mary, the one from Magdala we met last night, paid for all of us."

"How can that be? People aren't that generous."

"With Jesus, they are."

The long night's sleep had given Mary renewed energy, and she and Salome scrambled to keep up with Josey as they climbed the Adummim route. Holiday crowds sang beside them, rejoicing in the Sabbath that would begin that evening.

"I'm planning to stay at Samuel's in Bethlehem, but I didn't receive a reply, we left so quickly. Do you remember Josef's brother Jacob? He and his family still live in Bethlehem too, so maybe we can stay with them if we can't stay with Samuel."

"Isn't his wife the one from Emmaus?"

"No, that is Mary, Cleopas's wife. I imagine we won't meet those two until Passover."

Mary stopped to study the gleam the afternoon sun made on Jerusalem's temple. Mary's breathing quickened. *Why did this always happen? Was she always anticipating this final moment the angel promised her, the moment when her son would be declared king?* The announcement the angels gave the shepherds of a Savior, the Anointed One, once again was fresh in her mind, and Bethlehem was where the stargazers found her little boy. The King of the Jews, they called him.

"There's no time to rest. We still have a few hours to reach Bethlehem before nightfall," Josey reminded her.

Mary straightened her shoulders.

"I wish we were staying in Bethany with those other families," Sali said.

"My hope, Sali, was to celebrate Passover with Jesus. He needs to be with family more than ever now, and we need to be with him." She turned to Josey, and a tilted smile swept her face. "I'm finally learning how big that family is. When I asked the women in Jericho if I could help serve at Passover, I was told Jesus had made other plans."

"With so many followers, he can't leave a meal like that to chance, Mary."

In Bethlehem, Samuel pulled Mary and Salome into his arms and grasped Josey's arm. "You bring delight to this old merchant. These are precarious times; I am relieved you arrived safely."

"You've heard of all Jesus has been doing?"

"Most members of the Sanhedrin regard his idolization with disdain, if not murderous intent," said Samuel.

"That's what we've tried to tell you, Mama."

Mary frowned at Josey.

Salome fluttered her hands at Samuel. "Doesn't anyone read what the prophets foretold? Jesus fulfills several prophecies; Mary is witness to that."

"Few Pharisees would know about Jesus' birth, Sali."

Salome turned to her sister. "But it's true, Mary, and you know it."

"No arguments. We'll partake of supper now, but it behooves us to spend our Sabbath in prayer and fasting." Samuel led them inside and pointed to the feast spread across his table.

"I know the Lord of Hosts will protect Jesus, but prayer and fasting will be a good way to prepare for his victory procession the next day." Mary straightened her shoulders. "What a joy to come to Jerusalem now. If only my husband could have been here."

Salome faced her grizzled uncle. "Don't worry, Uncle Samuel. Jesus has begun establishing his kingdom right. He has already assigned two faithful men to implement it."

...

"I see them." Josey trotted down the road to meet his uncle Cleopas and his wife at the junction of the Emmaus road. Mary paced herself with Samuel's plodding while Salome pranced ahead toward Cleopas and Mary. Even from a distance away, Mary heard her sharing how Jacob and John would be Jesus' main assistants.

"Uncle Samuel, how can the priests and Pharisees reject him anymore?" Mary wondered. "They must not take out their scrolls anymore. King David sang, and I believe it. 'Let your priests be clothed with righteousness. Let your saints shout for joy! This is my resting place forever. I will live here, for I have desired it. I will also clothe her priests with salvation. Her saints will shout aloud for joy. I have ordained a lamp for my anointed.' What a privilege to be alive at this moment. Israel's true king has come."

Once together, Samuel led them along the Kidron Valley. Crowds streamed out of the Holy City toward the Bethany road, where it emerged past an olive grove. The crowd of people became one throbbing wave, surging and pulling. Mary clung to Samuel. Sali and Josey were shoved against Cleopas and Mary, who scrambled to keep from being trampled.

The shouting swelled as Jesus appeared at the top of the hill. Mary gasped. "Why is he riding a donkey? He should be on a stallion."

"I recollect there's a reference in the holy writings," said Samuel.

The memory of sitting beside her uncle in Ein Karem, following his fingers across the scroll of the prophet Zechariah, flashed in her mind. "Now I remember; it reads, 'Behold, your King comes to you! He is righteous and having salvation, lowly and riding on a donkey.' I didn't understand, and your sister explained it means he has humility."

"It seems disgraceful to me." Josey muttered, and Mary glared at him.

"Jesus is humble, isn't he, Mary." Salome turned to explain to Cleopas, but the people flocking to see this rabbi who had the Pharisees fuming were pushing him and his wife further away.

A young boy selling palm branches was squeezing through the crowd, dragging two ragged branches.

"I'll take those." Samuel handed the boy some shekels and gave Mary and Salome each a branch.

Samuel's bulk wasn't enough to get them a spot at the edge of the road. Mary stood two rows back, squeezed between Sali and a man who kept elbowing her from the side. Josey was somewhere behind them. All she glimpsed of Jesus as he rode past her toward the temple was the top of his head. It was enough.

She waved her branch wildly and shouted along with the mass of people. "Save us now, we beg you, Yahweh! Yahweh, we beg you, send prosperity now. Blessed is he who comes in Yahweh's name!"

Joy overwhelmed her, and she stood still while Sali, Josey, Samuel, and Cleopas and his wife joined the mob pursuing Jesus as he crossed the valley and climbed the road to the temple. Mary pictured the priests welcoming him inside the courtyard. She closed her eyes and sobbed with relief.

A chilly breeze ruffled her headscarf, and a tingle ran down her back. Mary shook it off and ran to join the others. "I did it," she called to the clouds. "Thank you, Holy One, for letting me be the caretaker old Anna prophesied: the caretaker of God's temple, to raise this wonderful son. Within a week, he'll be wearing a crown!"

BIBLICAL REFERENCES

Biblical Passages are from World English Bible translation, also called the WEB

Chapter 4
- Psalm 18:14
- Psalm 136

Chapter 6
- Psalm 42:1
- Psalm 71:14
- Luke 1: 28-38
- Proverbs 12:4

Chapter 7
- Luke 1:41-45
- Luke 1: 46-55
- Isaiah 11: 1-12
- Zechariah 3: 8-9; 6:12-13; 9:9
- Zechariah 14:9
- Deteronomy 6: 4-5, 7

Chapter 8
- Luke 1:76-77
- Isaiah 40:31
- Psalm 31:20

Chapter 9
- Psalm 46:1-2
- Psalm 12:1-3, 7-8
- Psalm 122:1

Chapter 11
- Luke 2:1-14
- Isaiah 7:14
- Isaiah 49:13
- Luke 2:25-32
- Luke 2:33-34
- Luke 2:38

Chapter 12
- Matthew 2:13
- Proverbs 28:15
- Psalm 140: 4 & 8
- Proverbs 4:18

Chapter 14
- Hosea 11:1, 11-12

Chapter 17
- Matthew 3:17
- Luke 1:47-48

Chapter 19
- Luke 1:47-48
- Luke 1: 48b-49, 51-53

Chapter 20
- Isaiah 40: 3, 5
- John 1: 29, 36
- John 2:4
- John 2:5
- Matthew 12: 47-50

Chapter 22
- Luke 1:47-49, 51
- Luke 8:18
- Mark 9:7
- Matthew 14:13-36
- Isaiah 9: 6

Chapter 24
- Isaiah 40:31
- Psalm 132: 9, 14, 16b-17
- Zechariah 9:9
- Psalm 118: 25-26a

About the Author

Langley, a mother of three children and grandmother of six, is a happily married former high school English teacher. She has been a bible study teacher for over 30 years, most of those years lived in arid high desert much like Israel. She has participated in Christian ministry trips to Europe, as well as Mexico, Colombia and Brazil. A trip to the Holy Land piqued her curiosity about Mary, prompting a second trip to absorb the landscape and culture. Along with many other fascinating and purposeful women of Scripture, Langley believes Mary is a mother struggling to raise her family in unusual and threatening circumstances, a woman to whom many can relate. More information is available at kclangleywrites.com.